Candyfloss

Candyfloss

JACQUELINE WILSON

ILLUSTRATED BY NICK SHARRATT

SQUARE
FISH

SQUARE
FISH

An Imprint of Macmillan

Wilson, Jacqueline.
Candyfloss / Jacqueline Wilson.
p. cm.
Summary: When her mother plans to move to Australia with her new husband and baby, Floss must decide whether her loyalties lie with her mother or her father, while at the same time, her best friend begins to make fun of her and reject her.
ISBN-13: 978-0-312-38418-0 / ISBN-10: 0-312-38418-1
[1. Divorce—Fiction. 2. Fathers and daughters—Fiction. 3. Friendship—Fiction. 4. Schools—Fiction. 5. England—Fiction.]   I. Title.
PZ7.W6957Can 2007
[Fic]—dc22
2006019923

First published in Great Britain by Doubleday,
an imprint of Random House Children's Books.
Originally published in the United States by Roaring Brook Press
Square Fish logo designed by Filomena Tuosto
First Square Fish Edition: September 2008
10 9 8 7 6 5 4 3 2 1
www.squarefishbooks.com

To Robbie and Callum

One

I had two birthdays in one week.

My first birthday was on Friday. Mom and Steve woke me up singing *"Happy Birthday to you."* They'd stuck candles in a big fat croissant and put a little paper umbrella and a toothpick of cherries in my orange juice.

My little half brother, Tiger, came crawling into my bedroom too. He's too tiny to sing but he made a loud *he-he-he* noise, sitting up on his padded bottom and clapping his hands. He's really called Tim, but Tiger suits him better.

I blew out all my candles. Tiger cried when the flames went out, so we had to light them all again for him to huff and puff at.

I had my birthday breakfast in bed. Mom and Steve perched at the end, drinking coffee. Tiger went exploring under my bed and came out all fluffy, clutching one of my long-forgotten socks. He held it over his nose like a cuddle blanket, while Mom and Steve cooed at his cuteness.

Then I got to open my presents. They were wrapped up in shiny silver paper with big pink bows. I thought they looked so pretty I just wanted to hold them for a moment, smoothing the silver paper and fingering the bows, trying to guess what might be inside. But Tiger started ripping them himself, tearing all the paper and tangling the ribbon.

"Tiger, stop it! They're *my* presents, not yours," I said, trying to snatch them out of the way.

"He's just trying to help you unwrap them, Flossie," said Steve.

"You need to get a bit of a move on, darling, or you'll be late for school," said Mom.

Tiger said *He-he-he*. Or it *could* have been *Ha-ha-ha*, meaning *Ya boo sucks to be you*.

So I lost my chance of savoring my five shiny silver presents. I opened them there and then. I'll list them. (I *like* making lists!)

1. A pair of blue jeans with lots of little pockets fastened with pink heart-shaped buttons. They matched a pink heart-patterned T-shirt with a cute koala motif across the chest.
2. A pink shoebox containing a pair of sneakers, blue with pink laces.

3. A little package of gel pens with a stationery set and stickers.
4. A pink pull-along trolley suitcase.

I left number 5 till last because it was big but soft and squashy, and I hoped it *might* be a cuddly animal (any kind, but not a tiger). He had torn off half the paper already, exposing two big brown ears and a long pointy nose. I delved inside and found two *tiny* brown ears and a weeny pointy nose. It was a mother kangaroo with a baby kangaroo in her pouch.

Tiger held out his hands, trying to snatch the baby out of the pouch.

"No, Tiger, he wants to stay tucked in his mommy's pocket," I said, holding them out of his reach.

Tiger roared.

"Just let him play with the baby kanga a minute. He won't do him any harm," said Steve, going off to the bathroom.

Steve talks a lot of nonsense sometimes. Tiger grabbed the baby kangaroo and shoved him straight in his mouth, first the ears, then the snout, and then his entire *head*.

"Mom, Tiger's *eating* him!" I protested.

"Don't be silly, Floss. Hang on!" Mom hooked her finger into Tiger's bulging mouth and rescued the poor little baby kangaroo.

"He's all covered in Tiger's slobber!" I said.

"Just wipe it on the comforter. Don't be such a baby, Birthday Girl," said Mom, giving me a little poke. "Do you like your presents, Floss?"

"Yes, I love them," I said, gathering them all up in my arms away from Tiger.

I supposed I loved my little half brother, but I wished we could keep him in a cage like a real tiger.

"There's actually another extra present," said Mom. Her eyes were shining as brightly as my birthday candles. She raised her voice, shouting to Steve in the bathroom. "Shall I tell Floss now, Steve?"

"OK, yeah, why not?" he said, coming back into my bedroom, shaving cream all over his face.

He put a little blob of shaving cream on the tip of Tiger's chin and pretended to shave him. Tiger screamed delightedly, rolling away from his dad. He wiped shaving cream all over my special cherry-patterned comforter. I rubbed at the slimy mark, sighing heavily.

"So, OK, what's my extra present?" I asked warily.

I very much hoped Mom wasn't going to announce she was going to have another baby. One Tiger was bad enough. Two would be truly terrible.

"It's a present for all of us. The best present ever, and it's all due to Steve," said Mom. She was looking at him as if he were a Super Rock Star/Professional Soccer Player/Total God, instead of a perfectly ordinary actually quite boring guy who picks his nose and scratches himself in rude places.

Steve smirked and flexed his muscles, striking a silly pose.

"Steve got a promotion at his work, Floss," said Mom. "He's being made a manager—isn't that incredible? There's a sister company newly starting in Sydney and Steve's been asked to set things up there. Isn't that *great*?"

"Yeah, I suppose. Well done, Steve," I said politely, not really taking it in at all. The stain on my comforter wasn't budging.

"*Sydney!*" Mom said.

I blinked at her. I didn't quite get the significance. Sydney was just an old-fashioned guy's name.

"She doesn't have a clue where it is," said Steve, laughing. "Don't they teach kids geography nowadays?"

Then I got it. "Sydney in Australia?"

Steve clapped and he made Tiger clap his little pink fists too. Mom gave me a big, big hug. "Isn't it exciting, Floss! Think of all the sunshine! You just step out of the city and there you are, on a fabulous beach. Imagine!"

I *was* imagining. I saw us on a huge white beach, with kangaroos hopping across the sand and koalas climbing palm trees and lots of beautiful skinny ladies like Kylie Minogue swimming in the turquoise sea. I saw Mom and me paddling, hand in hand. I sent Steve way, way out to sea on a surfboard. I stuck Tiger in a kangaroo's pouch and sent them hopping far off into the bush.

"It's going to be so wonderful," said Mom, lying back on the bed, arms and legs outstretched, as if she were already sunbathing.

"Yeah, wonderful," I echoed. "Wait till I tell Rhiannon and everyone at school!" Then I paused. "What *about* school?"

"Well, Steve reckons we'll be in Sydney a good six months, though we're not permanently emigrating. You'll go to a lovely new Australian school while we're out there, darling," said Mom. "It'll be a fantastic experience for you."

My heart started thumping. "But I won't know anyone," I said.

"You'll soon make lots of new friends," said Mom.

"I like my *old* friends," I said.

Rhiannon and I had been best friends for almost a whole year. It's the most wonderful thing in the world to be Rhiannon's best friend because:

1. She's the most popular girl in the class and always gets voted to be monitor and the lead part in any play and first on any team.
2. She's the prettiest girl in the class too. No,

the prettiest girl in the whole *school*. She's got long dark black hair, utterly straight and very shiny. She's got delicate black arched eyebrows and long thick black eyelashes but her eyes are bright blue. She is quite tall and very slim and could absolutely definitely be a fashion model when she's older. Or a rock star. Or a television presenter. Or *all three*.

3. Everyone else wants to be Rhiannon's best friend, especially Margot, but she's my best friend, so there. Margot's never ever going to break us up. No one can ever come between Rhiannon and me.

I loved Rhiannon to bits even though she could be a bit bossy at times. She generally told me what to do. But I didn't really mind because mostly I just wanted to please her.

I tried to imagine this big new Australian school. I'd watched the soaps on television. I made the girls wear funny checkered dresses and smile a lot with their big white teeth. They all spoke together. "G'day, Flossie, can we be your friends?" they chorused.

"Well, I'd normally say yes. But I'm Rhiannon's friend," I explained.

"Hey, daydream Birthday Girl!" said Mom, giving me a kiss. "I'm going to pop in the bathroom after Steve. Keep an eye on Tiger for me."

You needed two eyes looking out for Tiger. Plus another pair at the back of your head.

I gathered up all my birthday presents and put them up on top of my bookshelf, out of his reach. I pictured myself wearing my new T-shirt and jeans and sneakers, pulling my trolley-case, kangaroo under one arm, bouncing off to Australia. I saw how cleverly Mom had chosen my presents.

Then I looked at the stationery set. I fingered the writing paper and envelopes and the gel pens all the colors of the rainbow. Why would I be writing lots of letters?

Then my heart thumped harder. I dropped the stationery and the pens and ran to the bathroom. "Mom! Mom!" I yelled.

"What?" Mom was joking around with Steve, splashing him like a little kid.

"Mom, what about Dad?" I said.

Mom peered at me. "I expect your dad will phone you tonight, Floss. And you'll be seeing him on Saturday, same as always."

"Yes, I know. But what's going to happen when we're in Australia? I can still see him, can't I?"

Mom's brow wrinkled. "Oh, come on, Flossie, don't be stupid. You can't pop back from Australia every weekend, obviously."

"But I can go sometimes? Every month?"

"I'm doing very nicely, thank you, but we're not

made of money, kiddo," said Steve. "It costs hundreds and hundreds of pounds for a flight."

"But what am I going to *do*?"

"You can write to your dad," said Mom.

"I *knew* that's why you got me that stationery set. I don't want to write to him!"

"Well, if he'd only join the modern world and get a cell phone and a computer, you could text and e-mail him too," said Mom.

"I want to be able to *see* him like I do now," I said.

"Well, we're not going to be in Australia *forever*," said Mom. "Those six months will whiz past and then we'll be back. Unless of course it's so wonderful out there that we decide to stay! Still, if we *did* decide to stay for good we'd come back on a visit."

"Your dad could maybe come out to Sydney to see you," said Steve.

He said it nicely enough but there was a little smirk on his face. He knew perfectly well my dad was having major money problems. He had barely enough for the bus fare into town. If flights to Australia cost hundreds of pounds, there was no hope whatsoever.

"You're mean, Steve," I said, glaring at him.

"Oh, Floss, how can you say that? Steve's the most generous guy in the whole world," said Mom, deliberately misunderstanding. "He's planned for us to go to TGI Friday's as a special birthday treat for you tonight."

"I'd sooner have a birthday meal at home. A little party, just Rhiannon and me."

"I haven't got the time, Floss. I've got one million and one things to get organized. Come on, you know you love TGI Friday's. Don't spoil your birthday making a fuss about nothing."

I stomped back to my bedroom.

My dad wasn't *nothing*! I loved him so much. I missed him every week when I was at Mom and Steve's.

I'd forgotten I'd left Tiger in my bedroom. He'd gotten at my new gel pens. He'd decided to decorate my walls.

"You are a *menace*," I hissed at him. "I wish you'd never been born. I wish my mom had never met your dad. I wish my mom was still with *my* dad."

Tiger just laughed at me, baring his small, sharp teeth.

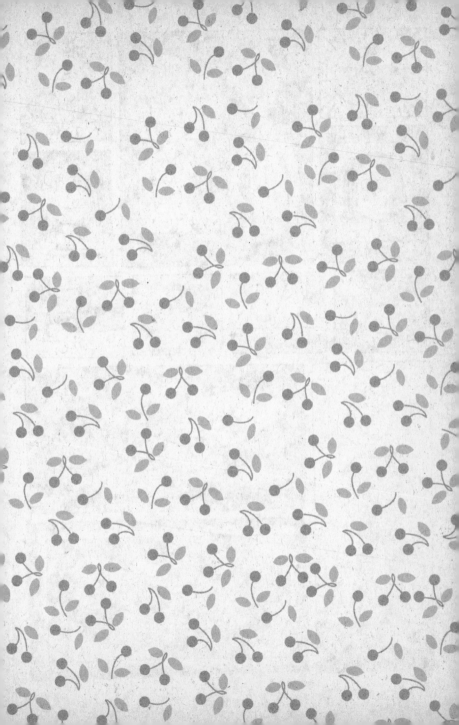

Two

I cheered up just a little bit when I got to school. I love Mrs. Horsefield, my teacher. She gave me a great big smile when I came into the classroom and said, "Happy birthday, Floss." She gave me an iced bun to eat at snack time. She gives each child in her class a bun when it's their birthday, but mine was a special big one with pink icing and a cherry on the top.

Rhiannon was looking at it enviously. She especially likes cherries.

"Want half my birthday bun?" I offered.

"No, it's yours," she said, but she looked hopeful.

I gave her the biggest half of the bun with the cherry.

"Yum!" said Rhiannon, sucking it like a candy. "OK, open your present from me, Floss."

She gave me a pink tissue package tied with pink ribbon, and a special card. I really wanted us to go off together so that I could open my present privately, but Rhiannon seemed to want me to open it with everyone gathered around. She'd given me a proper shop-bought card of two girls hugging. It said at the top in pink lettering, YOU ARE MY BEST FRIEND. I started to be glad that Margot and Judy and all their gang were lurking. *See!* I wanted to say. *Rhiannon's my best friend*.

"Open your present, Floss. You're such a slow-poke," said Margot.

She meant slow*coach*. She's got this irritating habit of talking in a fake American accent and using silly American expressions. She thinks it makes her sound sophisticated but *I* think she sounds plain stupid.

I could make a l-o-n-g list of reasons why I can't stand Margot. She used to be ordinary—in fact I can barely remember her back in the baby classes—but *this* year she's pretending she's all grown up. She's always giggling about boys and sex and pop stars. Judy giggles too. She looks as babyish as me but she's got an older brother who tells her all these really rude jokes. I don't understand most of them. I'm not sure Judy does either.

I was determined to take my time, smoothing the satin ribbon, feeling the little knobs of my present under the pink tissue, trying to guess what it was, but Rhiannon was getting impatient too.

"Hurry up, Floss. I want to see if you like it!"

So I pulled the ribbon off and tore the tissue paper and held my present in my hand. It was a beautiful bracelet made of shiny pink beads.

"They're real rose quartz," said Rhiannon proudly.

"They're really, really lovely," I whispered.

I was scared they must have cost a lot of money. I'd given Rhiannon a bracelet for *her* birthday, but it was just a pink and blue and purple friendship bracelet that I'd made myself. I'd also given her a friendship bracelet braiding set and hoped she'd make one specially for me, but she hadn't got around to it yet.

"It's, like . . . awesome," said Margot. "Let's try it on, Floss."

She snatched it straight out of my hand and wound it around her own wrist.

"It's *my* bracelet!" I said.

"OK then, baby—I'm not *taking* it, I'm just trying it on," said Margot.

"You're trying it on all right," I said grimly.

"You've got, like, the most amazing taste, Rhiannon," said Margot. "Where did you get the bracelet? I wish I had one like that."

Rhiannon started going on about this jewelry shop in some mall, not really trying to help me get my bracelet back. I knew if I asked, Margot would just muck around, making fun of me. I wanted to grab it right back off her horrible bony wrist, but I was frightened of breaking it.

Susan shook her head at me sympathetically. She was standing right at the back, away from the others. She was new and hadn't really made any friends yet. People teased her because she always got the top grades, and she had a silly surname, Potts. Well,

Rhiannon said it was silly. She teased her too. Rhiannon was very good at teasing. (Or very *bad*.) I wished she wouldn't. I begged her not to, but she wouldn't listen. Rhiannon bosses me around but you can't *ever* boss her. But she *is* my best friend.

"Rhiannon," I said desperately.

Rhiannon held out her hand to Margot. "Give us the bracelet back then, Margot."

Margot handed it over reluctantly.

"There," said Rhiannon, winding it around my wrist and doing up the clasp. Her cheeks were the delicate pink of the rose quartz. She was obviously pleased her bracelet had been so admired. "What other presents did you get, Floss? What did your mom give you?"

"Clothes and one of those pull-along case thingies and a kangaroo cuddly toy," I said.

"A cuddly toy! How gross!" said Margot. "Imagine, still playing with teddy bears! What about *dolls*?"

I blushed, holding my breath. Rhiannon had seen my Barbie dolls when she came to play. I prayed she wouldn't tell on me.

"Come on, Rhiannon," I said, taking her by the arm. "I want to tell you this huge secret. Wait till you hear what my mom told me."

"What?" said Rhiannon, licking a little dab of icing off her finger.

"Yeah, what secret?" said Margot. "You always have to create, like, drama, Floss."

"Well, I guess this *is* pretty dramatic," I said, stung.

I decided to show her. I took a deep breath. "We're only going to Australia," I said.

They all stared at me. Rhiannon looked particularly impressed. "Wow, you're going on vacation to *Australia*!"

"Well, *I'm* going on vacation to Orlando," said Margot. "It's got Disney World. Australia hasn't got Disney World."

"It's got the Great Barrier Reef and Bondi Beach and Ayers Rock," said Susan, who had crept to the edge of the group. "Though actually we should call it by its Aboriginal name, Uluru."

"Nobody asked *your* opinion, Swotty Potty," said Rhiannon. She turned to me. "So when are you going on this trip, Floss? Any chance I can come too?"

"I wish you could," I said. I was regretting telling everyone now. It made it seem too real. I had to explain properly. "It's not a vacation. We're going to stay there for six whole months."

"*Really?*"

"Yes," I said miserably. "Only I don't think I want to. I like it here. I'll miss my dad so much. And I'll miss *you*, Rhiannon."

"I'll miss you too!" she said, and she hugged me tight.

I hugged her back.

Margot and Judy made silly noises and stupid comments but I didn't care. Susan hitched her glasses higher up her nose, gave me a wan smile and wandered off.

I felt bad that Rhiannon had called her names. Susan wasn't swotty, she was just smart. I *liked* her. I wanted to be kind to her but I knew if I started speaking to her nicely people would start teasing me too.

I started to think about the Australian school during lesson time. I would be the new girl. What if everyone started picking on me? I was *quite* clever but I didn't ever get the top grade, so they wouldn't tease me for being swotty, would they? I had a perfectly ordinary kind of name, Flora Barnes. My initials didn't spell anything silly or rude. I didn't mind being called Floss or Flossie for a nickname. Rhiannon once or twice called me Flopsy Bunny but that was when she was making a big fuss of me.

I'd never ever find a friend in Australia like Rhiannon.

"You will stay my friend when I'm out in Australia, won't you?" I begged her at lunchtime. "And still be best friends when I come back?"

"Yes, of course," said Rhiannon.

She wasn't really concentrating. She was looking over at Margot and Judy, who were huddled up looking at some stupid pop magazine. They were giggling and kissing their fingers and stroking all their favorite boy bands. Rhiannon giggled too, watching them.

"You won't make friends with Margot when I'm gone, will you?" I said anxiously.

"Give it a rest, Floss! Which part of Australia are you going to, anyway?"

"Sydney."

We went to the library and found a big book about Australia.

"Wow!" said Rhiannon, flipping through pictures of bush and beaches and orange rocks and weird white buildings. "You are so lucky, Floss, it looks fantastic."

It didn't seem like a *real* place. It was all too bright and highly colored and bizarre, like a cartoon. I looked down at the parquet pattern on the library floor and tried to imagine myself going down, down, down, for thousands of miles and then popping out in Australia.

I'd never quite got to grips with geography. I knew the people in Australia weren't *really* upside down, but it still seemed a little odd all the same.

We read a ballad about an Australian called Ned Kelly in our English lesson that afternoon. He was a sheep thief and he ended up getting hanged.

"You'd better not steal any little lambs out in Australia, Floss!" said Rhiannon.

Mrs. Horsefield asked me to read a ballad about a Tragic Maiden out loud. I read it dramatically, making the Tragic Maiden weep and wail. Margot and Judy started snorting with laughter. Even Rhiannon smirked a little. I could feel myself blushing.

"That was very good, Floss," said Mrs. Horsefield kindly. "You're very good at reading aloud."

I'd always liked reading to my mom when she

did the ironing or started cooking, but now she chatted to Steve instead. I'd tried reading aloud to Tiger, but he fussed and fidgeted and kept wanting to turn the page before I'd finished reading all the words.

"Now I want you to have a go at making up your own ballads," said Mrs. Horsefield.

"Does it have to be all silly and old-fashioned and tragic?" said Rhiannon.

"It can be about anything at all, as long as it's in ballad form and tells a story," said Mrs. Horsefield.

Everyone started groaning and scratching their heads and mumbling. Everyone except Susan, sitting by herself in front of us. She was scribbling away like anything.

"Look at Swotty Potty," said Rhiannon. "Trust her. Oh, yuck, I hate this ballad stuff. What have you put so far, Floss?"

> *The girl sat in an airplane,*
> *Watching the clouds with wonder,*
> *Worrying how she'd get on*
> *In her new life Down Under.*

"Down Under what?" said Rhiannon. "That sounds stupid."

"Well, I know. I want to say *in Australia* but I can't find a word to go with it."

"What about . . . *wailier?*" Rhiannon suggested. "*The girl went ever more weepier and wailier because she was missing her best friend Rhiannon now she was in Australia.* There!"

"It doesn't fit, Rhiannon. It's too long."

"Well, say it very quickly then. Now help me, Floss. So far I've got, *There was a pretty young girl called Rhiannon, who joined a circus and got shot out of a cannon.* Hang on, inspiration! *It hurt a lot when she got shot, that poor pretty young girl called Rhiannon.* There! Maybe I'm not so terrible at ballads after all. Even though I don't show off in a swotty way like *some* people." Rhiannon put her foot up and kicked Susan's chair.

Susan jumped and her pen squiggled right across her page. She sighed and tore it out of her notebook. Then she turned around. "If you were a little bit swottier, you'd realize that you've written a limerick, *not* a ballad."

"Who cares what you think, Swotty Potty? You think you're it just because you like writing this poetry nonsense. What have you put anyway?" Rhiannon reached out and snatched Susan's spoiled page.

"Oh, yuck, what kind of silly stuff is that? What's she on about? Listen, Floss."

She walked along the corridors,
Pacing each floorboard with care.

She didn't step on a single crack
But no one knew she was there.
She edged around the wooden fence
Tapping each post in turn,
She counted each one attentively
But she had a lot to learn.
She tried to do math magic,
Adding all the sums in her head,
But all the figures multiplied
Her loneliness and dread . . .

"What kind of weirdo nonsense is that? And it's not a ballad either because it doesn't tell a story, it's just a lot of nonsense about nothing, so ya boo sucks to be you, Swotty."

Rhiannon crumpled the page up and threw it at Susan's head.

Susan turned around and chopped her hand quick on Rhiannon's shins.

"Get off! That *hurt*," said Rhiannon.

"Good," Susan muttered. "Now get your feet off my chair."

"Don't you tell me what to do, Swotty Potty," said Rhiannon. She leaned forward on the edge of her seat, ready to kick Susan hard in the back. But Susan grabbed her by the ankles and pulled. Rhiannon lost her balance. She shot straight off her chair and landed with a thump on the floor. She shrieked.

"Rhiannon! Whatever are you doing! Get up and

stop clowning around," said Mrs. Horsefield.

"Ouch!" said Rhiannon. "I think I've broken my elbow. *And* my wrist. And my bum hurts horribly."

"I think you'll live," said Mrs. Horsefield. "It serves you right for messing about."

"It wasn't *my* fault, Mrs. Horsefield," said Rhiannon. She paused. We had a strict code about tattling. "*Someone* pulled me right off my chair."

Susan kept very still.

"Hmm," said Mrs. Horsefield. She came over and felt Rhiannon's arm carefully. Rhiannon moaned and whimpered.

"I think you're making a fuss about nothing, Rhiannon," said Mrs. Horsefield briskly. Then she paused. She was looking at Susan now. "However, it's very silly and very dangerous to pull anyone off their chair—even if they're being incredibly provoking. I'm surprised at you, Susan."

Susan said nothing but her face went very red.

I felt terrible. We'd gotten poor Susan into trouble.

I couldn't concentrate on my ballad anymore. I kept thinking about Susan's. I wondered if she really went around counting things in her head to make everything turn out all right. Only they didn't ever turn out right. We were all horrible to her. Especially Rhiannon.

I edged closer to Rhiannon. "Do you think we should maybe tell Mrs. Horsefield it was our fault, because we snatched Susan's ballad and made fun of

her?" I said. I delicately said "we" instead of "you" —
but Rhiannon was still outraged.

"Are you *joking*?" she hissed. "She really hurt me!
My arm aches awfully. I bet it *is* broken, or at the very
least badly sprained. Swotty Potty deserves to get into
trouble. She's turned into mad Psycho Girl, out to get
me."

"Oh, Rhiannon, you know that's not true," I said
anxiously.

"Are you calling me a liar?" said Rhiannon. She sat
up straight and looked me right in the eyes. "Whose
side are you on, Floss? Do you want to break friends
and go off with Swotty Potty and write sappy poems
together?"

"No! No, of course not. You're my best friend,
you know that."

"Yes, and I gave you the bracelet with real rose
quartz stones even though I really wanted it for
myself. But I gave it to you because that's what best
friends are for. Even though you're not even going to
be here soon, as you'll be flying off to Australia."

"But I don't want to go! You know I don't. I'd give
anything to stay," I said.

"Well, why don't you then?" said Rhiannon.

"Why don't I what?" I said, muddled.

"Stay here. Kick up such a big fuss that they have
to change their minds."

I thought about it. "I'm not really very good at
making a big fuss," I said.

"Yes, I know, you're hopeless." Rhiannon sighed irritably. "You're so gutless, Floss. You just try to be nice to everyone."

I felt wounded but I reached out and hooked my little finger around Rhiannon's.

"Ouch, watch out, that's my sore arm! What are you doing?"

"Trying to make friends properly. Because you're my best friend in all the world and I love my beautiful bracelet and I really will try not to go to Australia. Anyway, we probably won't be going until summer vacation and that's ages away, so let's not even think about it now." I hung onto Rhiannon's finger and she grinned at last and hooked her own little finger properly around mine and we vowed to make friends, make friends, never ever break friends.

Susan had her head bent over her notebook, writing her ballad out all over again. Her soft brown hair fell forward, showing the white nape of her neck. She sniffed once or twice, as if she might be trying not to cry.

I still felt very bad about her, but there was no way I could comfort her, not in front of Rhiannon.

* * *

I showed off my rose quartz bracelet to Mom when I got home from school. She was clearing out the kitchen cupboards, while Tiger bashed saucepans at her feet.

"Oh, trust Rhiannon and her mother. They always

have to show off how much money they've got," said Mom. "Hey, did you tell Rhiannon about Australia? I bet she was envious."

"Yes, she was. Ever so. Oh, Mom, I'm going to miss her so much."

"You sappy old thing," said Mom, giving me a hug. "I think it'll do you good to make some new friends. You let Rhiannon boss you around too much."

"I'd like to be friends with Susan, this new girl, but Rhiannon hates her. What do you think I should do, Mom? Should I try to be nice to Susan even if it makes Rhiannon mad at me?"

"I don't know, lovey. It's all a bit pointless, isn't it, seeing as we'll be in Sydney in two weeks' time."

I stared at Mom. "In two *weeks*?" I said. "Why didn't you tell me we were going that *quick*?"

"Quick*ly*, Flora—do speak properly. There didn't seem any point in telling you earlier, you'd have just got all worked up and excited and rushed around telling everyone."

I thought hard. "Telling *Dad*, you mean," I said.

"Yes, well, it's not really anything to do with him."

"He's my *dad*!"

"Yes, I know. Calm down. Don't shout like that. Honestly! If you must know, I was trying to be tactful to your dad. Steve's done so brilliantly to be given the chance to get the Australian branch up and running. He'll be earning twice the money—I just can't believe it! It felt like rubbing your dad's face in it because he's such a failure."

"Dad's not a failure," I said fiercely.

Mom cupped my face with her hands. "Oh, come on, Floss. I know you love your dad and he's a *good* dad in lots of ways. He's a very sweet, kind man, and I'd never deliberately bad-mouth him to anyone—but he's useless when it comes to business, even you must admit that. He's in debt up to his eyeballs and that awful café is fast running out of customers. I don't know why he doesn't call it a day and sell up altogether."

"Dad wouldn't *ever* sell the café!" I said.

"Yes. Well. Goodness knows what else he could do! Anyway, I just thank God *I* don't have to slave there anymore," said Mom. "Oh, Floss, isn't it wonderful!" She kissed me on the tip of my nose. "Aren't we lucky girls! In two weeks' time we'll be stepping out of that plane into glorious sunshine." She threw old rice packets and sauce bottles and jam jars with a *thump thump thump* into the garbage can as she spoke. Tiger accompanied her on saucepan percussion.

"You've got some serious sorting out to do yourself, Floss," said Mom. "We're going to put most of our stuff in storage. There's no point keeping any old trash though. It's time you chucked a lot of your old toys out."

"I suppose I could throw away my Barbies," I said.

"That's the spirit! *And* some of those old teddy bears. We'll make a start on your room tomorrow."

"I'll be at Dad's."

"Well, I'll do it for you. Now, you'd better get dressed up for our meal out. You can wear your new birthday clothes if you like. You get in the bathroom while I change Tiger."

"He's not coming too, is he?" I said.

Mom looked at me. "What do you think we're going to do with him, Floss? Leave him here and tell him to heat up his own milk and tuck himself up in bed?"

"Oh, ha-ha, Mom. Why can't he have a babysitter like when you and Steve go out?"

"Because this is a family outing, silly. Now go and get ready, Birthday Girl."

I thought about Mom's words as I wriggled out of my school uniform and put on my new jeans and T-shirt. I couldn't ever have a *real* family outing anymore. It was all so easy-peasy when we were just *our* family, Mom and Dad and me. But now when I went out with Dad, Mom was missing—and when I went out with Mom, Dad was missing and I was stuck with Steve and Tiger instead.

I stared out of my bedroom window down into the garden. Steve had landscaped it himself and made all these pretty flowerbeds and a pergola and a pond with goldfish, but now that Tiger was old enough to climb out of his stroller it was more like his own personal adventure park. OK, I had my lovely swing in one corner, but Tiger had his own small swing *and* his slide *and* his pedal car *and* his sandpit *and* his baby bouncer *and* his toddler gym climbing frame.

It was more like Tiger's birthday celebration than mine at TGI Friday's. He sat in lordly fashion in his high chair, giggling and kicking his legs whenever any of the waitresses went by. They all ruffled his silly sticking-up hair and tickled him under his chin, cooing and clucking. No one told him off when he ate his fries with his fingers or spilled his drink.

Mom ordered a special birthday cake for me with sparklers. Tiger screamed and squirmed so desperately to see them that they held them in front of him for ages. The sparklers had stopped sparkling by the time they put the plate on the table. I felt as if all my sparkles had gone out too.

I knew I shouldn't be jealous of my little baby brother. He didn't commandeer all the attention *deliberately*. It was very annoying all the same.

That was what was so great about my weekends with Dad. It was just Dad and me. He treated me like his very special little princess.

Three

My second birthday was on Saturday. I went to my dad's. Mom always took me. She usually stayed a little while and had a cup of coffee in the café. Dad often put a whole plate of cakes in front of her—jam doughnuts, apple turnovers, apricot Danish pastries, all her old favorites.

Mom could never be tempted to have so much as a mouthful. She'd just shake her head and pat her flat tummy. Sometimes she couldn't help looking at *Dad*'s tummy and shaking her head. She often gave Dad lectures about my food, saying she didn't want me eating any greasy café fry-ups, especially not his special french fry sandwiches, called chip butties. And I had to have lots of fresh fruit and vegetables and only one small cake at tea time. Dad and I would nod solemnly—and then wink at each other when she was gone.

Mom didn't drive me over to Dad's this Saturday. Steve did.

"Why can't you take me, Mom?" I said.

"I've got too much to do, Floss. I'm busy, busy, busy," said Mom.

She was rushing around in her jeans and an old flannel shirt of Steve's, sorting our things into three big piles: TAKE, STORE and CHUCK. Tiger was crawling around on his hands and knees, playing with the piles, draping old tights around his shoulders like a feather boa and waving a saucepan as a hat.

"Let's put Tiger in the CHUCK pile," I said.

"Oh, ha-ha, very droll," said Mom. "Go on then, off you go to your dad's."

"I still don't see why you can't take me, same as usual," I muttered, trailing after Steve.

But it wasn't the same as usual. I knew perfectly well why Mom didn't want to take me. She didn't want to face my dad when he found out about Australia. It was so mean of her. I sat in the back of Steve's fancy company car and glared at the back of his pink neck. He had a very short haircut. Mom said it was cute and loved running her fingers through it. I thought it looked plain silly. Who wants designer stubble on their *head*? Steve was wearing one of his special weekend sport shirts with very short sleeves, showing off his big muscles. He worked out at the gym most mornings before work.

Mom had joined the gym now too. She even took Tiger to a baby gym class, which was *totally* nuts.

Tiger crawled around at way too rapid a pace as it was. He was learning to climb up onto beds and wriggle right into corners. He needed to be restrained, not encouraged.

Steve started making general chitchat in the car. He never knew quite what to say to me. Ditto me him. He asked if I was looking forward to going to Australia. I said, "Mmm." He said wouldn't it be fabulous living in an exciting city like Sydney. I said, "Mmm." We gave up after that. Steve switched the radio on and we both listened to music. Steve hummed along. I kept quiet. I only do sing-songs with my dad. They played a Kylie song on the radio.

"*She's* Australian," said Steve.

"Mmm," I said.

"Maybe we'll all start talking Australian. *Isn't that right, cobber?*" said Steve in the most truly terrible Australian accent.

I didn't respond with so much as an "Mmm."

I needed to concentrate on what I was going to say to my dad. When should I tell him? I tried rehearsing the right words inside my head, but it was like when your computer screen freezes. I couldn't think up anything at all.

Steve turned into our road and pulled up outside the café. I looked up at the sign: HARLIE'S CAFÉ. It's named after my dad. It isn't called Harlie like the big motorcycles; he's Charlie, but the big *C* fell off ages ago. Mom always calls Dad a Right Charlie, like it's some kind of insult.

The café used to get lots of customers. My dad's chip butties were especially famous. Everyone came to eat them. Lots and lots of guys came from this big building site. The café was always crowded out at lunchtime because all the high school students spent their lunch money at our place. But then everyone got into this Healthy Eating and the students had to stay at school and eat salads. The guys finished building the big offices and moved on. The office workers had sandwiches and wraps sent in. They didn't want fry-ups and chip butties. We still had a few lunchtime regulars, but then a big pizza takeout opened up just down the street and they started going there instead.

Dad had lots of spare time to spruce up the café now but he never seemed to get around to it. The paint was peeling and the window was dirty. Some boy had written a rude word on it with his finger. The menu had slipped sideways and one of the limp curtains was drooping off its rail and someone had thrown their takeout pizza boxes right by the doorstep.

"Poor old Charlie," said Steve. "The café's starting to look like a real dump. Is he still getting any customers?"

"He's getting heaps and heaps," I said. "My dad's the greatest cook in the world. He's going to get his own big restaurant one day. I bet he'll get to be one of those famous chefs on television, with his own program and his own cookbooks."

"Mmm," said Steve.

"You wait. He's going to be *heaps* more successful than you are, Steve," I said, and I grabbed my bag and shot out of the car.

I hoped he wouldn't tell Mom I'd been cheeky. I dashed into the café, the bell ringing wildly. It was almost empty, the place settings undisturbed on the blue-and-white check tablecloths. There were just the three regulars.

Billy the Chip was eating a chip butty, hunched up over the table, listening intently to the sports channel on his crackly little transistor radio. Billy the Chip came and had a chip butty every single day, though he made his own chip butties every evening in his chip van outside the railway station. Dad used to go to his chip van when he was a little boy. Dad's *dad* went to his chip van when *he* was a boy. Billy the Chip had had his chip van forever. He was very old and very thin and very gray and he walked very slowly because he had to take it easy. He'd sleep late, eat his butty at my dad's, spend his afternoon in the betting shop, drive his van to the station, and then make french fries all evening until the pubs were closed and the last train had gone.

Old Ron sat at the next table eating his bacon and eggs, still in his raincoat and cap even though it was boiling hot in the café. Old Ron was old, but nowhere near as old as Billy the Chip. He nodded and winked at me, but as he had a nervous tic and nodded and winked continuously, I wasn't sure whether he was greeting me or not.

Miss Davis sat right at the other end, as far away from the two old men as she could manage. She saw them nearly every day in the café but she never spoke to them, or even glanced in their direction. She sat with her back to them, sipping her cup of tea. She had her pull-along bag by her side. She kept one hand on it, as if she were scared it would wheel itself off independently. It was lumpy with stale bread and birdseed. She fed all the pigeons in the town every morning, stopping off at my dad's café for refreshment halfway around.

"Hey, Dad!" I called.

He peered out of the little hatch in the kitchen and then came running. "How's my little birthday sweetheart?" he said, giving me a great big chip-smelling hug. He whirled me around and around so that my legs flew out behind me.

"Mind my bag," Miss Davis snapped, though we weren't anywhere near it.

"There's a horse called Birthday Girl in the big race at three thirty," said Billy the Chip. "I'll have a little bet and if I get lucky, I'll buy you a special birthday present, Flossie."

"Birthday, is it? Can't even remember when mine is," said Old Ron.

I wasn't sure whether he was joking or not. Old

Ron didn't seem too sure either. Still, he gave me a very fluffy toffee out of his raincoat pocket as a birthday treat. Dad thanked him very much but mouthed *Don't eat it!* at me. I said I'd save it for later.

"Oh, well, I suppose I'd better find you something too," said Miss Davis, scrabbling inside her bag.

I wondered if she was going to give me a packet of birdseed, but she found her purse and gave me twenty pence. I thanked her very politely because I knew weird old ladies like Miss Davis think twenty pence is a lot of money.

Dad smiled at me gratefully and then led me into the kitchen. He'd maneuvered one of the café tables into the corner and decorated it with tinsel and balloons and hung the Christmas tree lights up above. There was a silver place mat, and little silver bows on the knife and fork, and a banner with HAPPY BIRTHDAY PRINCESS in Dad's wobbly printing.

"Oh, Dad!" I said, and I started crying.

"Hey, hey, hey! No tears, sweetheart!" said Dad. "Now, sit yourself down on your special throne and open your presents."

He thrust three big red packages at me, and one little limp brown paper package tied with string.

"That one's from Grandma," said Dad. He rubbed his lip. "Don't get too excited."

I squeezed the soft brown paper. "I think she's knitted me something again," I said.

Grandma's presents were generally hand-knitted.

They were made especially for me but she couldn't quite keep up with how old I was. She knitted me weeny toddler-size pink sweaters with rabbits and ducks and teddy bears on the dinky pockets.

"It feels even littler this time," I said, sighing.

"Maybe it's knitted underwear!" said Dad. "Don't worry, I promise I won't make you wear it."

Grandma's present wasn't knitted underwear. It was almost as bad. She'd knitted me two droopy woolly animals, one gray, one sludge, with little blobby sewn eyes. It was hard working out which species they were. The gray one had big ears and a very long droopy nose. The sludge one had small ears and a tail.

"I think this one's an elephant," I said, fingering the gray one. Then I looked at the sludge creature. "Do you think this one's a dog or a cat?"

"Looks like it could be either," said Dad. "Perhaps it's a dat or a cog."

"Dad! What am I going to say to Grandma when I write a thank-you letter?"

"Just say thank you for the lovely woolly, cuddly toys," said Dad. "It doesn't do to specify. I once thanked her for a stripy scarf, though privately I thought it was much too small. It turned out it was a special knitted tie. Oh, well. She means well, bless her. Now, open your other presents, Princess."

The three red packages all said *Happy Christmas* in curly gold writing.

"Sorry, pet, I didn't have any proper birthday wrapping paper," said Dad. "Come on then, open them up. I'm dying to see what you think of them!"

The first package contained a homemade silver paper crown studded with gummy jewels. Silver glitter sprinkled my curls when I put it on, but Dad said it just made my hair look extra specially sparkly.

"You look like a real birthday princess with your crown on," said Dad. He bowed to me. Then he curtsied too, which made me giggle.

The second package contained a pair of silver high-heeled shoes.

"Real high heels, Dad! Wow!" I said.

They were secondhand ladies' shoes, much too big for me, but I didn't care. I kicked off my new sneakers and stuck my feet in my special silver shoes.

"Oh, dear, they don't really fit. Don't twist your ankle, for God's sake," said Dad. "You'd better just wear them indoors until you grow into them. Open the big package then."

It was a long pink satin dress with puff sleeves and rosebuds around the bodice. It had once been somebody's bridesmaid's dress. They were quite a big somebody. The dress hung off me and trailed down onto the floor, even when I was wearing my new high heels.

"Oh, dear, it's much too big," said Dad.

"No, it isn't. It's lovely! I've always wanted a really long special dress," I said quickly.

"And the shoes are too big too," said Dad.

"But you don't get high heels my size. I can always stuff them with socks or something. I feel like a real princess in them, Dad," I said.

"You're *my* princess," said Dad, grinning at me. "Right, I'd better prepare a royal feast for my little mini-queen."

I hadn't been able to eat any breakfast at Mom's. I wasn't sure I had the appetite for one of my dad's famous fry-ups either. My tummy was still so tense because I had to tell him about Australia. I decided I should do it there and then, the minute he made me my breakfast, so it was all over and done with, and then Dad would understand why I didn't feel like eating.

But Dad was so sweet serving me a plate with a funny food face—french fries for hair, two mush-rooms for eyes, a sausage for a nose, a curly piece of bacon for a smiley mouth and a spoonful of baked beans on either side as rosy cheeks. I couldn't spoil his fun. I shut up and ate my face as best I could, vowing to myself I'd tell him at lunchtime.

But at lunchtime a whole crowd of soccer fans came barging into the café for chip butties before the match. Dad was kept so busy that I couldn't stop him in his tracks with my news. He made the fries and but-tered the rolls and I served them and took the money.

Lots of the guys were in a good mood and left a big tip for the "weeny waitress."

I tried to give Dad the money but he wouldn't hear of it.

"It's yours, Floss. You've earned it fair and square. We make a great little team, you and me."

"When I leave school we'll have our own fancy restaurant, you and me, eh, Dad? Chez Charlie and Floss, yeah?"

It was one of our favorite games, but today Dad just shook his head sadly.

"I don't think you should tie yourself down to your old dad, little Floss," he said. "I think I'd just cramp your style. I'm hardly a success story."

"Yes you *are,* Dad. Look, I'm sure the café will pick up soon. Look how busy we've been this lunchtime."

"Ten chip butties aren't going to change my luck, sweetheart," said Dad. He took a deep breath. "Floss, maybe I should tell you something . . ."

I took a deep breath too. "Dad, maybe I should tell *you* something . . ."

We looked at each other.

"Is it bad news?" said Dad.

"Yes," I said.

"Mine's bad news too. But we can't have bad news on a birthday! We'll tell our sorry tales tomorrow, OK, sweetheart? We've got more important things to do today—like making your birthday cake!"

We only had a couple of customers for cups of tea all afternoon so we could concentrate on the cake. Dad let me take a turn mixing it, with a dish towel tucked around me so my princess dress wouldn't get splattered. He let me scrape out the bowl afterward. I even *licked* it. Dad just laughed.

The cake made the whole café smell beautiful when it was baking in the oven. Dad and I played catch with my birthday balloons and then he played loud rock music and we did a birthday dance. I kept falling out of my silver high heels so I took them off my feet and put them on my hands and made them do a tap dance on each tabletop.

Then the cake came out of the oven all golden brown and beautiful. We mixed up the buttercream in a bowl while the cake was cooking, and then spread it in the middle like a sandwich, with a layer of raspberry jam.

"Now we'll do the icing on the top," said Dad. "What decoration do you fancy? Rainbow sprinkles? Little silver balls? M&M's? Glacé cherries? Crystallized roses?"

I thought hard, pondering each choice.

"*All* of them?" said Dad, grinning.

"Yes, *please!*" I said.

"OK, there you have it," said Dad. "R-i-g-h-t! The Cake Decorator Extraordinaire will get cracking, assisted by the Birthday Princess herself."

We studded the cake with silver balls and sweets, sprinkling and dabbing and daubing until the entire cake was covered, with scarcely any room for candles.

"Shall we light your candles now and have a slice?" said Dad eagerly.

"You bet," I said.

Dad lit each candle, singing *"Happy Birthday"* very loudly and off-key. Then I closed my eyes and wished as hard as I could. *Please, please, please let me stay seeing Dad somehow!* I blew so hard I felt my chest would collapse. I opened my eyes—and every snuffed candle burst into flames again.

I blinked at them, bewildered. I blew again. They flickered, they faded—and then flamed.

"Blow a bit harder, Floss," said Dad.

"I *am*," I said, struggling, nearly in tears. I so wanted my wish to come true.

"Hey, hey, don't get upset, pet. It's only silly old Dad having a bit of fun. They're just joke candles, look." Dad blew them out too, and they instantly relit themselves.

"It's so you can have *lots* of birthday wishes," he said. "I'll make a wish too." He shut his eyes and muttered under his breath.

"What are you wishing for, Dad?"

"I can't tell you or it won't come true," said Dad, giving my nose a tiny flick. "Come on, here's the cake knife. Let's have a huge hunk each, eh?"

We chomped our cake. Whenever one of Dad's customers drifted in, we gave them a slice too. There was still a semicircle of cake left when Dad locked up the shop.

We usually cuddled up on the sofa and watched an old video on TV. Dad hadn't got around to buying a DVD player yet. In fact the television itself was on the blink. You often had to hit it before it would work. So instead, Dad read to me and I read to him or we played funny paper games like Tic-Tac-Toe and Hangman and Battleships.

"We'll sofa-slouch tomorrow," said Dad. "We've got a hot date tonight, Birthday Girl. Get your jacket."

"Where are we going, Dad?"

He winked at me. "There's a traveling funfair up on the common this week."

"Oh, wow!"

Mom never let me go to fairs. She said they were horrible noisy, rough places. She said she couldn't stand all the fried-onion food smells, they were a horrible reminder of the café. Mom and Steve took me to Chessington World of Adventures and Thorpe Park and Alton Towers. They all cost a lot of money so Mom said you didn't get riffraff. But I wasn't with Mom, I was with Dad. We both *loved* fairs.

"Better change out of your fancy silver shoes, sweetheart. Fairs can be muddy places," said Dad.

I knew it would be sensible to change out of my princess dress too, but Dad said quickly, "No, no, you can still stay a birthday princess in your frock, sweetie."

I knew perfectly well I looked like an idiot in my secondhand bridesmaid gown, my denim jacket, and my new sneakers. Still, I knew Dad wanted me to act like I couldn't bear to take my dress off because it was so special. So I wore the entire bizarre outfit, silver paper crown and all.

I prayed I wouldn't meet anyone from school at the fair. Especially Margot and Judy!

Four

The fair was crowded. There were quite a lot of big boys milling about, the sort Mom would call riffraff. Dad put his arm around me.

"You stick close to your old dad, sweetheart," he said. "Now, what shall we go on first?"

"The carousel!" I said.

"Good choice!" said Dad. "Come along then, Princess, select your steed."

Dad let me take my time, circling the carousel so that I could see every single horse and work out which one I liked the best. I spotted a snow-white horse with a pink mane and tail and a big pink smiley mouth. Her name was written in magenta around her neck. She was called Pearl.

I ran for her the minute the carousel slowed down, but it was difficult in my long bridesmaid dress. Another girl elbowed me out of the way and clambered on first.

"Never mind," said Dad. "We'll wait."

So we waited, and at long last the carousel slowed down again and this time *Dad* ran too, and he got to Pearl and saved her for me.

"You ride with me, Dad," I said.

I hitched up my skirts and sat in front of the golden butterscotch pole coming out of Pearl's back, and Dad sat behind me, his arms around my waist. We paid our money and the lovely old music started up and we rode round and round until the whole fairground was just a mosaic of colored lights. I wished Pearl would kick her silver hooves and rear up off her stand and gallop away with us forever.

"Would you like another ride on Pearl, Princess?" Dad asked.

"Oh, please!"

So we went round and round and round again, and when we at last got off Dad let me pat Pearl's nose and stroke her long mane.

"She's so pretty," I said. "I just love her pink mane. It matches my dress, Dad, look."

"We'd better make sure our refreshments match your dress too," said Dad. "Candy for my Floss!"

He led me to a candyfloss stall. It was decorated with roses, and a great pink teddy bear in a frilly dress dangled from the awning.

"Mom never ever lets me have cotton candy because it's so bad for my teeth," I said.

"You can give your teeth an extra thorough brush tonight," said Dad, and he nodded at the big blond lady in the candyfloss van. "We'll have one each please. *My* teeth are pretty decayed already."

"I wouldn't say that," said the candyfloss lady. "You've got a lovely smile, sir."

Dad gave her a big grin then. I grinned too. I love it when people like my dad.

"You take after your dad, darling," said the candyfloss lady. "You're looking very gorgeous in that pretty pink frock. Have you been a bridesmaid?"

"No, it's her birthday. She's my birthday princess," said Dad.

"*Dad!*" I said, feeling silly.

"Aah, isn't that lovely. Well, we'd better make you an extra big birthday special."

I watched, fascinated, as she poured sugar into the middle of her metal cauldron and then set it spinning. Wisps of cotton candy formed as if by magic. She took a stick and twirled it around and around until it bore an enormous pink fluffy cloud of candyfloss.

"Here you are, sweetheart," she said, handing it over.

"Oh, yum!" I said.

I held it in awe, approaching it gingerly, not quite sure how to bite into it. Then someone behind jostled me and my nose went deep into the pink fluffy cloud and stuck there.

"Watch out, mate! Mind my little girl," said Dad, turning around.

It wasn't just one mate. There were six or seven big lads, all of them holding cans of beer. They were strutting around, saying stupid things. Very, very rude things. They didn't take any notice of Dad at all.

"Give us one of them big scoops of peanuts," the biggest guy said to the candyfloss lady.

"Yeah, one for me too, I've got the munchies."

"I'll have popcorn—the big carton," said another.

"You wait your turn, boys. I'm serving this gentleman," said the candyfloss lady.

"Here, we don't wait turns. We tell you, you serve us—*get it*?" said the biggest.

"This is my stall, and I don't have to serve anyone, so you can all get lost—*get it*?" said the candyfloss lady.

They paused, taking it in.

"You don't talk to me like that," said the big guy. Then he called her a terribly rude word.

"Don't you dare bad-mouth the lady," said Dad. "You need your mouth washed out with soap, lad."

"You need your mouth shut, you fat jerk," said the boy, and he punched Dad straight in the face.

Dad hit him back, but then all his friends jumped in. I screamed and someone shoved me and I ended up flat on my face in the mud. I lay there, stunned. There was a lot of shouting, a lot of struggling.

I lifted my head. "Help! They're hurting my dad!" I yelled.

"It's OK, sweetheart. Your dad's OK now. Here, let me help you up, you poor little darling." It was the candyfloss lady herself, sitting me up gently and wiping my sticky face. My silver crown fell off, all torn and crumpled.

I peered around desperately for my dad. I saw a lot of figures in the distance—big burly guys dragging the horrible drunk lads away from the fair.

"They're not taking my dad away too, are they?" I said.

"No, no, of course not. He's over there, by my stall, see?"

Dad was leaning against the stall, with a big fairground guy offering him a cloth for his bleeding lip.

"Don't give him that dirty old rag, Saul! Here, mind the stall for ten minutes while I get these two properly cleaned up in my caravan," said the candyfloss lady.

She helped me stand up, tutting sympathetically when she saw the state of my dress.

"Dear, oh, dear! Still, it's not ripped—I wish I could say the same for your poor dad's jeans! I'm sure all that mud will wash off easily enough. Did those idiots hurt you, lovey?"

"I don't *think* so," I said. I still couldn't understand what had happened. One minute they'd all been hitting my dad, and then the next they were all limping away, escorted by the fairground guys.

"Dad! Dad!" I said, stumbling over to him. "Dad, did you beat them all up, those horrible lads?"

Dad laughed and then winced, because it stretched his sore lip. "*Me?*" he said. "I was blooming useless, Floss."

"No, you weren't. You were wonderful, sticking up for me like that," said the candyfloss lady.

"He stuck up for me too," I said.

"Yes, he's very gallant and brave, your dad," said the candyfloss lady. "Now, you two come with me and we'll get you cleaned up properly."

"So how come they all stopped fighting?" I asked, as we followed her in and out of the stalls and trailers to the circle of caravans.

"Our guys keep an eye out for hassle," said the candyfloss lady. "One hint of trouble and they all come running. And they're tough lads too."

"I'll say," said Dad. "Especially the one with the fair hair and all the skull rings, the one who gave me the rag for my nose. He felled three of the boys with one blow!"

"Ah, Saul. He's *my* lad," said the candyfloss lady. "He's a real softie, especially with the girls, but you don't want to get on the wrong side of him."

"I'm certainly glad he was on *my* side," said Dad.

"Right, this is my van," said the candyfloss lady.

It was a beautiful bright pink, with red roses carefully painted above the door.

"I love the roses," said Dad.

"That's my name. Rose. It was my mom's name and my gran's. They claimed we were related to the fortune-teller Gypsy Rose. They used to read palms and peer into the crystal ball and all that jazz."

"Can you tell fortunes?" I asked excitedly.

"Oh, I can read the tea leaves with the best of them," she said, smiling at me. "Come on, up the steps."

We climbed the neat golden ladder and went through the pink door.

"Ooooh!" I said.

It was the most wonderful magical strange room ever. The inside walls were bright pink too, with lots of paintings of flowers and country cottages and little children in nighties. Great glittery glass mirrors doubled and tripled all the images, so you weren't quite sure what was real and what was reflection. There was a big red velvet sofa with needlework cushions, and a polished table with a lace cloth, and a cabinet in one corner containing lots of china crinolined ladies. A gold clock ticked and tocked on a sideboard, with a big china dog on either side.

"It's so beautiful!" I said.

"I'm glad you like it, duckie," said Rose, going into her tiny kitchen and running water into a red bowl.

"How come you've got running water?" said Dad.

"Oh, we get it piped wherever we pitch up."

"So do you travel all over the country?"

"Well—just the southeast. We set up at a new site each week during the summer." She got a cloth and started washing my face and hands. She did it very gently, going carefully around my eyes and nose and mouth, not scrubbing splish-splosh the way some grown-ups do. Then she started dabbing at the stains on my dress.

I had another peer around the beautiful red room while she was mopping me.

"How come all your lovely ornaments and pictures don't get broken when you move on to the next site?" I asked.

"I'm magic. I just go *zap!*"—she waved her long silver fingernails—"and fix them to the walls with my occult powers."

I blinked at her. So did Dad.

Rose burst out laughing. "No, of course I don't! I bundle them all up carefully in Bubble Wrap each time," she said.

"And where do you sleep? I can't see a bed anywhere," I said.

"Floss, stop being so nosy," said Dad. "It's rude to ask so many questions."

"I don't mind a bit," said Rose. "See that sofa. You lift the seat part—and there's my bed, all lovely and cozy, neatly stowed out of sight."

"What about Saul? Where's his bed?"

"He's got his own trailer now. He's way too big to share with his old mom."

"What about Saul's dad?" said my dad.

Rose chuckled. "Now who's being nosy!" she said. "Oh, he cleared off a long time ago. Last spotted with a tassel-twirling circus girl half his age."

"Oh. Right. I'm sorry," said Dad, going a bit pink.

"Don't be sorry, dear. I like my independence. There!" She held out my pink skirts. They were wet, but nearly all the mud had come out.

"You've done an expert job there," said Dad.

"I've had enough practice! My Saul used to come back covered in mud every single time he went out to play," said Rose.

She rinsed out the bowl and got a clean cloth. "Now, sir, let's sort you out."

"I'm not a sir! I'm Charlie," said Dad. "And this is my little girl, Floss."

"How do you do, Charlie. OK, let's get you cleaned up properly. That little toerag gave you a nasty split lip as well as a bloody nose. No kissing for you for a day or two!"

"The chance would be a fine thing," said Dad.

She mopped Dad *very* gently. Dad can be a bit of a baby when he cuts himself, but he didn't wince once, not even when she dabbed his cuts with anti-septic.

"Now, what about your legs? Are they cut too?"

she said, peering at the great rips in the knees of Dad's jeans.

"Just skinned. They're fine," said Dad.

"Oh, you're such a stoical chap," said Rose. "Still, it must have been a nasty shock. I think we could both do with a nip of brandy, don't you?"

She poured two drinks in pretty crimson glasses, and she gave me a lovely lemonade in a green glass goblet.

"White wine, madam?" she said, serving it with a flourish.

"Delicious!" I said. "But could I possibly have a cup of tea too?"

"You don't like tea, Floss!" said Dad.

"No—but I want Rose to read the tea leaves."

"Well, to tell you the truth, lovey, I've only got tea bags in my caddy. But I'll read your palm, how about that?"

"Oh, yes, please!"

I thrust it at her eagerly. She sat down beside me and took my palm in hers, looking at it intently.

"Aaah!" she said.

"What? Oh, please, what is it?"

"Rose is going to tell you that you bite your nails and you've just had a birthday and you're the apple of your dad's eye!" said Dad, laughing.

"Oh, *Dad*," I said.

"Yes, shush, Dad," said Rose. She delicately traced the lines on my hand. "Now, this line is broken—

which tells me you've had a little heartache, and you've felt torn in two—is that right?"

"Oh, yes!"

"Don't worry though, darling, I can see very happy times ahead. Yes, there are going to be a few changes in store."

"I don't think I like changes," I said. "I've had too many."

"No, no, these are good changes, you wait and see."

"What are they?" I said warily.

"Ah, that's for you to find out in the future!"

"Can't you give me a hint or two?"

"They're changes to do with your home, your family, your friends—"

"Oh, no! Is Rhiannon going to break friends with me and go off with Margot?"

"You wait and see." She gently tapped me under the chin. "Don't look so worried. You wait—there are all sorts of signs and portents. This is your lucky break, Floss."

"Is it mine too? I could certainly do with my luck changing," said Dad.

"Do you want me to read your palm too?"

"Mmm, maybe not! I'm not sure I'd like what I heard," said Dad, downing his drink. "Well, you've been so kind to us, Rose. We'd better not keep you away from your candyfloss stall any longer. Come on, Floss, it's ages past your bedtime."

"Well, if you change your mind, come back and find me," said Rose, smiling at him. "Now, the least we can do is give you both a free ride on something. What do you fancy? The Ferris Wheel? The Waltzer? The Rotunda?"

Dad looked at me. I looked at him.

"Another go on Pearl?" said Dad.

"Oh, please!"

So we had one more magical ride on the merry-go-round. Pearl galloped round and round on her silver hooves, pink mane and tail flying. We flew with her, and as the hurdy-gurdy music played, I sang in my head, *Our luck is changing, our luck is changing, our luck is changing!*

Five

I decided to tell Dad that night, but I was too tired to do more than scrub candyfloss off my face, brush my teeth, and then collapse into bed.

I decided to tell Dad over breakfast instead, but he made special croissants, putting a funny black beret on his head and hanging a string of plastic onions around his neck, pretending to be French. I couldn't tell him when he was prancing around singing "Frère Jacques" and calling me his little cabbage.

I decided I'd tell Dad before lunch, but we went to the park and fed the ducks all the stale bread left over from the café. There was so much, the ducks had a veritable banquet, quacking appreciatively whenever I shook the bags and it started snowing chunks of bread. I didn't want to spoil their fun—or ours.

I decided to tell Dad during lunch, but he sat me down in the café and pretended I was a very special customer. He served me a funny little salad in the shape of a clown's face—lettuce hair, hard-boiled egg eyes, and a cherry tomato nose.

"There! Tell your mom I give you ultrahealthy grub," said Dad. "OK, now for dessert."

It wasn't quite as healthy. Dad garnished big slices of birthday cake with whipped cream and ice cream and raspberry sauce, making a totally heavenly birthday sundae. I couldn't possibly spoil it by blurting out my news.

We were so full afterward we flopped at either end of the sofa and watched our ancient old video of *The Railway Children*. It jumps around a lot and sometimes gets stuck but we know it so well it's not a problem. We chanted along with it half the time. At the very end, Bobbie goes to the station and she sees her father and goes running to him, calling, "Daddy, oh, my daddy."

My dad is a big silly softie. He always cries at this bit and I tease him rotten. Only this time I thought what it must really have been like to be poor Bobbie, parted from her father all that time—and I was the one who burst out crying.

"Hey! No blubbering allowed! That's *my* job," said Dad, giving me a little loving poke. Then he looked at me properly. "You're not *really* crying, are you, Flossie? What's the matter, eh? You can tell your old dad, can't you?"

That was just the trouble. I *couldn't* tell my dad, it

was just too awful. I wound my arms around his neck and clung to him tightly.

"I'm going to miss you so, Dad," I sobbed into his old gray jersey.

"I'm going to miss you all week too, sweetheart. I just live for our weekends together, especially now . . . Well, I've got in a bit of a muddle with money, and things are a bit tricky at the café. Still, as long as I've got you, that's all that matters," said Dad, rubbing his bristly cheek against the top of my head.

I sobbed harder.

"Hey, hey, don't cry so, little Floss. Your curly mop feels so silky. You're like my own special candy-floss. Watch out I don't eat you all up." He made funny slurping noises, pretending to nibble my curls.

I couldn't help giggling, even though I was still crying hard.

"That's it, start cheering up, my darling. Wonder-boy Steve will be calling for you soon in his flashy car and I don't want him telling your mom you've been miserable with me. You've got to be the all-singing, all-dancing happy little girl who thinks her parents splitting up is a piece of cake. And *talking* of cakes, better not tell your mom we scoffed a whole birthday cake between us or we'll really be in for it!"

"Dad? Oh, Dad!"

"What is it, little pal? Spit it out."

"I don't know *how*," I wailed.

Then I heard a car pull up outside. I jumped up off the sofa. It was Steve, far too early. Steve and Mom and Tiger, all come to collect me.

I had to spit it out now. It torrented out like a waterfall.

"Dad, I can't bear it, but we're going to Australia, Steve's got this new job and we're moving there next month, they've only just told me and I've been trying to tell you all weekend and I haven't been able to and they say it's not forever, just six months, but it will feel like forever and I feel like I'm being cut in half because I love you so, Dad."

The doorbell rang. Dad shook his head, looking dazed. For one terrible moment his face crumpled up. Then he took a deep breath and tried to smile.

"That's really exciting news, Floss," he said. "Australia, eh? Well, sport, we'll have to buy you one of them funny hats with corks on it."

"Do you mind terribly, Dad? Are you mad at me?"

"Of course I'm not mad at you, silly girl. I do *mind*, obviously. I'll miss you dreadfully. Just you make sure you don't forget your old dad."

"Oh, Dad, as if!" I said.

The bell rang again. Someone knocked loudly with their knuckles on the café door.

"Come on, sounds like your mom's getting impatient," said Dad.

I clung to him like a baby monkey, unable to let him go. He staggered with me to the door and opened it with difficulty.

"What are you playing at, Charlie? We've been ringing and knocking for ages," said Mom. She looked at me. "Oh, Floss, you've got yourself in a silly state!" Then she looked properly. "What on earth's that pink thing you're wearing? And whose silver shoes are those? They're *way* too big for you!"

Dad gently put me down. I wobbled on my high heels.

"They're my birthday princess clothes," I sobbed. "I think they're beautiful."

"Yes. Well. Get your things together then, we've got to be off. We're going to Steve's mom's for dinner." Mom caught Tiger's fist. He was trying to pick peeling paint off the café door. "Don't, pet! Dirty! Yes, we're off to see Granny, aren't we?"

"She's not *my* granny," I said. "I want to stay with Dad." I wound my arms as far as I could around Dad's large waist and leaned my head against his chest. I could hear his heart going *thump-thump-thump* underneath his shirt.

"Don't start behaving like a baby, Floss. You'll be able to see your dad again before . . . before . . ."

"Before you all go to Australia," said Dad, patting me on the shoulder.

"Yes, Australia!" said Mom, looking Dad in the eyes for the first time. "So Flossie's told you?"

"Yes, she has. She's a bit upset about it, as you can see," said Dad.

"Well, you've obviously been stirring her up. She's really thrilled to bits. It's a fantastic opportunity," said Mom. "Steve's done so well, getting this job."

"I'm *not* thrilled," I mumbled to Dad. "I wish she'd just shut up about Steve."

"What was that?" said Mom.

"Why didn't you tell me before?" said Dad.

"Well, we're telling you now," said Mom. "Steve's going to be in charge of this whole new Australian branch at double his current salary, and—"

"Yeah, yeah," said Dad. He obviously wanted Mom to shut up about Steve too. "What I mean is, how is it going to affect Floss? And me, for that matter. It's going to kill me not seeing my little girl."

"Sorry about that, pal," said Steve. He's *not* Dad's pal, not in a million years. "It wasn't deliberate, you know. I didn't even put in for the job in Sydney, they simply offered it to me." He shrugged and smirked to show us he couldn't *help* being so brilliant and clever and in demand.

"It's all very well saying sorry," said Dad. He looked at Mom. "What about my right to see Floss? I've got joint custody, you know that."

"You can come and see her any time you want," Mom said calmly.

"How am I going to get there? Walk?" said Dad.

"I can't help it if you can't afford it," said Mom.

"We can't miss this golden opportunity. There's nothing you can do about it, Charlie."

I felt Dad sag a little.

"I don't suppose there is," he said, so sadly. "Well, I hope it all works out for you. And don't you worry, little Floss, we'll write lots. You never know, I might win the lottery and then I'll come flying over to see you straight away . . . or I'll put on my Superman pants and soar all the way to Sydney under my own steam."

He was trying to make me laugh but it just made me cry harder.

"Come on, Flora, don't be such a little drama queen," said Mom. "Change out of those silly shoes, take that frock off, and let's get going."

I unhooked myself from Dad. I wiped my eyes and took a step backward. I looked at him. He had tears in his eyes too, though his mouth was stretched into a wide clown smile. Then I looked at Mom and Steve and Tiger. My two families.

I suddenly knew where I belonged.

"I'm not going," I said.

Mom sighed. "Look, Granny Westwood's expecting us, and Tiger's getting restless. I want to give him his bottle in the car and settle him off to sleep."

"I'm not going *at all*," I said. I took a deep breath. "I'm not going to Australia. I've decided. There's nothing you can do to change my mind. I'm staying with my dad."

Six

It was as if I'd thrown a bomb at Mom. She exploded. She told me I was being ridiculous. She insisted I had to go with her. I was part of her family.

"I'm part of Dad's family too," I said.

Dad gave me this great big hug—but then he held me at arm's length and looked into my eyes. "Are you sure you know what you're saying, Floss? I think maybe you'd be much better off in Australia with your mom. You don't have to stay with your old dad, you know. I'll miss you heaps and heaps but I'll manage fine, I promise."

"*I* won't manage, Dad," I said. "I want to stay with you."

"Well, you *can't*, so you can stop this silly act right now," Mom said. "You're my daughter and you're coming to live with me."

"No, I'm not."

"Yes, you are."

"No, I'm *not*."

"Yes, you *are*."

"Oh no, I'm NOT."

"Hey, hey, hey, you two! You sound like a bad pantomime act," said Dad.

"Don't you tell me what to do," said Mom. "I'm sure this is all your fault. You put Floss up to this. I tell you, she was absolutely thrilled to be going to Australia, as anyone in their right mind would be."

"Well, she seems in her right mind now to me—and it's clear what she wants to do," said Dad. "She wants to stay with me."

"She can't! A daughter's place is with her mother," Mom insisted. She turned to me. "Floss?" Her voice cracked as if she were going to cry. "You do really want to be with me, don't you, darling?"

She waited. Dad waited. I waited too.

I didn't *know* what I really wanted.

Yes, I did. I wanted Steve and Tiger to disappear in a puff of smoke. I wanted our family to be just Mom and Dad and me. It would be like it used to be long ago, when Dad called Mom his big princess and she laughed at all his silly jokes and we had breakfast in bed on Sunday mornings and cuddles all together on the big sofa in the living room.

I shut my eyes for a second and wished for what I wanted.

I knew my wish couldn't possibly come true. I

opened my eyes again. There was Mom, her forehead pinched with two sharp lines above her nose, her carefully outlined shiny lips pressed hard together in a straight line. There was Dad, gnawing at a piece of loose skin on his thumb, his hair sticking up sideways, his sweatshirt too tight over his tummy. I could wish and wish until I blew up like a giant balloon, but Mom and Dad weren't ever going to get back together.

Tiger started whining because Mom was holding him too tightly. Steve reached over and took him, swinging him up onto his broad shoulders. Tiger chuckled with delight. He loved his dad.

I loved *my* dad. I loved him even more because he wasn't tall and fit and handsome and clever like Steve. Mom had Steve and Tiger. Dad didn't have anyone but me.

"I really want to stay here with Dad," I said quietly to Mom. "Please, please, please let me."

Mom's face screwed up. Her glossy lips disappeared as her mouth contorted. Tears started rolling down her cheeks. "All right," she whispered. She clutched her stomach as if she'd just been punched.

Steve pulled her close, Tiger still perching on his shoulders.

Dad put his arms right around me. I could feel him shaking. I think he was crying too.

* * *

It would have been easier if we could have all split up there and then, but I stayed with Mom and Steve and Tiger until they went to Australia.

It was awful. Mom and I didn't know how to act with each other. One day Mom would act all cold and distant, and whenever I looked up she'd be staring at me reproachfully. The next day she would be brisk and bossy, telling me she was damned if I was going to mess up all their plans and if I didn't want to go to Australia it was my loss, not hers. But the day after that she suddenly burst into floods of tears and I did too. I sat on Mom's lap and cuddled in close and she rocked me as if I were as tiny as Tiger.

"I'm going to miss you so, my baby," said Mom.

"I'm going to miss you too, Mom," I said.

"*Please* come with us," she murmured into my curls.

I wanted to so much. Mom looked like she'd really, really miss me, maybe even as much as Dad. I didn't see how I could *bear* to be without my mom. I thought of all our cuddles, all our girly talk, all our shopping trips, all the secrets she told me about growing up and girls-and-boys.

As the days wore on I got so cast down that I even started to feel I was going to miss Tiger. Whenever I went near him he held out his chubby arms to be picked up. When I whirled him around or blew a raspberry on his fat little tummy, he chuckled and snorted and kicked his bendy legs like a little frog. He was even starting to say my name, though he couldn't quite manage the *l*, so I was his "Fossie."

I suddenly got into the whole big-sister thing. I sat him on my lap and read him all his boring little books about tractors and tank engines. I drew him pictures of dogs and cats and cows so that he could *woof-woof* and *mew-mew* and *moo-moo* for hours. I fed him his chopped-up chicken and carrots, pretending the spoon was an airplane flying through the air and docking in his drooly little mouth. I gave him his bath, making all his plastic ducks bob up and down and nibble his tummy with their orange beaks. I tucked him in at night with his pacifier and his stripy teddy bear and my baby kangaroo.

"You can have Baby Kangaroo if you like, Tiger," I whispered. "Seeing as you've taken such a shine to him."

Tiger clasped Baby Kangaroo happily.

"Maybe you'd better have Mother Kangaroo too," I said. "I don't think they'd like being separated."

I knew I wasn't going to like being separated from *my* mom. I couldn't help hoping that she'd suddenly change her mind and decide she couldn't bear to go to Australia without me. Steve didn't *have* to take this new job. We could all go on living in our house and I could go on staying with Dad on weekends and we could still be a kind of family even if Mom and Dad weren't living together.

But Steve brought home lots of cardboard boxes

and started packing everything up. Tiger played happily in this new cardboard city, plopping himself down on sheets of Bubble Wrap and squealing with laughter when they went *pop*.

Mom started packing her stuff too, selecting all her favorite clothes and consigning her fun fur coat and big boots to the boxes going into storage, as it wasn't really cold in Australia even in their winter. She started going through all my things too, packing all the good stuff to be taken to Dad's and putting all my old clothes and toys in a big garbage bag.

I stared at all my special dolls and cuddly teddy bears. I loved them so—but Rhiannon now said they were just for silly babies. I rounded up all my Barbie dolls, twirled each one around on her tippy toes, and then made them jump one after the other into the plastic bag.

"Are you sure about your dolls, Floss? Won't you want to play with them at your dad's?"

"They're just for babies," I said firmly.

"Well, at least they look attractive. Why chuck them and keep all these moth-eaten old teddy bears?"

"I'm not," I said, and I tumbled them all into the bag too, until it was bulging with soft yellow and fawn fur.

"Good for you, Floss," said Mom. "But you'd better keep Kanga and Baby Kanga for yourself, as your best toys. They were actually very expensive. Tiger will just mess them up."

"No, I want him to have them, Mom. As a special present from his big sister."

"Well, that's very sweet of you, dear. You're right, you're getting too grown-up for cuddly toys."

But then Mom suddenly seized hold of a droopy pink poodle with the embarrassing name of PP huddling at the bottom of my old toy box. (I'd simply shortened Pink Poodle to her initials, but I knew her name would make Margot and Judy chortle—and maybe Rhiannon.)

"Chuck her, Mom," I said.

"No, we have to keep PP," Mom said, stroking her.

"Mom! PP's *ancient*." She was more gray than pink now, her fur was very matted, and she had only one glass eye, which gave her face a baleful, lopsided expression.

"You used to lug her around everywhere with you when you were little," said Mom. She looked at me. "You're *still* little," she said, and she started crying.

I'd seen Mom cry lots of times before, but never like this. She sat back on her heels and sobbed, her mouth like a mailbox because she was howling so hard. It was so scary that Tiger stopped crawling around her wardrobe playing with shoes, and huddled down into her pashmina pile, sobbing too.

I wanted to cry as well, but Steve was out playing a farewell round of golf with all his boring buddies, so he wasn't around to comfort Mom. I had to be the grown-up. I put my arms around Mom and I rocked her and she clutched me tight and wept against my chest until my T-shirt was sodden.

"Please don't cry, Mom," I begged. "I'm not little, I'm big now. I'll be fine with Dad while you're away, and then when you come back from Australia, we'll go back to me living with you during the week, and we'll get back to normal again, you'll see."

"Oh, darling," Mom sobbed. "I think I've gone crazy. What am I *doing*? I *can't* leave you behind, I simply can't."

Seven

I started to hope that she'd really changed her mind. She'd stay in this country after all and forget about Australia.

The next day she stopped all her frantic packing and consulted a lawyer. I wasn't allowed to go into his office with her. I had to stay in the reception room minding Tiger. He wouldn't stay on my lap. He prowled around on his hands and knees, his sticky hands scrabbling at all the leather-bound law books on the shelves. The receptionist tried cooing and clucking at him, but Tiger wasn't in a mood to be charmed. He was yelling his head off when Mom came out of the lawyer's office. She looked in a yelling mood too.

"As if I'm going to hang around and let the courts sort it out!" she exploded the moment we got outside. "We've got the tickets, we're all set to go. We can't hang around now! Steve has got to start working at the Sydney branch this month. I can't let him go off on his own. He needs my support—and if I'm not careful, some silly young thing will bat her eyes at him and turn his head. What am I going to *do*?"

Mom glared at me as if it were all my fault. "Why can't you jump at this fantastic chance, Floss? I was nuts to let you dictate to me. Look, you're coming with us, whether you like it or not!"

"What are you going to do, Mom? Kidnap me? I'm a bit big to bundle under your arm. Are you going to lock me in one of the suitcases?"

"Stop being so cheeky!" Mom said, giving me a shake.

"Well, you stop bossing me around! Ouch, you're *hurting* me. I've told you and told you, I'm not coming, I'm staying with Dad."

"*Why* do you want to stay with him?"

"I love him."

"More than you love me?"

"I love you *both*," I said, crying. "Mom, he needs me."

"So you care more about his feelings than mine? All right then, stay with him. I won't try and persuade you anymore. Happy now?" Mom snapped.

Of course I wasn't happy—and neither was she. It was exhausting. It looked like we were going to go on like this forever, best friends one day and snarling enemies the next.

The day before Mom and Steve and Tiger flew off,

we were all mixed up. Mom and I were hugging one minute and shouting the next. But that night Mom left Steve alone in his big bed, edged her way around the last of the boxes, and came and clambered into my single bed beside me. She held me tight and I nestled in to her. Neither of us slept much. Mom told me stories about when I was a very little girl. I told Mom stories about what I planned to do when I was a big girl. We held on to each other, Mom's hands gripping my arms fiercely, as if she could never bear to let me go.

Dad came to collect me in his van, so that he could carry all my extra stuff. It's a big white van and I'd always loved riding in it, feeling so special strapped up high beside my dad, but I saw the way Steve shook his head at the dents and scratches on the paintwork. Dad saw too, and must have minded, but he shook Steve's hand nevertheless and wished him luck with his new job. He patted Tiger on the head. Then he gave Mom a great clumsy hug.

"Let's stay friends, Sal. I swear I'll take the greatest care of our Floss. You enjoy Australia and your new life, but don't forget to come back home, babe."

Mom always twitched with irritation when Dad called her babe, but now she sniffled tearfully and gave him a big hug back.

I held my breath as my parents embraced. Maybe now, at the very, very last minute, they would realize that they really loved each other after all. Then Mom moved away and the moment was over.

It was our turn to hug, Mom and me. We hugged and hugged and hugged. It hurt so much. It seemed like I was making the biggest mistake of my life.

"I want you to have this, Floss," said Mom, handing me an envelope. "It's an open airline ticket to Sydney. You can use it anytime in the next six months. It'll be strange traveling such a long way on your own, but the stewardess will look after you. Or, of course, you can change your mind now and come with us after all."

I wanted to cling to Mom and say *Yes, yes, yes!*

But I saw Dad's face. He was nodding and trying to smile. I *couldn't* say yes. I just shook my head sadly, but promised I'd take great care of the ticket.

Dad opened the van door. Steve lifted me in. Mom gave me one last kiss. Then we were driving away from my mom, my home, my whole family . . .

I waved and waved and waved long after we'd turned the corner and were out of sight. Then I hunched down in my seat, my hands over my mouth to stop any sound coming out.

"It's OK to cry, darling. Cry as much as you want," said Dad. "I know it must be so awful for you. You're going to miss your mom so. *I'll* miss her, in spite of everything. But she'll be coming back in six months, and the time will simply whiz by. If I can only win the lottery, we'll both jet out to Sydney for a month's vacation, just like that. Yeah, if I could win the lottery, *all* our problems would be solved." Dad sighed heavily. "I feel so bad, little Floss. I should have insisted you go with your mom."

"I want to be with you, Dad," I murmured, though I wasn't sure it was true now.

We went back to the café. Dad opened it up and got the tea and coffee brewing. There wasn't much point. We had no customers at all, not even Billy the Chip or Old Ron or Miss Davis.

"I might as well shut it up again. I doubt anyone will be in until lunchtime, if then," said Dad. "Come on, kiddo, let's go out for a bit. What would you like to do?"

That was the trouble. I didn't really want to do *anything*. We wandered around the town for a bit, peering in some of the shops. There wasn't much point getting excited about anything because I knew Dad didn't have any money. He tried to start up this game of what we'd buy if we won the lottery. I didn't feel like joining in much.

"I suppose your mom's Steve could buy you any of this stuff with a flash of his credit card," Dad said.

"I don't want any of it," I said.

"That's my girl. The simple things in life are best, eh?" Dad said eagerly. "Come on, let's go to the park and feed the ducks. You like that, don't you?"

I wondered if I was getting too old for feeding the

ducks, but we picked up a bag of stale sliced bread back at the café and headed down to the park, even though it had started raining.

"It's only a little drizzle," said Dad.

By the time we reached the duck pond we were both wet through and shivering because we hadn't bothered to bring our proper coats.

"Still, nice weather for the ducks," said Dad.

They were swimming around in circles, quacking away. Mother ducks and ducklings.

I threw them some bread, large chunks for the mothers and dainty bite-sized morsels for the ducklings, but they seemed full to bursting already. There were large chunks of bread bobbing all around them but they couldn't be bothered to open their beaks. They'd already had so many visitors. Mothers and toddlers.

"Never mind, let's take the bread back home and make chip butties, eh?" said Dad. "Two for you and two for me. Yum, yum in the tum!"

I wasn't listening properly. I was looking up at an airplane flying high in the sky, as small as a silver bird.

"Your mom won't be on her plane yet," Dad said softly. "They aren't going to the airport till this evening. It's a night flight."

I had crazy thoughts about packing my case, running like mad to Mom's, and begging her to take me after all.

Maybe that was why I was so fidgety when I got

home. I flopped around on the sofa, I lolled about the floor, I watched ten minutes of one video, five of another, I read two pages of my book, I got out my felt pens and started a drawing and then crumpled up the paper. I ended up rolling the pens all over the floor, flicking them moodily from one side of the room to the other.

One went right under the sofa. I had to scrabble for it with my fingers. I found little balls of fluff, some old potato chips, a tissue, and a screwed-up letter. I opened it up and saw the word *debt* and the word *court* and the word *bailiffs* before Dad snatched it away.

"Hey, hey, that's *my* letter, Floss," he said. He crumpled it up again, screwing it tighter and tighter in his hand until it was like a hard little bullet.

"What is it, Dad?"

"Nothing," said Dad.

"But I thought it said . . . ?"

"It was just a silly letter sent to try to scare me. It's not going to, OK?" said Dad. "Now, you just forget all about it, there's a good girl. Come on, let's have our chip butties!"

Dad made two each, and one for luck. I could only eat half of one, and that was a great big effort. It turned out Dad didn't have much of an appetite either. We looked at the chip butties left on the plate. It was as if Dad had made enough for both my families. I wasn't sure I could stand to be in this very small family of two now. I wasn't sure how we were going to manage.

The Apple Café

Eight

I was swimming in an enormous duck pond, gigantic birds with beaks as big as bayonets swooping toward me. I opened my mouth to scream for help and started choking in the murky green water. I coughed and coughed and went under. I got tangled in long slimy ropes of weed. I couldn't struggle free. The huge ducks swam above my head, their great webbed feet batting me. I was trapped down there, my lungs bursting. No one knew, no one cared, no one came to rescue me . . .

I woke up gasping, soaked through. I thought for one terrible moment I might have wet myself—but it was only a night sweat. I staggered up out of my damp bed, mumbling, "Mom, Mom"—and then I remembered.

I stopped, shivering on the dark landing. I couldn't run to Mom for a cuddle. She was six miles up in the air, halfway across the world.

I started crying like a baby, huddled down on the carpet.

"Floss?"

Dad came stumbling out of his bedroom in his pajamas and very nearly tripped over me. "What are you doing *here*, pet? Don't cry. Come on, I'll take you back to bed. It's all right, Dad's here. You've just had a bad dream."

It seemed as if I were stuck in the bad dream. Dad tucked me in gently but he didn't know how to plump up my pillow properly and smooth my sheet. He didn't find me a big tissue for my runny nose. He didn't comb my hair with his fingers. He did kiss me softly on the cheek, but his face was scratchy with stubble and he didn't smell sweet and powdery like Mom.

I tried to cuddle down under the comforter but it smelled wrong too, of old house and french fry grease. I wanted to go to *Mom's* house, but it was all changed. Our stuff was all packed up. Soon there would be strangers renting it. I imagined another girl my age in my white bedroom with the cherry-red carpet and the cherries on the curtains. I saw her looking out of my window at my garden and my special swing and I couldn't bear it.

Three months ago Steve had fixed up the baby swing for Tiger, all colors and bobbles and flashing lights. I'd done the big-sister bit and patiently pushed him backward and forward, but I couldn't help remarking that I wished *I'd* had a swing when I was little.

I didn't think Mom and Steve had taken much notice, but the next weekend when I was at Dad's, Steve rigged up this amazing proper traditional wooden swing, big enough for an adult—certainly big enough for *me*.

"My swing!" I sobbed now.

"What? Please don't cry so, Floss, I can't make out what you're saying," said Dad, sounding really worried. "Listen, I know how badly you're missing your mom. I've got your airline ticket safe in the kitchen drawer. We can book you onto a flight and you can join up with them. It will be like a big adventure flying all that way."

"No, no. I want my *swing*," I said.

Dad missed a beat before he understood. "Well, that's easy-peasy," he said. "We'll drop by your mom's place tomorrow and take your swing. Don't upset yourself, darling. Your old dad will sort things for you."

We went around to the house early Sunday morning, before Dad opened up the café. Dad parked the van outside the house. It looked so absolutely normal I couldn't believe Mom and Steve and Tiger weren't there behind Mom's gathered curtains.

We didn't have a key, but we didn't need one to wiggle open the bolt of the side gate and walk around into the back garden. Tiger's swing wasn't there. It had been dismantled and packed up. The only trace of it was the four square marks in the grass where the legs had been.

My swing still stood there sturdily. Too sturdily. Dad tried and tried to take it down. He even broke into the garden shed and bashed at the swing's supports with Steve's tools. The swing didn't budge but Steve's stainless-steel spade got horribly dented.

"Oh, darn," said Dad. "Now I suppose I'll have to pay for a new blooming spade on top of everything else."

"Never mind, Dad."

"But I *do* mind. Why am I so useless? Look, I'm going to collapse that swing if it's the last thing I do."

Dad battered and bashed a lot more. He tugged and tussled with the swing. He even tried digging around it with the bent spade, but the supports went way, way down—almost to Australia.

Dad stood still, wiping his brow, his face damp and scarlet.

"It doesn't matter, Dad, honestly," I said.

"It matters to me," said Dad grimly.

I peered up at the swing, wishing I hadn't said a word. Dad stared too, his brow furrowed, as if he were trying to fell the swing by sheer willpower. Then he suddenly clapped his hands and ran and got Steve's scary long pruning shears.

"Dad! What are you going to do?"

"It's OK, Floss. I've just worked it out. We'll liberate your swing. We just need the rope and the seat. We don't *need* the stupid supports. It's going to be a *portable* swing now, you'll see."

Dad reached up and snipped at the top of each rope. They came thumping down with the wooden seat attached. "There!" he said, as if he'd perfected the most astonishing trick.

I blinked doubtfully at the severed swing and said nothing.

When we got back home Dad took the swing out in the backyard. He's never actually gotten around to turning it into a proper garden. There's not really room, anyway. There are big Dumpsters for taking the trash from the café, and all the cardboard boxes of old stuff that Dad's going to sort one day lurking under tarps, and bits and pieces of very old bikes, and an electric scooter that never worked properly.

There's a tiny flowerbed of pansies because Dad says they've got smiley faces, and an old sandpit I used to play Beaches in when I was very little, and an ancient gnarled apple tree that's too old to produce any fruit, although it was the reason Dad bought the café long ago. He was going to make our own apple pies and apple cake and apple chutney and applesauce. He painted a big new sign to go above the door—THE APPLE CAFÉ—and he painted the walls and window-sills bright apple green.

He changed the name to Charlie's Café long ago, but the apple-green paint's still there, though it's faded to a yellowy lime and it's peeling everywhere. Mom always nagged Dad to chop down the apple tree because it wasn't doing anything useful, just causing shadows in the yard, but Dad reacted as if Mom had asked him to chop *me* down.

"We'll hang your swing on the apple tree!" Dad said now.

He spent all afternoon putting it up. He tested the branches first, swinging on them himself, yelling like Tarzan to make me laugh. I still didn't feel a bit like laughing but I giggled politely.

Then Dad went up and down a ladder, fixing one end of the swing rope here and the other end there. He had to take an hour's break hunting down an ancient encyclopedia in a box of books in the attic to find out how to do the safest knots.

When at last he had the swing hanging we found it was too low, so that my bottom nearly bumped the ground. Dad had to start all over again, shortening the ropes. But *eventually*, by late afternoon, the swing was ready.

"There you are, Princess! Your throne awaits," Dad said, ultraproudly.

I put on my birthday princess gown over my jeans to please him and sat on my swing. Dad beamed at me and then went wandering off again to find his old camera to commemorate the moment. He didn't come back for a long time.

I had to stay swinging. I didn't *feel* like swinging somehow. I wouldn't have told Dad for the world, but you couldn't really swing properly now that it was attached to the apple tree. The swing shook around too abruptly and hung slightly lopsided, so you started to feel queasy very quickly. It wasn't very pretty out in the backyard, staring at the tarps and bike parts, and the Dumpsters were very smelly.

I sat there and sat there and sat there, and when Dad came back eventually clutching his Polaroid, I had a short burst of swinging and smiled at the camera.

"It's a great swing, isn't it!" said Dad proudly, as if he had made it all himself. "Hey, why don't you phone Rhiannon and see if she wants to come around and play on it too?"

I hesitated. I'd asked Rhiannon over to play heaps of times, but always at Mom's. I'd wanted to keep my time over the weekend especially for Dad. But now *all* my time was with Dad.

"Go on, phone her," said Dad. "Ask her around to tea. Does she like chip butties?"

I wasn't sure. We always ate salads and chicken and fruit at Rhiannon's. Her school packed lunches were also ultrahealthy: wholemeal rolls and carrot sticks and apples and tiny boxes of raisins. But maybe chip butties would be a wonderful wicked treat?

I knew I was kidding myself. I suspected it would be a big, big, big mistake to invite her over. But I felt so weird and lonely stuck here with Dad with nothing to do. If Rhiannon was here, we could goof around and do silly stuff and maybe I'd start to feel normal again.

I phoned her up. I got her mom first.

"Oh, Flora, I'm so glad you called! How *are* you?" she asked in hushed tones. "I was so shocked when Rhiannon told me about your mother."

She was acting as if Mom had *died*.

"I'm fine," I lied. "Please can Rhiannon come over for dinner?"

"What, today? Well, her grandma and grandpa are here. Tell me, Flora, do you see your grandma a lot?"

"My grandma?" I said, surprised. "Well, she sends me birthday presents, but she doesn't always remember how old I am. Dad says she gets muddled."

"What about your mom's mom?"

"She died when I was a baby. There's Steve's mom, but I don't think she likes me much."

"You poor little thing. Well, listen to me, sweetheart. Anytime you need to discuss anything girly, you come and have a word with me, all right? I know your dad will do his best, but it's not the same, not the same at all. A growing girl needs her mother. I just can't understand how *your* mother . . ." She let her voice trail away.

I clutched the phone so tightly it was a wonder the plastic didn't buckle. I couldn't stand her going on like that, as if Mom had deliberately abandoned me. I decided I didn't want Rhiannon to come over after all, but her mom was busy calling to her and asking for details of the address.

I heard Rhiannon saying stuff in the background. It didn't sound as if she wanted to come over.

"You've got to go! It's the least you can do. Poor little Flora will be feeling so lonely," Rhiannon's mother hissed.

"I'm fine, really," I said.

"Yes, dear, I'm sure you are," she said, in a *don't-think-you-can-fool-me* tone of voice.

I couldn't fool Rhiannon either when she came over. She was wearing a lacy blue top and white jeans. She had one little braid tied with blue and white thread in her long glossy black hair. She looked beautiful. She seemed so out of place in our café.

"Oh, Floss, you poor thing, your eyes look so sore, all red and puffy," she said.

"It's an allergy," I said quickly.

Rhiannon sighed at me. She turned to Dad. "My mom says you must call her if you've got any problems."

Dad blinked. "Problems?"

"You know. Over Flossie," said Rhiannon. She was acting like she was my social worker or something. Even Dad looked a bit irritated.

"We haven't got any problems, Floss and me, have we, doll-baby? But it's very kind of your mom to offer all the same, so thank her very much. Now, would you two girls like to go and play on Floss's swing?"

He led the way through the café, out into the kitchen, and opened the door to the backyard dramatically, as if Disneyland beckoned.

Rhiannon stepped warily into the backyard, walking

as if she were wading through mud. She peered at the Dumpsters, the tarps, the bike parts. It was definitely a mistake inviting her over. I suddenly saw Rhiannon telling her mother all about our dismal backyard. Worse, I saw her telling Margot and Judy and all the girls at school.

I looked at her anxiously.

"Oh, there's your swing. How . . . lovely," she said.

"I know it's not lovely," I whispered. "But Dad's fixed it all up for me especially."

"Sure. OK. I understand," said Rhiannon. She raised her voice so that Dad could hear in the kitchen. "Oh, Floss, your swing looks great hanging on the apple tree," she said, enunciating very clearly, as if Dad were deaf or dumb.

She hopped on it, had one token swing, then hopped off again. "So, shall we go up to your bedroom and play?" she said.

"Maybe we should swing a bit more," I said.

"But it's, like, boring," said Rhiannon. "Come on, Floss, I've been nice to your dad. Now let's go and do stuff."

"OK."

We went back indoors. Dad had started peeling potatoes in the kitchen. He looked baffled to see us back so quickly.

"What's up, girls?" he said.

"Nothing's up, Dad. I—I just want to show Rhiannon my bedroom," I said.

I didn't, didn't, didn't want to show her my bedroom.

She looked around it, sucking in her breath. "Is *this* your bedroom?" she said. She wrinkled her brow. "But I don't get it. Your bedroom's lovely, all red and white and clean and pretty."

"That's my bedroom at my mom's, you know it is," I said.

I sat on my old saggy bed and stroked the limp comforter, as if I were comforting it.

"So, OK, where's all your stuff? The cherry curtains and the red velvet cushions and your special dressing table with the velvet stool?"

"I've got all my clothes and books and art stuff here. The curtains are still at Mom's and the other things have been put into storage. They wouldn't fit in my bedroom here."

I scarcely fit in my bedroom at Dad's. It was not much bigger than a cupboard. There was just room for the bed and an old chest of drawers. Dad had started to paint it with some special silver paint, but it was a very small can and it ran out before he could cover the last drawer. He'd propped a mirror on top of the chest and I'd laid out my brush-and-comb set and my china ballet dancer and my little cherry-red glass vase from my dressing table at home. They didn't make the chest look much prettier.

"Dad's going to finish painting the chest when he can find some more silver paint," I said. "And he's going to put up bookshelves and we're going to get a new comforter—midnight-blue with silver stars—and I'm going to have those glow stars stuck on the ceiling *and* one of those glitter balls like you get at dances—and fairy lights—and—and—" I was running out of ideas.

Rhiannon looked at me pityingly. "What sort of house is your mom going to have in Australia?" she asked.

"They're just renting. It's just some little apartment," I said.

I was lying. Mom had shown me a brochure with pictures of beautiful modern apartments with balconies and a sea view. They'd deliberately chosen an apartment with three big bedrooms so that I could have the room of my dreams.

"It couldn't be littler than this place," said Rhiannon. "You must be a bit nuts to want to stay here rather than go to Australia."

"I want to be with my *dad*," I said.

"Do you love your dad much more than your mom then?"

"No, I love them both the same. But Dad needs me more," I said.

"Well, it still seems crazy, if you ask me," said Rhiannon, sitting down on the bed beside me. It creaked in protest. She peered down at it, shaking her head in disgust.

"Well, I'm *not* asking you," I said. "And anyway, *you* were the one who said I didn't have to go. I thought you wanted me to stay so we could be best friends forever. Don't you want to be my best friend now, Rhiannon?"

"Of course I do."

"We're best friends forever?"

"Yes, like, forever and ever, dummy," said Rhiannon, sighing and shaking her long hair over her shoulders.

She was saying all the right words but she was saying them in this silly American accent.

Nine

I had more bad dreams that night. I wished I'd kept my great big Kanga to cuddle in bed. I couldn't believe I'd actually thrown away all my old teddy bears. All I had was the limp lopsided elephant and dog that Grandma had knitted me. I reached out of bed and tucked one on either side of my head. They didn't look very fetching but they *felt* warm and soft, like a special scarf.

I lay awake worrying that the bad dreams would come back the minute I closed my eyes. It helped that every time I wriggled around on my pillow a soft little knitted paw patted me.

I fell asleep just as it was starting to get light—and then woke with a start. Something was ringing and ringing and ringing. The telephone! I stumbled out of bed and ran to answer it. Dad lumbered behind me in his pajamas, huffing and puffing.

"Hello?" I said into the phone.

"Oh, *there* you are, Floss! I've been calling for ages!" said Mom. "I thought you and Dad must have left for school already. What are you doing, having breakfast?"

"Um—yes," I said, not wanting to tell Mom we'd slept in. She sounded so *close*, as if she were back in our house across town. "Oh, Mom, have you come back?" I said breathlessly.

"What? Don't be silly, darling, we only just got here. My Lord, what a journey! Do you know, Tiger didn't sleep a wink the entire flight. Steve and I were just about going demented."

"I can imagine," I said.

"But never mind, we're here now, and you should just see the apartment, Floss. I feel like a film star! We've got a fantastic sea view and even though it's winter here it's so bright and sunny. I just can't believe how beautiful it all is. It would all be so perfect if only you were here too. Oh, Floss, I miss you so!"

"I miss you too, Mom. So, so much," I whispered. I didn't want to be tactless to Dad, but he patted my shoulder reassuringly to show me he understood.

"I just *know* you'd love it here. If you could just see for yourself how lovely everything is, you'd jump on a plane tomorrow, I know you would. Oh, darling, are you all right? Is Dad looking after you OK?"

"Yes, Mom, I'm fine, really."

"He's giving you proper food, not endless fry-ups and cakes and chip butties?"

"Yes, Mom," I said.

I was still feeling queasy from last night's chip butties. Rhiannon had been a little bit rude about them when Dad served them up for our dinner. *Very* rude, actually. I'd felt so sorry for Dad I'd said quickly, "Well goody-goody, if you don't like them, that means there's all the more for me." I'd ended up eating all of my chip butty *and* Rhiannon's.

Dad boiled eggs and ran down to the corner shop and bought tomatoes and cucumber and lettuce to make Rhiannon her own special salad, but she only ate two mouthfuls, and she didn't appreciate him turning them into a funny face for her.

"Does your dad think I'm, like, a baby?" she said.

"Dad's bought special salad stuff," I told Mom truthfully. "And he's fixed up a new swing in the garden and I've had Rhiannon over to play."

"That's good," said Mom. "Well, I don't want to make you late for school, sweetheart. You take care now. I'm going to send you lots of photos of our apartment and the beaches and the parks and the opera house. Once you see them I just know you'll be dying to come and join us."

I swallowed. I didn't know what to say. Most of me *ached* to be in Australia with Mom. But not without Dad.

"Do you want to speak to Dad, Mom?"

"Well, I'll have a little word, yes, please. Good-bye then, Floss. I love you so much."

"Good-bye, Mom. I love you too," I said.

I leaned against Dad while Mom questioned him. She sounded like a nurse taking a full medical history. She asked:

1. Is Floss looking mopey?
2. Has she cried much?
3. Is she biting her nails a lot?
4. Is she as chatty as usual?
5. Is she really eating properly?
6. Is she having trouble getting to sleep?
7. Did she wake up at all in the night?
8. Is she having bad dreams?

I started to expect her to ask how many times I'd been to the bathroom.

"She's *fine*," Dad kept saying. "For pity's sake, you've only been gone five minutes. She's not likely to have had a nervous breakdown already. Now, we'd better be leaving for school. What? Of course she's had breakfast," said Dad, crossing his fingers in front of my face. He said good-bye and then put down the phone .

"Phew!" he said. "Oh, dear, Floss, let's shove some breakfast down you quick. I'm not sure there's time for eggs and bacon—"

"I don't want breakfast, Dad, there's not *time*. I'm going to be late."

"No, no, you've got to have something inside you. Cornflakes? I'll shove my jeans on and sort something out while you run and get washed and dressed."

I hadn't properly unpacked my pink pull-along suitcase or my cardboard boxes of clothes. My school blouses were horribly screwed up and my skirt was so creased it looked like it was pleated.

"Dad, can you iron these?" I said.

"What? Oh, God, I'm not sure my old iron works anymore. I don't really bother with my stuff, I just drip them dry."

I had to go to school all crumpled. I couldn't find my good white socks, so I had to wear an old pair of navy woolly winter ones, and my sneakers were all muddy from the garden. I couldn't even get my hair to go right. I'd been tossing and turning all through the night and now all my curls stuck straight up in the air as if I were plugged into an electric outlet.

Dad didn't seem to notice as he drove me to school. We arrived at the exact time Rhiannon was jumping out of her mom's Range Rover. *They* noticed.

"Floss! Oh, dear!" said Rhiannon's mom. "You look a bit bedraggled, darling."

"I'm fine," I said.

"Why have you got those funny socks on? Like, *navy*?" said Rhiannon. "And yuck, what's that on your *shoes*? It's not dog poo, is it?"

"No, it's just a bit of mud," I said, blushing.

Dad was peering out of the van anxiously, biting his lip. He frowned as Rhiannon's mom leaped out of her Range Rover and went over to him.

"Look, Mr. Barnes, I know it's difficult for you now you're a one-parent family—"

"Flossie's got two parents," said Dad. "I'm simply the one currently in charge."

"Whatever. I was wondering . . . You could always pop a bag of laundry into my house once a week. My cleaning lady often irons for me, I'm sure she wouldn't mind—"

"It's very kind of you, but we'll do our own washing and ironing," said Dad.

"Well, if you think you can cope!" said Rhiannon's mom, making it plain by her tone that she didn't feel Dad could cope at all.

"Bye, Dad," I said, waving, so he had an excuse to escape.

He waved back worriedly, obviously seeing now how scruffy I looked. I gave him a big beaming smile to show him I didn't care, stretching my mouth unnaturally wide, as if I were at the dentist's.

"You look like you're going to take a bite out of someone, Floss," said Rhiannon.

Margot and Judy were sitting on the wall. They heard what Rhiannon said and started snorting with laughter. Then they took in my appearance and laughed all over again.

"Oh. My. God," said Margot. "What happened to you, Floss? Has there been some major disaster so you've been, like, buried alive? Even your hair's exploded! Look at it, all fluffed out and standing on end."

"And what's that funny smell?" said Judy, wrinkling her nose. "It's like . . . french fry grease!"

"Well, that figures," said Margot. "Her dad runs this greasy-spoon café."

"It's *not* greasy," I said fiercely. "It's very special. My dad's chip butties are *famous*."

Margot and Judy cackled so much they very nearly fell off the wall. Rhiannon got the giggles too. She put her hands over her mouth but I could still see she was sniggering.

"Don't laugh at me!" I said.

"Well, you do look funny. But I know it's not your fault," said Rhiannon. "Mom said I've got to make special allowances for you."

"Why have you got to make special allowances for old Smelly Chip?" asked Margot.

"Because her mom's walked out on her."

"No, she hasn't! Don't say that!" I protested.

"OK, OK, don't get all touchy. I'm trying to be extra *nice* to you."

She might *say* she was being extra nice but she certainly wasn't acting it. I was scared I was going to start crying in front of them, so I ran into school.

I hoped Rhiannon would run after me. I wanted her to put her arms around me and tell me I didn't really look funny and she didn't care what I looked like anyway because she was my best friend.

She didn't run after me. She stayed smirking in the playground with Margot and Judy.

I locked myself in a bathroom stall and had a little private cry. Then I heard someone else come in. I clamped my hand over my nose and mouth to stop all the little snorty-snuffly sounds leaking out. I sat very still. Someone seemed to be standing there, waiting. Waiting for me?

"Rhiannon?" I called hopefully.

"It's Susan."

"Oh!" I blew my nose as best I could on school toilet paper, flushed the toilet, and emerged, feeling foolish.

Susan looked at me. I glanced at myself in the mirror above the sinks. I looked even worse than I imagined — and now I had red eyes and a runny nose too.

"I've got a cold," I said, splashing water on my face.

"Yes," said Susan solemnly, although we both knew I was fibbing.

I tried wetting my hair while I was at it, to smooth it down. It went obstinately fluffier, springing up all over the place.

I sighed.

"What?" said Susan.

"I hate my hair," I mumbled.

"I think you've got lovely hair. I'd give anything to have fair curls."

"It's not pretty yellow fair. It's practically snow white and much too curly. I can't grow it. It grows *up* instead of down."

"I'm trying to grow mine, but it's taking forever," said Susan, tugging at her soft brown hair. "I'd love it to grow down past my shoulders but I'm going to have to wait two whole years, because hair grows only a quarter of an inch each month. Vitamin E is supposed to be good for healthy growth, so I'm eating lots of eggs and wholemeal bread and apricots and spinach, but it doesn't seem to be having any noticeable effect so far."

"You know such a lot of stuff, Susan."

"No, I don't."

"You do—you know about the rate hair grows and vitamin E and all that."

"I don't know how to make friends," said Susan. We looked at each other.

"I want to be your friend, Susan," I said. "It's just . . ."

"I know," said Susan. "Rhiannon."

"I'm sorry she's so mean to you. Susan, your ballad— I thought it was so good."

"Oh, no. Rhiannon was right about that. It was terrible."

"Maybe . . . maybe you could come over and play

sometime, at my dad's?" I said. "It's not fancy or any-thing. It's just a funny café and we live over the top. I haven't got a very nice bedroom but—"

"I'd *love* to come," said Susan.

She smiled at me. I smiled back. I thought hard. Rhiannon would see if Susan came home with me after school.

"What about Saturday?" I said, glancing over my shoulder, scared that Rhiannon had crept up somehow and was standing right behind me, listening.

"Saturday would be wonderful," said Susan.

"Great!" I swallowed. "The only thing is . . ."

"Don't worry, I won't tell Rhiannon," said Susan.

I blushed. "*This* Saturday?" I said.

"Yep, this Saturday."

"You could come for tea. Only it might not be very . . . Do you like chip butties?"

Susan considered. "What are they?" she said.

I stared at her in surprise. How could she know a million and one facts and figures and yet be so clueless about chip butties?

"I know what a chip is," said Susan. "Fried potato."

"Well, you put a whole batch of chips in a big, soft white buttered roll—that's a chip butty."

"Fries in a roll?" said Susan.

"It's not exactly healthy eating," I said humbly. "But my dad specializes in *un*healthy eating, I'm afraid."

"It sounds like a delicious idea," said Susan.

Then Margot and Judy came barging into the bathroom. My heart started thudding. But it was all right: Rhiannon wasn't with them.

Margot narrowed her eyes at me. "Were you, like, talking to Swotty Potty?" she asked.

"What are you, the Rhiannon private police force?" said Susan. "No, she wasn't talking to me. No one talks to me, you know that."

She marched out of the bathroom, with Margot and Judy making silly whistling noises after her. Then they turned to me. Margot still looked suspicious.

"So what are you, like, doing here? Rhiannon's looking for you."

"Is she?"

I ran past them. Susan was halfway down the corridor. I ran past her too. I ran all the way to our classroom and there was Rhiannon, sitting on her desk, swinging her legs impatiently. She had such lovely slender lightly tanned legs. Mine were like spindly white matchsticks.

"There you are! What did you run off for? You are so *moody* now, Floss." Rhiannon sighed. "And if you don't mind my saying so, you really do look awful. I bet Mrs. Horsefield tells you off. You know how fussy she is, always going on about the boys not tucking their shirts in and telling all the girls off for rolling up their sleeves. You won't be her special teacher's pet today."

"Don't be so mean!"

"I'm not. I'm just pointing out the truth. You are, like, *so* paranoid."

And you are, like, so stupid talking like Margot, I thought, but I didn't dare say it.

When Mrs. Horsefield came into the classroom, I hunched low at my desk, desperately smoothing my blouse and skirt, as if my hands were little irons. I was fine until halfway through math, when Mrs. Horsefield asked me to come up to the front of the class to do a sum on the board.

I stared at her, agonized, slumping so far down in my seat my chin was almost on the table.

"Come on, Floss, don't look so bashful," she said.

"I—I can't do the sum, Mrs. Horsefield. Can't you pick someone else?" I suggested desperately.

"I know math isn't your strong point, but let's see what you can do. It's really quite simple if you work through it logically. Up you go!"

I had no option. I walked up to the board in my crumpled clothes and navy socks and muddy sneakers. Mrs. Horsefield looked startled. Margot and Judy giggled. I felt my cheeks flaming. I waited for Mrs. Horsefield to start shouting at me. Astonishingly, she simply handed me the chalk and said quietly, "OK?"

I was anything but OK. I tried to do the stupid sum, my hand shaking so that the chalk stuttered on the board. I kept getting stuck. Mrs. Horsefield gently prompted me, but I was in such a state I couldn't think of the simplest answer.

I looked around helplessly—and there was Susan, mouthing the numbers at me. I wrote them quickly and then rushed back to my seat. Mrs. Horsefield let me go, but when the bell went for break she beckoned me.

"Can we have a word, Floss?"

"Uh-oh," said Rhiannon.

"Wait for me?" I said.

"Yeah, yeah," said Rhiannon, but she was drifting off as she spoke.

I stood at Mrs. Horsefield's desk. She waited until the last child had left the classroom. Then she tipped her head to one side, looking at me.

"So why are you in such a sorry state? Dear oh dear! Did your mom sleep in this morning?"

"Mom's not here anymore," I said, and I burst into tears.

"Oh, Floss!" said Mrs. Horsefield. She put her arm around me. "Come on, sweetheart, tell me all about it."

"Mom's gone to Australia for six months. She *hasn't* walked out on me, she's coming back, she badly wanted me to go with her but I said I wanted to stay with my dad and I *do*, but I want Mom too!" I sobbed like a silly baby.

Mrs. Horsefield didn't seem to mind. She reached into her handbag and found me a couple of tissues, one to wipe my eyes and one to blow my nose.

"We could use a whole handful of tissues for your shoes too," said Mrs. Horsefield. "So you and Dad are finding it a bit difficult just now?"

"Dad's going to get an iron. We didn't have time to clean my shoes. And I've lost all my white school socks," I wailed.

"I'm sure you'll get into a routine soon enough. Try to get your school things ready and waiting the night before. Don't just rely on Dad. You're a sensible girl, you can sort yourself out. It's really quite simple—like the math sum! You worked it out eventually, didn't you? Well, with a little help from Susan."

I blinked.

"Susan's such a nice girl," said Mrs. Horsefield. "She could do with a friend right now."

"I know," I said. "I want to be her friend." I lowered my voice in case anyone was hanging around the classroom door. "We *are* friends in secret. She's coming over to my place this weekend. It's just we can't be friends at school because . . ."

Mrs. Horsefield raised her eyebrows, but didn't comment. "Oh, well, I'm sure you girls will sort yourselves out, given time. Do come and have a little chat with me whenever you're feeling upset or there's some little problem at home. I'm not just here to teach you lessons, you know. I'm here to help you in any way I can."

She paused, and then opened her desk drawer. There was a big paper bag inside. She opened it up and offered it to me. I saw one of her special pink iced buns with a big cherry on the top.

"Go on, take it," she said.

"But it's not my birthday."

"It's an *un*birthday bun for a little midmorning snack."

"Isn't it *your* midmorning snack, Mrs. Horsefield?"

"I think I've been having far too many snacks, midmorning or otherwise," said Mrs. Horsefield, patting her tummy. "Go on, off you go."

I took the bun and went out into the corridor. Rhiannon had said she'd wait but there was no sign of her. So I took my pink bun out of the paper bag and ate it all up myself. I especially savored the cherry.

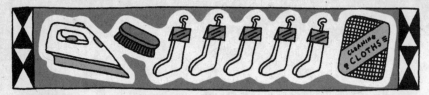

Ten

Dad was waiting for me when we got out of school. Rhiannon's mom was standing next to him, obviously giving him advice. He was nodding politely, but when he saw me running across the playground, he rolled his eyes, making a secret funny face at me.

"Thank goodness," he said, giving me a big hug. "That woman's been talking my ear off for the last ten minutes. The stuff she was saying! Some nerve! She even suggested I try Internet dating to get myself a girlfriend!"

"Oh, Dad, you're not going to, are you?" I asked anxiously.

"There's only one girl in my life, sweetheart. She's very little and she's got masses of curly hair and big blue eyes and she goes by the name of Princess," said Dad, whirling me around. "Come on, let's get home. I've been shopping!"

"I thought we were short of money, Dad."

"We are. Desperately. But we might as well spend what little we've got."

"Who's looking after the café?"

"Billy the Chip is supposed to be keeping an eye on things." Dad paused. "Though I doubt he'll be run off his feet."

There wasn't a single customer in the café. Billy the Chip was glued to his radio, listening to the races at Newmarket.

"Is Birthday Girl running again, Mr. Chip?" I asked.

"Don't talk to me about that silly filly! She went all flighty and finished second to last," said Billy the Chip. "Still, let's see if you can bring me luck on the last race, sweetheart. Here are the runners. What do you fancy?"

I peered at the list in his newspaper and then stabbed my finger at a name. "Iced Bun! That's the one. I had a lovely iced bun today, with a cherry on the top. Bet on Iced Bun, Mr. Chip."

"It's a complete outsider, but I suppose I could risk a fiver if you're feeling lucky."

"Put a fiver on for me too," said Dad.

"All right, I'll run down to the betting shop right this minute."

Billy the Chip was so old and skinny and frail he couldn't really *run*. He crept in slow motion, having a rest and mopping his brow every few seconds.

Dad shook his head. "Poor old Billy. I don't know how he keeps going. I worry about him still running that chip van. There are so many thugs in town now, especially late at night. He needs someone there if any of them start trouble. He's got a son but he's in Australia."

We looked at each other.

"It's obviously the *in* place, Floss," Dad said, sighing.

"Who wants to be one of the *in* crowd?" I said, taking his hand. "I'd sooner be us."

Dad squeezed my hand back. "You mean all the world to me, little Floss. Now listen here, lovey, I've bought a brand-new iron from Argos and five pairs of white socks from the market and a shoebrush and some cleaning rags too, so tomorrow we'll send you off to school super spic-and-span, I promise. And I've got a *salad* for your dinner, and oranges and apples. You'll be absolutely vibrating with vitamins, the picture of health and beauty! I don't need that Rhiannon's mom muscling in. I'm going to be a brilliant dad from now on."

"You've always been a brilliant dad, silly," I said.

"No, darling, I've been a terrible dad, in all sorts of ways." He took a deep breath. "I'm in a bit of a pickle with the café, Floss."

"I know, Dad. Don't worry. I'm sure business will pick up soon. And you've got me to help you now. I can be the waitress on the weekend. I promise you can keep all my tips."

"Oh, Floss, you're such a sweet kid. If only it was that simple. No, darling, I'm afraid I'm down and almost done for. I didn't spell it out before because I needed to sort out what I was going to do. Only I still haven't got a clue and time's running out."

"Don't worry, Dad. Maybe Iced Bun will win its race and we'll make a fortune!"

"The odds would have to be ten thousand to one to sort things out for me, pet," said Dad.

I tried to work out in my head how much we'd win at those odds. I needed Susan to help me with the math.

It was a waste of effort anyway. Iced Bun came in last. Billy the Chip trailed back from the betting shop looking defeated.

"Well, that was a waste of time and money," he said.

"I'm ever so sorry, Mr. Chip," I said, feeling responsible. "Let me get you another cup of tea."

Billy the Chip smiled at me, patting me on the head with his shaky old fingers. "Little Miss Curlymop. You're a dear girl. No wonder your dad's so fond of you. Here, I still owe you a birthday present."

"No, you don't. Birthday Girl came second to last. I'm terrible at choosing horses, Mr. Chip. Take absolutely no notice of me in the future!"

Dad fixed me my special salad for my dinner and then spent hours ironing all my clothes with the brand-new iron. He wasn't very good at it. The collars kept rumpling up and he pressed odd sideways lines in the sleeves.

"Maybe I could try, Dad?" I suggested, but he wouldn't let me in case I burned myself.

He sent me to bed early so I wouldn't oversleep in the morning. He sat beside me, one arm around me, while he read me a chapter of a story about a girl and a magic toad. The girl didn't have a mom; she just lived with her dad.

"Maybe *we* need a magic toad," said Dad. "*And* a magic iron that does the ironing all by itself. *And* a magic money box that's always stuffed full of fifty-pound notes."

"Dad, what *is* going to happen to the café? Will we have to sell it?"

Dad swallowed. He closed his eyes. His lips puckered up. I thought for one terrible moment he was going to start crying.

"The café isn't really mine to sell now, Floss. I had to borrow money on it. Lots of money, just to keep things going. And try as I might I haven't been able to keep up with the payments. So—so it looks as if they might close us down."

"Will someone else come and run our café?" I asked.

"I'm not sure, pet. Maybe."

"But—but will they come and live upstairs in the apartment with us?"

"The thing is, Floss, the apartment is all part of the café. And if I'm pushed out of the café, I'll be pushed out of the apartment too."

I saw us both being shoved into the street by a giant bulldozer. "Oh, Dad!" I said, clutching him.

"Oh, Lordy, I shouldn't have told you, especially now, when you're just going to sleep. I am so *stupid*. I've kept quiet for months, mostly because I couldn't face up to it myself. I've just kept hoping something would turn up, that they'll give me another loan—*anything*. I just can't believe they'll make us homeless."

"But what will we *do*, Dad?" I thought about the homeless people I'd seen on a trip to London. "Will we . . . will we live in a cardboard box?"

"Oh, Floss!" Dad spluttered. I didn't know whether he was laughing or crying. Maybe he didn't know either. "Of course we won't be living in cardboard boxes. No, love, you'll be fine. I'll get in touch with your mom and then pop you on the plane to Australia. I should have made you go in the first place. It was so bad of me, but it meant so much to me that you wanted to stay with your old dad. I kept desperately hoping that business would somehow pick up—but no such luck."

"I'm not going to Australia, Dad! I'm staying with you, no matter what. Even in a cardboard box." I put my arms tight around his neck. "Anyway, I *like* cardboard-box houses. Remember, I used to sit in one when I was little, with all my dolls and teddy bears squashed in beside me, playing Mothers and Fathers."

"You were such a sweet little kid," said Dad, kissing the top of my curls. "Now, you'd better settle down. Night-night, darling. You're not to worry, promise me?"

Of course I worried. I didn't sleep for ages and ages, and when I did I dreamed that our café and apartment had turned into cardboard. It started to rain and all the walls sagged and the floor split and I barged through the cardboard door yelling for Dad. When I found him he looked so old and frail, and when I hugged him he bent in half and crumpled in my arms as if he were cardboard too.

I woke up crying and ran to Dad. But he wasn't in his bedroom even though it was now the middle of the night. I peered under his comforter, I lifted his pillow, I even looked under his bed. Then I heard little creaking sounds coming from the kitchen.

I found Dad ironing away, my school blouses all around the room, hanging off doors and pegs and racks as if a flock of weird white birds were roosting in our kitchen.

"Dad?"

"Hello, little sweetheart," said Dad, acting like it was the most normal thing in the world to be up ironing at three in the morning.

"What are you doing? You've already ironed all my school blouses."

"Yes, and I made a real mess of them, so I've damped them all down and I'm doing them again. And *again*. This is my third time and they're *still* a bit sad and crumpled."

"They're fine, Dad. Leave it. Come back to bed, please!"

"I can't seem to sleep when I do, yet I'm exhausted in the daytime. I'm keeping Australian time. Maybe I should go and live there too!"

I thought about it, my heart thumping. "Well, if we have to leave the café, why can't we *both* go to Australia? Maybe Steve would lend you the money for the fare? You could pay him back once you'd started working. And I could still live with you but I could see Mom too. Maybe we could all stay there!"

"You're being so brave, Floss, about missing your mom," said Dad. "There's no chance of me going to Australia though, pet. I'd never take a penny off old Steve for starters. And I wouldn't be allowed into the country to work because I've no money and no skills."

"Yes, you have, Dad! You're great at running the café."

"Come off it, pet! I doubt I'd even get a job as a dishwasher. I'd *certainly* not get a job in a laundry. Look, I've scorched your blouse!" He held it up despairingly and showed me the brown mark.

"Never mind, Dad. Please. Stop ironing."

"Maybe the mark will come out if I wash it again," said Dad. Then he saw my face. "Sorry, pet! Your old dad's gone a bit nuts, that's all. Right. I'll stop ironing." He switched off the iron and stood in the middle of the kitchen in his old stripy pajamas. "Shall I tuck you up in bed, Floss?"

"I'm not sleepy now either."

"So . . . what shall we do?" said Dad. He shifted his weight from one bare foot to the other, considering. "I know!" he said suddenly. "Let's go and have a swing!"

"But it's the middle of the night, Dad," I said, wondering if he really *had* gone crazy.

"There's no law that says you can't have a night-time swing in your own garden," said Dad. "Put your coat on, sweetheart, and stick your feet in your boots."

Dad put a thick jersey over his pajamas and pulled on his own boots. Then we went downstairs, through the sad, silent café and out into the backyard. I thought it would be dark and scary, but there was a bright full moon making the yard look silvery and magical. We threaded our way through the bike parts and all the other junk. The Dumpsters had been emptied that day, so they hardly smelled at all. A little cat circled them wistfully, mewing for food.

"Oh, Dad, look, isn't she sweet?" I said. I bent down, a little clumsy in my boots. "Here, puss."

She looked at me, considered, and then approached me cautiously.

"Come on, then. I won't hurt you."

I reached out my hand and she came right up to me. She sniffed my palm hoping for scraps but seemed happy enough when I stroked her instead.

"She's a very thin little cat. Can we feed her, Dad?" I asked.

Dad was peering at her. "She's black, isn't she? Black cats are meant to be lucky, aren't they? Even skinny little stray ones! OK, if she hangs around a while I'll see if I can find a can of tuna."

"There, puss! You're so clever, coming calling to a café. That's my dad over there. He's going to fix you a perfectly lovely meal in a minute. Purr-fectly. Hey, Dad, purrfectly—do you get it?"

"Oh, ha-ha, funny Floss," said Dad. He sat himself down on the swing, kicking at the ground with the heel of his boot.

The cat rubbed against me, nuzzling in and purring when I stroked the side of her neck. Her bones felt so tiny and delicate underneath her soft fur.

"I wonder if you belong to anyone, little cat," I said. "You haven't got a collar on, have you? You don't look as if you've been fed for days. Dad, if she's really a stray, can we keep her?"

"We can't even keep ourselves, Floss," said Dad.

"Well, we can all three be strays, you, me and the cat," I said. "We can call her Lucky. You never know, Dad, maybe our luck is changing right this minute."

"Yes. Whoops! What was that? A big pink pig just flew past my head, flapping its wings."

"You wait and see, Dad," I said, gently lifting Lucky up in my arms. She nestled in to me as if she'd known me since she was a kitten.

"*We should be so lucky—lucky, lucky, lucky,*" Dad sang, kicking off and swinging. "Hey, this swing's lop-sided! Oh, Floss, why didn't you tell me?"

"It's fine, Dad, really."

"No, it's not—but I'll fix it for you tomorrow. Oh, dear, did Rhiannon remark on it when she came over?"

"Not really," I fibbed.

"I'm sorry I let you down with Rhiannon. I know she's your best friend."

"She *is*, but I've got another friend too now. Dad, can my new friend Susan come over on Saturday?"

"Is she very fancy and fussy like Rhiannon?" said Dad, swinging wildly, waving his boots.

"No, she's very clever but she's quiet, not a bit fussy or bossy," I said.

"I like her already!" said Dad.

* * *

It was lovely having Susan as my secret friend at school. We smiled and nodded at each other whenever Rhiannon wasn't looking. Most days we managed to meet up in the girls' restroom for a minute or two. We fixed it that she'd come at three o'clock on Saturday and stay for dinner.

"Chip butties! Promise?" said Susan.

I promised.

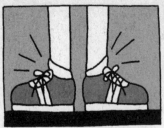

MY DAD

BY FLORA

My Dad

FLORA

IMPORTANT

Eleven

I was so looking forward to Susan coming on Saturday. Then on Friday Rhiannon ruined everything.

She'd been hanging around with Margot and Judy a lot of the time. They often looked in my direction and whispered and giggled.

"What's the joke?" I asked.

"You're the joke," said Margot "Like—your socks!"

Dad had tried hard with my new white socks. He was worried my birthday-present dress and shoes were far too big, so he'd bought extra-small children's socks. They were so extra small they were Tiger-size. It took me ages to pull them over my toes, and the heel came uncomfortably under my instep. The top of the sock kept getting sucked under my shoes each time I took a step, so every few seconds I had to bend down to pull them up. I'd have been much better off in my old navy socks, but I didn't want to hurt Dad's feelings.

He'd mastered the ironing now, but our laundering system was a bit of a problem. We didn't have a tumble dryer, so Dad hung all my clothes on a rail in the kitchen.

"Yuck! Fry grease!" said Margot, pretending to sniff me and then holding her nose.

Judy held her nose too. Rhiannon didn't, but she smirked and spluttered.

I knew my clothes *did* smell of café cooking. I didn't know what to do about it. I tried sprinkling my school blouses with a little leftover bottle of Mom's special perfume, but that made them hold their noses even more. They wafted their hands in the air and went "Pooh" and "Phew."

I felt like twisting their noses right off their faces.

I also wanted to cry because the perfume made me miss Mom so much. I ran away, and this time Rhiannon came after me.

"For goodness sake, don't be such a baby, Floss. They're just *teasing*," she said.

"I'm tired of being teased. I can't stand Margot and Judy," I said.

"Oh, don't be silly. They're good fun, so long as you don't take them seriously. Margot's soooo cool. Do you know, she's got a diamond stud in her belly button! I wish my mom would let me get my tummy pierced."

"I bet she just stuck it on," I said. "And it's probably not a *real* diamond."

"Well, so what? It still looks great. And she's got,

like, *such* a flat tummy too. I wish *my* tummy didn't stick out so. Still, I'm going to stay on this special diet and get super slim, you wait and see."

"You're super slim now, you know you are. Anyway, dieting's stupid at our age."

"You're just saying that because you're still so skinny. But you keep on eating all those chips and fry-ups at your dad's café and you'll be, like, ginormous." Rhiannon waved her arms in the air to demonstrate.

"No, I won't," I said—though I knew my dad was a *little* bit ginormous.

"Still, my mom's got this special healthy eating recipe book. She'll give it to your dad when he comes over to get you on Saturday," said Rhiannon.

I blinked at her. "Get me from where?" I said.

Rhiannon sighed impatiently. "From my place, stupid."

"But you haven't asked me over to your house on Saturday," I said, my heart thumping.

"Well, I'm asking you now," said Rhiannon. "Mom says you're to come for lunch and tea *and* bring a bag of all your clothes and she'll put them in the washing machine and iron them for you. Don't look like that, Floss. There's no need to feel embarrassed. Mom doesn't mind, really."

"I—I can't come, not this Saturday," I stammered.

"Why can't you come? It's all fixed," said Rhiannon.

"I've got to help my dad in the café," I fibbed.

"You're not supposed to work in the café. That's child labor. He can't make you."

"He doesn't *make* me do anything. I want to help."

"Well, you'll have to help some other time, because my mom's especially canceled her new highlights appointment at the hairdresser's just so she can be at home to look after you. Like I said, it's all fixed."

I didn't know what to do. I couldn't possibly tell Rhiannon the truth. She'd never forgive me if she knew I'd invited Susan over.

I mulled it over miserably during the next lesson. I couldn't concentrate during history, and when Mrs. Horsefield suddenly asked me a question, I didn't have a clue what she was talking about. She called me up to her desk when the bell rang.

"You're a little Dolly Daydream today, Floss. What's the matter, dear?" She was smiling at me sympathetically, not a bit angry.

I hung my head and made one foot do a tiny little pointy dance on the floor.

"Missing your mom?" Mrs. Horsefield said softly.

"Mmm," I said, because I *was* missing her dreadfully. Sometimes when Dad wasn't around I went and looked at the ticket in the kitchen drawer. I was determined not to use it—but it was good to know it was there.

"But you're getting on well together, you and your dad?" said Mrs. Horsefield.

"Oh, *yes*. Dad's being lovely. He always is," I said.

"That's good. Well, you certainly look a lot sharper today," said Mrs. Horsefield, looking at my newly washed hair, my clean blouse, my pressed skirt, my very small white socks and my spotless shoes.

I made the other shoe do a little dance, trying to work up the courage to ask Mrs. Horsefield what I should do about seeing Rhiannon on Saturday.

"Yes?" Mrs. Horsefield prompted.

I swallowed. I couldn't. I asked her something else instead.

"Mrs. Horsefield, do I smell?"

Mrs. Horsefield looked startled. "Oh, Floss! You're as clean as clean. You look as if you've just jumped out of a bath today."

"Yes, but do I *smell*?"

"Not of anything unpleasant," she said evasively.

I sighed deeply.

"Has someone been saying nasty things?" said Mrs. Horsefield, sounding angry.

"No. Well. They were just teasing," I said quickly.

"Teasing can be horribly cruel. I don't suppose you're going to tell me who it was?"

I shook my head, gazing at my feet.

"You don't need to tell me. I'm sure I can guess. Don't you take any notice of them." She paused. "Oh, well. You'd better run out into the sunshine. I love sunny days like this. I put my washing out on a line and it dries beautifully and smells of fresh air."

I nodded gratefully and walked to the door.

"Will you watch out for Susan for me, Floss? I think she's still a bit lonely. She could really do with a kind girl like you to be her friend."

"Yes, Mrs. Horsefield," I said.

I so, so, so wanted to be Susan's friend. But I was too scared to be a kind girl.

I ran to the girls' restroom. Susan was standing in a corner, counting the tiles up and the tiles down, muttering each number. Then she saw me and her mouth stretched into a smile.

"Hi, Floss!" she said happily. "I can't wait till Saturday."

I took a deep breath. "Oh, Susan, I'm ever so sorry, but I can't make Saturday after all."

Susan stared at me. It was as if I'd taken the smelly floor mop in the corner and shoved it in her face, smearing the smile away.

"Did Rhiannon find out?" she said, her voice wobbling a little.

"No! No, it's nothing to do with Rhiannon," I lied. "No, it's just I've got to do stuff with my dad, that's all. But you can come the Saturday *after.* That will be OK, won't it?"

"Yes, probably," said Susan, but her voice still sounded funny.

"We'll still have chip butties," I said.

"Yes. Great," said Susan flatly.

It was as if she knew. I told myself she couldn't possibly know. I pretended that everything was still perfectly fine. I would go to Rhiannon's on Saturday. She was my best friend after all. I'd wear my rose quartz bracelet and play in Rhiannon's beautiful blue bedroom and maybe I'd teach her how to make a friendship bracelet. Then the *next* Saturday I'd see Susan at my house and we'd play on my swing and eat chip butties and maybe she'd do all the things Rhiannon thought were babyish or boring, like playing pretend imaginary games or drawing pictures or making tiny dollhouses in cardboard boxes.

Rhiannon was busy planning Saturday too. *This* Saturday.

"My mom's going to take us shopping at Green Glades when you come this Saturday, Floss," she said loudly.

"Ssh!" I hissed.

Susan sat right in front of us. She was writing her comprehension—but her pen paused in midair.

"It's OK. Mrs. Horsefield's over there helping Dumbo Diana," Rhiannon said. "Anyway, she won't pick on us. You're total teacher's pet now. *Anyway*, Mom's going to get you some new socks and stuff, seeing as yours are, like, so weeny and weird."

"Please, ssh!" I whispered.

"It's OK. We all know it's not *your* fault. Mom's going to do it very tactfully. She's going to pretend *I* need new stuff and then she's going to say, 'Oh, look, why don't I get a jumbo pack or whatever, and then they'll be for both of you.' She's got it all planned. We're probably going to do shoe shopping too. I told her you just have those crazy silver high heels to wear at home and she says you'll ruin your feet."

Susan hadn't restarted her comprehension. She was too busy comprehending the situation.

"We're going to this fabulous new restaurant for lunch. I'm going to have a mango smoothie, yum, and then you get to choose all these different salads—it's, like, soooo delicious. Mom says she owes it to *your* mom to help you eat healthily, seeing as you have to live on those chip butties most of the time."

Susan's head bent low when Rhiannon said chip butties. Her hair fell forward. The nape of her neck looked white and forlorn.

I wanted to reach forward and pat her on the shoulder, maybe put my arm around her. I stayed stuck beside Rhiannon. She went on and on and on about seeing me on Saturday.

There was still a tiny little bit of me that somehow hoped Susan couldn't *quite* hear.

The bell rang for the end of class. Susan stood up, starting to pack her bag. Rhiannon jumped up, barging past her, scattering her books on the floor. She didn't try to pick them up or even say sorry.

"See you tomorrow, Floss," she bellowed, right in Susan's face.

Susan dodged down, gathered her books, and hurried out of the classroom. She clicked her fingers as she went, counting under her breath.

"That Swotty Potty gives me the creeps," said Rhiannon. "She's totally nuts, isn't she, Floss?"

I stared after Susan until my eyes blurred.

"*Floss?*" said Rhiannon. "What's up *now*? Don't you go all wimpy and weepy on me tomorrow—it's going to be a fun day, right?"

It didn't feel like it was going to be a fun day at all. I told Dad about the change of plan. He raised his eyebrows when I said I was going to Rhiannon's.

"I'll deliver you there and I'll pick you up whenever you want, but *please* don't make me come and talk to that wretched woman!" said Dad. "So what about your new little friend Susan? Is she going to Rhiannon's too?"

I sighed at the impossibility of ever being able to explain to Dad the complications of the situation. I didn't really want him to know all the ins and outs anyway. He probably wouldn't say anything, let alone tell me off, but I'd feel bad anyway. I was feeling very, very, very bad as it was.

I hung my pink birthday T-shirt and special jeans over my swing seat as we didn't have a washing line in the backyard. I hoped the cool night air would make them smell fresh and beautiful the next morning.

When I woke up I heard pattering on my window. It was raining hard.

"Oh, no!" I threw my raincoat over my nightie, stuck my feet in my boots, and rushed out to the backyard.

My clothes were sodden. My jeans had fallen right off the seat and were all muddy on the ground. My T-shirt had curled itself around and around like a Swiss roll, as if some little night creature had used it as a blanket.

"Lucky?" I called hopefully, momentarily distracted from the Wet Clothes Disaster.

I had *so* wanted her to stay with us. When she turned up in the middle of the night I'd fed her a whole tin of tuna and given her a saucer of milk to lap. She'd mewed at me gratefully. She'd even given me a little lick of appreciation. I'd squatted beside her and stroked her from her neat little head to the tip of her tail, and she'd wriggled happily and started purring. I thought she was making it as plain as could be that she wanted to live with me. But when I tried to pick her up gently and carry her indoors she cried and struggled, scratching me. I had to let her go. She flew away from me, back behind the Dumpsters.

I'd tried to wheel one out of the way so I could get at her, but she mewed at me indignantly and crammed herself into the farthest corner behind the biggest one.

"Don't fuss her, Floss," said Dad. "It looks like she wants to stay outside."

"But it's all dark and smelly by the trash. She'd be so much happier indoors. She could share my bedroom. I could make it so safe and cozy for her," I said.

"You can't force her in if she doesn't want to come," said Dad. "She's not our cat."

"I so want her to be ours, Dad."

"Well, leave her be for now. She'll hang around if she feels like it. *She'll* decide whether she's going to be our cat or not."

"Our Lucky," I said.

I'd checked up on her ten minutes later. I peered behind every Dumpster. I peeped under every tarp. I scoured the entire backyard. There was no sign of Lucky.

"She probably went for a little prowl around, Floss. That's what cats do," said Dad.

"But she will come back?"

"Well. Probably," said Dad. "In her own good time."

"Probably isn't definite enough!" I wailed. "Oh, Lucky, where are you? You will come back, won't you? You really badly want to be our little lucky black cat, don't you?"

I listened hard for a tiny mew. If Lucky could hear me, she kept quiet.

I'd paced the backyard all the following evening, but there was still no sign of her. I got Dad to open a fresh tin of tuna and I poured out another saucer of milk and waited tensely, hour after hour.

A big ginger tomcat came prowling past but I hid Lucky's gourmet meal from him. Lucky herself didn't come near. I left her food out overnight and it was nearly all gone in the morning—but I couldn't tell if Lucky herself had eaten it, or whether the ginger tom-cat had come back.

On Friday Dad had said gently that maybe we couldn't count on Lucky returning.

"Maybe she's gone back home to her real owners. Or maybe she's happy fending for herself, being a little street cat."

"She'd be much happier with us," I said. "She'll come back, Dad, in her own good time, like you said."

If she *had* come back during the night and had a nap cuddled up in my T-shirt, she hadn't hung around to say hello this morning.

I picked up my sodden jeans and T-shirt and squished my way back into the house. Dad was in the kitchen in his bathrobe, yawning and scratching.

"Floss? Have you been out to play in the pouring rain?" he said. He held up my clothes. "For goodness sake! We'll have to put them straight back in the wash. You should have kept them clean for visiting Rhiannon."

I leaned against the kitchen table, helping myself to cornflakes straight from the box. "Lucky might just have been in the backyard last night," I said.

"Hmm. Well, we could do with some luck right this minute," said Dad, looking through his mail.

There was a handful of bills and one scary white envelope with IMPORTANT stamped in big red letters.

Dad opened it up, read it quickly, shoved it in his bathrobe pocket, and then slumped beside me. He reached in the cornflakes box for a snack. His hand was trembling and cornflakes spilled onto the kitchen floor.

"What's the matter, Dad?" My voice sounded croaky because my throat was so dry. I swallowed hard but the cornflakes in my mouth wouldn't go away.

"It's our eviction notice," said Dad. He breathed out, so hard that the cornflakes box wavered and nearly fell over. "I wrote to them begging for more time, explaining I'm now looking after my daughter full-time. I thought that might just sway them. I mean, what sort of heartless monsters would render an innocent little kid homeless? Well, now I've found out. We've got two weeks, Floss. Two flipping weeks and then we have to hand over the keys or they'll send in the muscle." Dad bent forward, resting his head on the table.

"Dad?" I whispered.

I lowered my own head, staring at him. His eyes were closed.

"Please, Dad! Sit up. It'll be all right," I said, stroking his head.

Dad groaned. "I've let you down, darling."

"No, you haven't! Here, Dad, let me make you a cup of tea."

I bustled around, boiling the kettle and fetching a

mug and milk and tea bags. I knew Dad would look up when it came to me pouring the boiling water, just in case I wasn't doing it safely enough. Just as I'd thought, he sat up straight the second the kettle switched off.

"Here, I'll do it," Dad said, sighing.

He made us both a cup of tea and then sat sipping his, staring all around the kitchen. He looked at the greasy walls and the ancient stove and the higgledy-piggledy cupboards and the cracked linoleum tiles on the floor. He stood up and stroked some silly old paintings I'd done at nursery school, each a red blobby figure with a big smiley mouth, all bearing the same title: *My Dad*. He picked up my clay rabbit models on the windowsill and my lopsided plaster ashtray and the plate I'd painted with big purple pansies because Dad said they were his favorite flower.

"All my treasures," Dad mumbled, as if the kitchen were crammed with wondrous antiques.

"We'll pack everything and take it with us, Dad," I said.

"To decorate our cardboard box?" said Dad. He shook his head. "Sorry, sorry, I'm getting maudlin. No, I'll manage. Maybe one of my old biker friends will let me sleep in a corner of his living room for a bit, just till I get myself sorted out."

"Will they let me have a corner too, Dad?" I asked anxiously.

"You're not sleeping on floors, darling. No, I'll

wait till this evening, when it's morning in Australia, and then I'll phone your mom. We'll whiz you over to Sydney."

"No, Dad!"

"Yes, Floss," said Dad firmly. "Now, you go and find yourself some decent dry clothes and forget all this nonsense for the moment. You're going to have a lovely day with Rhiannon."

I wasn't at all sure about that. I dressed myself in my old jeans and my old stripy T-shirt, after burying my head in them to see if they smelled. It was so difficult to tell at home in the café because it *all* smelled so cozily of cooking.

I brushed my hair and I brushed my teeth and I brushed my shoes. I did this varied brushing ultra-thoroughly, and at each stroke of the brush I made a wish that our luck would change and that somehow or other Dad could stay cooking his chip butties forever.

Billy the Chip came in to mind the café while Dad was taking me to Rhiannon's. He was clutching his *Racing Post*.

"Come on, young Flossie, pick me a winner," he said.

"Oh, Mr. Chip, I'm terrible at picking winners. Birthday Girl was hopeless, and Iced Bun was worse."

"Have another go, darling."

"What, you think it'll be third time lucky?" I said.

"Yes!" said Billy the Chip. "Look! Third Time Lucky is running at Doncaster! We've got to back it now. What about you, Charlie? Shall I put something on for you?"

"I haven't got anything left to bet with, mate. I think it might be a bit of a waste anyway. Look at the odds. It hasn't got a chance."

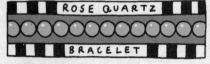

ROSE QUARTZ

BRACELET

FRIENDSHIP

BRACELET

Twelve

Rhiannon was especially sweet to me. She was almost like the *old* Rhiannon, before she started thinking Margot was wonderful. And I felt almost like the old Floss, when I still had two homes and I could see Mom whenever I wanted.

We went to play in Rhiannon's beautiful blue bedroom, and it was so *peaceful* lying back on her soft flowery comforter and seeing the clean white paint and fresh blue ruffles. It felt as if we were floating up into the sky. Rhiannon let me shake all her snowglobes and wind up her Cinderella musical box and flick from channel to channel on her own little white television.

She let me try on all her coolest clothes. She even let me try walking in her brand-new boots with pointy toes and real heels. She didn't want to try on my jeans and T-shirt, so I let her wear my birthday-present rose quartz bracelet. It looked very pretty on her slim white wrist. I asked her where her friendship bracelet was.

"I don't know," she said, shrugging. "Think I must have lost it."

"Oh. Well. Never mind," I said. "I'll make you another if you like. Tell you what, we could use that kit I gave you and make each other a friendship bracelet now."

Rhiannon wrinkled her forehead. "Like, boring!" she said. "No, we're going shopping—I *said*. Mom's taking us to Green Glades."

Rhiannon's mom drove us there in her big Range Rover. Rhiannon and I knelt up in the backseat and made faces at people in the cars behind.

"I bet you wish you had a big car like our Range Rover," said Rhiannon.

"It's lovely—but actually my dad's van is just as big," I said.

"Yeah, but, like, that's just a transit van," said Rhiannon.

They obviously didn't compare so I kept my mouth shut. I was starting to feel a bit sick. I hadn't realized Green Glades was so far away. I wriggled around in my seat and stared straight ahead. My jeans were starting to be a bit too small for me. They pressed uncomfortably into my tummy. I closed my eyes, praying that I wasn't going to disgrace myself.

"Hey, don't go to sleep on me, Floss!" said Rhiannon.

"No, no, leave her be, darling," said Rhiannon's mother. "She looks as if she could do with a good sleep. She's looking so peaky, poor lamb. I know her dad is doing his best but I bet he doesn't get her to bed on time."

I wanted to argue, but I knew if I sat up and opened my mouth I would actually start spouting vomit. I stayed still as a statue, eyes shut, tummy clenched, sweat trickling down inside my T-shirt with the effort of keeping my breakfast in place.

Seemingly many, many years later we got to Green Glades and parked the car. I rushed to the nearest ladies' room, and when the stall door shut me away from Rhiannon and her mom, I threw up as silently as possible.

"Oh, darling, you do look weak and feeble," Rhiannon's mother cooed when I staggered out. "You haven't been sick, have you?"

"No!" I said emphatically, because she'd only start on about my dad's chip butties. I suddenly soooo wanted my mom, who would know exactly how to deal with Rhiannon's mother. I hated being the poor, sad, sickly girl, especially when I was *feeling* so poor and sad and sickly.

I wanted to talk to her on the phone. Dad was going to phone her tonight to tell her that he thought I should go to Australia. My stomach started churning again. I wanted Mom but I wanted Dad too. I couldn't bear the thought of leaving him. He'd said the muscle would move in. I didn't really know what the muscle were. I pictured an army of huge red-faced, prickly-headed guys, all of them punching my poor dad and then kicking him out of our café with their big heavy boots as if he were a bag of trash. I saw him sitting in the gutter, crawling inside his cardboard box.

I had to run right back to the bathroom and throw up all over again. I didn't even have anything to be sick with anymore; it was just horrible bile stuff. I couldn't fool Rhiannon and her mother this time. I suffered a lecture about suitable diet for the next half hour, though I told them truthfully I'd simply had a small bowl of cornflakes for my breakfast.

"Margot has the most amazing mango and pineapple smoothies for her breakfast. We made them ourselves. It was *so* cool," said Rhiannon.

"When were you having breakfast with Margot?" I said.

"When she had this sleepover," Rhiannon said airily.

I was stunned. I had been so scared of upsetting Rhiannon by having Susan over for tea, and yet here she was casually telling me that she had actually *stayed the night* at Margot's.

"What?" said Rhiannon, seeing my expression. "Oh, Floss, lighten up. It's *OK*. You don't have to be, like, *jealous*." She actually laughed at me.

"I'm *not* jealous," I mumbled foolishly.

"Don't worry, dear. You're still Rhiannon's special friend," said Rhiannon's mom.

She didn't say "best" friend. "Special" made me sound embarrassing and needy, the poor little loser you had to be nice to because you felt so sorry for her.

I felt my cheeks burning. I didn't *want* Rhiannon as my friend anymore, best or special. I wished, wished, wished I'd made real friends with Susan.

I was stuck with Rhiannon and her mother. We went up and down every single arcade and walkway of the Green Glades shopping center. I'd have liked it if I was there with *my* mom. We'd look at things together and try on different stuff and strike crazy poses like fashion models and tell each other we looked drop-dead gorgeous.

Rhiannon and her mother took their shopping *seriously*. They tried on outfit after outfit, reciting the designer labels as if they were magic charms.

"You must try on anything you fancy too, Floss," said Rhiannon's mom. "I'm determined to treat you, darling. We can't have you wandering about like a sad little scarecrow."

She bought me new white socks. She wanted to buy me new shoes too, but I said that my sneakers had been a special birthday present from my mom and I wanted to wear them all the time.

"They're starting to look a bit shabby already, dear," said Rhiannon's mom, but she didn't press it.

She *did* press me to choose some new clothes. She didn't *say* anything disparaging about my jeans and T-shirt, but she shook her head and sighed, so it was clear what she thought of them.

I didn't want her to buy me anything. I didn't even

want the socks, though I needed them badly. But there was no way I could keep saying no without seeming rude and ungrateful. I tried picking out the cheapest top and jeans I could find on the bargain racks so that they would cost as little as possible, but this didn't please Rhiannon or her mother.

"Oh, God, Floss, you can't possibly like that tacky old T-shirt. It looks like something out of a flea market," said Rhiannon. "And those jeans! I wouldn't be seen dead in them. Look at the cut of the leg. They are, like, *so* old-fashioned."

"You're not really into fashion, are you, dear?" said Rhiannon's mother. "Don't worry, Rhiannon's always been a bit forward—she could spot a designer label when she was still in her stroller. We'll help you, darling. You don't need to dress in that little girly-wirly get-up just because you're so small. We'll find you an outfit with a bit of oomph."

I didn't know what oomph was. I didn't much like the sound of it.

I was right to be wary.

Rhiannon went rushing around collecting armfuls of clothes, including a denim outfit studded with rhinestones, with a matching cap.

"Oh, darling, that's so cute. Hey, pick one out for Floss in a smaller size. I'm sure she'll look wonderful in it."

Rhiannon looked *sort of* wonderful in the tiny tight

skirt and little studded bomber jacket and the sparkly skimpy vest that showed her tummy. She slipped the cap on at a jaunty angle and struck a pose, as if a million cameras were flashing.

I didn't look at all wonderful. The little skirt looked weird way up my spindly legs and I hardly dared move in it in case my underwear showed. The bomber jacket hung on me oddly and the vest looked as if it had shrunk in the wash. The cap wouldn't stay on unless I clamped it down hard over my curls.

"You look so sweet, Floss," said Rhiannon's mother, tugging at the cap and pulling the jacket. "There, that's the ticket. You and Rhiannon look just like sisters. We have to buy it for you."

"No, please. It's very kind of you but it's much too expensive," I protested, truthfully enough. The price of each designer outfit would have clothed an entire orphanage of children from head to foot in ordinary denim. Besides, I hated the whole outfit, only I couldn't really say so when Rhiannon and her mom thought it was so wonderful.

I let them buy it for me. I said thank you over and over again. Rhiannon and I wore our brand-new outfits then and there. Rhiannon swished and strutted around the shopping center and nearly everyone turned and smiled and stared at her. They stared and smiled at me too, but they also raised their eyebrows. It was like they had thought bubbles over their heads.

They thought, *What a beautiful child* when they looked at Rhiannon. They thought, *What a sad little weirdo* when they looked at me.

I hoped we were done. We weren't. We went in heaps *more* shops before we went for lunch in the Green Glade Grotto. It had grass-green velvet chairs and a fake grass carpet and rocks instead of walls, with real trickly waterfalls. Rhiannon's mother ordered Rhiannon and me a Green Glade Super Special Drink (lemonade and lime juice with slices of real lime, little green flowers cut out of cucumbers, and tiny green umbrellas).

"You can eat the lime and the cucumber, but not the umbrella!" said Rhiannon's mother, as if I were Tiger's age. "Now, what would you like to eat, dear? I know you love your chips, and they *do* do very nice French fries here, but I think Rhiannon and I will be having a Green Glade Super Special Salad. Would you like to try one too?"

So I tried one. It came on a green glass plate patterned like lettuce. The food was very prettily set out like a flower, with strawberries in the center, pink grapefruit petals, and arugula leaves.

"There! You're really enjoying it, aren't you?" said Rhiannon's mother, as if she were introducing me to the concept of salad for the very first time.

"It's delicious," I said, as limply as the lettuce.

"What's *up* with you?" said Rhiannon, kicking me under the table.

I didn't really know. If I'd been spending the day with my best friend Rhiannon last month, being treated to new clothes and lovely meals, I'd have been over the moon, the stars, orbiting in outer space. But now I wanted to be anywhere else. I wanted to be in Australia with Mom and Steve and Tiger. I wanted to be back home in the café with Dad and Billy the Chip and Old Ron and Miss Davis. I wanted to be playing on my swing with Susan.

Oh, Susan.

I looked at Rhiannon. I realized I really didn't like her anymore.

"What?" said Rhiannon, tipping her cap at an even cuter angle. My rose quartz bracelet slid prettily up and down her arm. "Why are you looking at me like that? Honestly, Floss, you are, like, soooo moody at times."

"Now now, Rhiannon," said Rhiannon's mom. "What did I say about being kind to Flossie? Imagine how you'd feel if I went off and left you."

"My mom *didn't* leave me. She's coming back in six months—just over *five* months—and I feel *fine*. I've got my dad," I said.

"Yes, dear," said Rhiannon's mother, but the expression on her face made it obvious she didn't believe a word of it.

Rhiannon yawned and picked up a magazine. "Oh, wow! Look! It's Purple!" she said.

"Purple what?" I said.

"Purple! They're just the coolest boy band ever, especially Danny. He is, like, fantastic," said Rhiannon, kissing her fingertip and pressing it to Danny's pouty photo mouth.

"I bet Margot likes him," I said.

"She's only got tickets for their latest tour! Her dad's taking her, and she can choose a friend to come too and she said she wants me to come instead of Judy."

"Can't Flossie come too?" said Rhiannon's mother.

"Floss isn't into cool bands like Purple. She'd never even *heard* of them," said Rhiannon. "Hey, can we go to HMV, Mom? Can I get their latest album? *Please!*"

"What sort of music do you like, Flossie?" said Rhiannon's mother.

I shrugged. I liked all the golden oldies Dad played on the van radio, and we sang them together. Dad often sang the women's songs, making his voice very high-pitched, putting in lots of oohs and coos. I sang the guy parts in a deep growl. We could rarely reach the end of any song because we kept cracking up laughing.

Rhiannon would *certainly* crack up laughing if I said I liked "Crazy Little Thing Called Love" and "Stand by Your Man" and "Dancing Queen." So I just kept shrugging, like I was doing shoulder exercises.

"Rhiannon, you should tell Flossie all about these boy bands," said Rhiannon's mom. "Don't worry, Floss, we'll take you in hand."

I felt I was growing smaller and smaller and smaller and they were scrunching me up in their hands. I didn't *want* to be turned into a little replica of Rhiannon.

"Now, dear, what would you like to do most of all?" said Rhiannon's mother.

Go home! I longed to say, but I knew that would sound very rude indeed, especially as she was trying to be so kind to me. So I said I'd like to go to HMV too and Rhiannon smiled at me and went "Yay!"

We spent the rest of the afternoon at Green Glades doing Rhiannon things. I was good at suggesting all the right places. We went to heaps more clothes shops and a special perfume shop, spraying on samples until we reeked, and then we spent hours trying all the testers on Boots's makeup counters.

All the time I played a game in my head choosing the places that Susan and I might like. We'd both want to spend ages in the bookshop, and we'd maybe like the art shop too, and *perhaps* Susan wouldn't laugh if I wanted to go to the Bear Factory. We wouldn't necessarily have to spend any money. We could have fun choosing our best books and our favorite set of coloring crayons, and we could each decide on a factory bear and name it and choose different outfits for it.

I could list our choice of books and crayons and little bear clothes and Susan could count them all up in her head. We'd wander off to the swankiest restaurant and pretend to choose a special meal in celebration. But before we ordered Susan would say, "I don't know, this all sounds totally delicious but do you know what I *really* fancy?" and I'd say, "Mmm, yes, I think there's only one possible choice," and then we'd both laugh and shout, "CHIP BUTTIES!"

But Susan wouldn't ever want to come back to the café with me to have chip butties because I'd betrayed her. Dad was being thrown out of the café anyway. He wouldn't be able to make his special chip butties.

I couldn't stop the tears welling in my eyes. I kept my head bent and blinked hard but Rhiannon still saw. She edged up very close so that her mother wouldn't hear.

"*Baby!*" she hissed in my ear.

I sniffed and tried to stop crying. It didn't work.

"Oh, Floss, don't cry," said Rhiannon's mother. "Come here, you poor little thing." She put her arms around me and gave me a powdery hug. She used the same perfume as my mom. I cried harder.

"Oh dear, oh dear. Maybe we'd better take you home now," she said.

I was still a bit sniffly when we got back. I rubbed my eyes hard and straightened my stupid cap.

"Thank you very much indeed for the lovely day out," I said as politely as I could. "And thank you for the green meal and the socks and the fantastic out-fit too."

"You're very welcome, dear. I just wish you'd let me do more for you."

We drew up outside the café. Rhiannon's mom looked at the HARLIE'S CAFÉ sign and sighed.

"I think I'll come in and have a little word with your Dad," she said.

"Oh, no. Don't, please. He'll be too busy serving all his customers," I said quickly, though I knew there'd be only Billy the Chip, Old Ron, and Miss Davis sitting there, stirring their tea at separate tables.

"Oh, well . . ." said Rhiannon's mom doubtfully.

"Bye, Rhiannon," I said, climbing out of the car.

Rhiannon waved her arm. The rose quartz bracelet slid up underneath the sleeve of her denim jacket.

"My bracelet—" I said, and then I stopped.

"Oh, Rhiannon, give poor little Floss her birthday bracelet back," said Rhiannon's mother.

"No, it's all right. I'd like her to have it," I said.

"But we gave it to you," said Rhiannon's mother, sounding faintly irritated.

"You've given me much too much. Rhiannon can keep it now. She lost the other bracelet I gave her."

"Which bracelet?" Rhiannon's mother asked. "I didn't know you gave Rhiannon a bracelet."

"Just some old thready thing," said Rhiannon. "Are you *sure* I can keep the rose quartz bracelet?"

"Yes," I said.

I didn't want it anymore. I didn't even care that Rhiannon obviously hadn't liked my friendship bracelet, even though it had taken me hours to make it, and I'd chosen Rhiannon's favorite colors, pink and blue and purple, and fastened it with a little silver heart. There was no point having a friendship bracelet if you didn't want to be friends anymore.

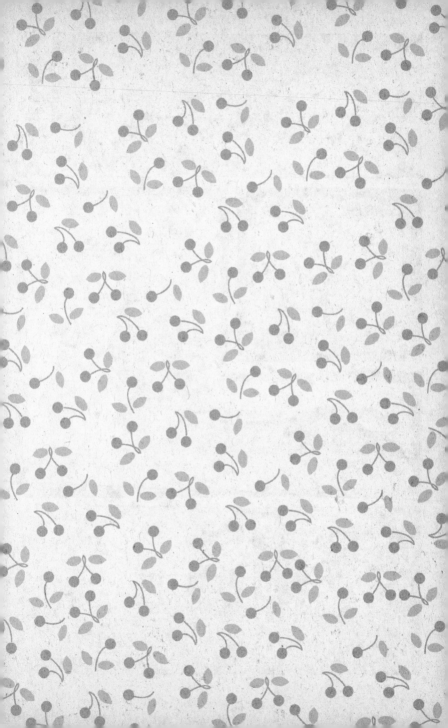

Thirteen

I walked into the café. I knew at once that something strange had happened. We didn't have any new customers, but Billy the Chip, Old Ron, and Miss Davis were all sitting at the same table. They weren't drinking tea. They were drinking from dinky little glasses, filling them from a big green bottle. Champagne!

Dad had a glassful too. He raised his glass at me, and then nearly spilled his champagne when he saw what I was wearing.

"Oh, Floss, what has that woman done to you! Here, darling, come and have your first weeny little sip of champagne."

"What are we celebrating, Dad?" I asked.

"It's our dear old Billy. He's the one who's celebrating!" said Dad, raising his glass to Billy the Chip.

"Is it your birthday, Mr. Chip?" I asked, taking a small sip out of Dad's glass. The bubbles fizzed up my nose and made me giggle.

"You can't give alcoholic liquor to the child. Look at her, she's drunk already!" said Miss Davis.

"Oh, liven up, you old biddy. It would do you good to get drunk yourself for once," said Old Ron.

"It's not my birthday, sweetheart," said Billy the Chip. "But it feels like it. I backed Third Time Lucky in the four thirty at Doncaster—a fifty-to-one outsider, no less—and guess what, the darling little filly grew wings and flew home, first past the finishing post!"

"Oh, well done!" I said, clapping my hands. "Oh, Dad, *did* you have a bet too?"

"I thought I was being so sensible," said Dad, shaking his head. "Still, I'm thrilled for Billy, and very grateful too."

"It's me that should be grateful to little Flossie here. I'll buy you a big dolly or teddy for a belated birthday present—and do your dad a little favor into the bargain."

"Mr. Chip's doing us a great big favor, Floss," said Dad, sipping champagne. He took my cap off and ruffled my curls back into place. "There! Call me old-fashioned, but I don't really care for the trendy outfit on you, pet."

"I hate it, Dad. I didn't want her to buy it for me. Don't worry, I won't ever, ever, ever wear it again. *But what's the big favor?*"

"Well, you know the whole sad situation about the café—" Dad started.

"Oh, Dad, oh, Dad! Is Mr. Chip going to give you some of his winnings so we can keep the café?" I burst out.

"Of course not, Floss! We owe far too much. No, I'm afraid we've got to go by Monday next week. But I've got somewhere to go now. *And* I've got a job for the next few weeks!" Dad beamed at Billy the Chip. "It's so good of you, Billy. You're a great friend."

"Think nothing of it, Charlie. You're the one doing me a favor, taking over the van and keeping an eye on my place while I'm off gallivanting." Billy the Chip nodded at me. "I'm off to Australia, young Floss. I'm going to spend my winnings on a ticket to go and see my boy. I can't wait!"

"Isn't that great, Floss! You can travel with Billy, keep each other company."

"I'm staying with you, Dad," I said firmly, though inside I was as wobbly as a jelly.

"No, Floss, that's completely nuts and we both know it."

"Then I'm completely nuts," I said, making a funny face.

They all chuckled, while Dad shook his head.

"So you're going to run Mr. Chip's chip van, Dad?"

"That's right, little darling."

"And is that where we're going to live . . . in the chip van?" I said. I tried to say it casually, but my voice came out all squeaky as I said it.

Dad burst out laughing. Billy the Chip laughed too, his pale potato face flushing pink. Old Ron roared. Even Miss Davis chirped and cooed, sounding like her birdy friends.

"It might be a bit of a squash, sweetheart," said Billy the Chip. "I don't think you could squeeze even your little bed inside my old van. No, you and your dad can stay at my house. You can be my house sitters—and feed my cats too. Your dad says you like cats. Is that right, Flossie?"

"Yes, especially little skinny black ones," I said wistfully.

Dad wouldn't let me have any more champagne, but he poured lemonade into a special glass for me so that I could join in the party too.

"I'm a bit hungry from all the excitement," said Billy the Chip. "How about a chip butty, Charlie?"

"They're on the house, pal," said Dad. "Hey, little Floss, come and be my Number One Kitchen Assistant."

When we were out in the kitchen and Dad had set the chips sizzling, he bent down till our faces were level and cupped my cheeks with his big hands.

"Are you sure you're serious about staying with me, darling? I truly think you'd be so much better off joining up with your mom. Billy's offer is a godsend but he's only going for a month. He says we can still stay at his place after he comes back but that doesn't seem very fair. I've no idea what his house is like, though I shouldn't think it's very big."

"It'll be bigger than a cardboard box, Dad," I said. "I'm staying."

Dad laughed, but his eyes went all watery. "You're a great little kid, my Floss," he said. "So, we'll have to get your toys all packed up again. We'll take your swing with us too. Let's hope we can tie it up in Billy's garden somewhere, though I can't promise. Run and have a little swing now, sweetie, make the most of it. I'll call you when the fries are done."

I went into the backyard even though I didn't really feel like swinging. I felt as if I'd been on a giant swing for far too long as it was. I was dizzy with all the changes in my life. Rose was wrong. All the changes that had happened so far had been horrible. She'd got her good luck signs wrong too. My lovely little lucky black cat had sloped off to live somewhere else. She probably hadn't been snacking on the plates of tuna. I was fattening up that ginger tomcat, or a stray squirrel or fox was licking its chops and coming back for more at this newly opened animal annex to the café.

I leaned over the swing seat, moodily propelling myself backward and forward with the tips of my toes. The seat was hard against my tummy. I hung my head right down, staring at the scrubby grass. I sent messages through the earth all the way down to Australia.

"*I miss you so, Mom,*" I whispered.

I shut my eyes and thought about the airline ticket. Everyone thought I was nuts not to go to Australia, even Dad. He'd be all right now. He had a job and a place to live. It wasn't as if I'd be leaving him *forever*. In five months I'd be back.

I could have my own bedroom in Australia, not a camp bed in a corner of some funny old man's house. I could have fresh clean comfy clothes, not creased smelly stuff or embarrassing designer denim. I could make new friends and I could be a proper friend back. I could play on the beaches and swim in the sea, I could go into the bush and see all the animals, jump with the kangaroos, cuddle the koalas . . .

"Mew!"

I opened my eyes. Lucky was sitting right in front of me, her green eyes shining, her little mouth open wide.

"Mew, mew, mew!" she said, for all the world as if she were saying hello.

"Oh, Lucky!" I nearly fell right off the swing, onto my head. I caught hold of the rope, wriggled free, and then bent down in front of Lucky, holding out my hand.

"Hello, darling," I whispered. "You've come back!"

"Mew!" she said, padding softly toward me until her lovely little head was right by my palm. She let me tickle her chin, arching her neck and stretching her whole body. She wasn't quite as skinny now, and her fur seemed softer and thicker.

"Have you been eating all the food I've left for you?"

Lucky gazed at me with her beautiful emerald eyes, a *wouldn't-you-like-to-know!* expression on her face.

"Would you like something to eat now? Some nice brown slurpy slimy specially bought cat food?"

"Mew," said Lucky. It was a definite yes.

"So what am I going to do? If I go and get your food will you promise, promise, promise to stay here? Or will you come indoors with me? We've got a lovely café with lots of milk. Won't you come and see it while we still live here? Please?"

Lucky stretched, considering. Then she leaned against me docilely. I slipped my hands gently around her. This time she let me lift her up, her whole body relaxed.

"Oh, Lucky, Lucky, Lucky," I said, rubbing my cheek against her silky fur. Then I walked very carefully into the house, Lucky clasped to my chest.

Dad was concentrating on lifting the golden chips out of the sizzling pan. "Good swing, sweetheart?" he said.

"Yep. Dad, *look*!"

Dad looked—and nearly dropped the chips. "Oh, Floss, your little cat! She's come back!"

"She doesn't mind coming in this time, does she, Dad? She wants her dinner!"

"OK, you give her something to eat while I make us all chip butties."

I had to put Lucky down to fill one little bowl with cat food and another with water. I was worried she'd try to scoot straight out of the back door but she waited patiently, licking her lips at the smell of the food.

"Eat up, little Lucky," I said.

"You eat up too, little Floss," said Dad, giving me a chip butty.

Dad went off with a big plateful of butties for Billy the Chip and Old Ron and Miss Davis. I stayed in the kitchen, sitting cross-legged beside Lucky. When we'd both finished eating, she went to the back door, looking at me expectantly.

"You want to go away already?" I said. "Look, I know this is a café, but you don't have to rush off the minute you've finished your meal."

Lucky took no notice. She lifted one paw, pointing it at the door as if she could zap it open by magic.

"OK," I said, sighing. "But you'll come back? Promise?"

I opened the door. Lucky shot out . . . to the nearest bush. She squatted in the earth, concentrated, then carefully scattered earth with her paws, covering everything up.

"Did you just want to go to the *bathroom*?" I said.

Lucky looked at me coyly, as if she didn't really

want to talk about it. She let me pick her up and carry her back indoors. I showed her to Billy the Chip and Old Ron and Miss Davis.

"There we go! A lucky black cat. This is a day and a half all right," said Billy the Chip. He smacked his lips appreciatively after eating his last bite of butty. "I don't know how you do it, Charlie. You make tip-top fries. I've been in the chip business all my life, and my dad before me, but my fries pale into insignificance beside yours."

"When's my luck going to change, then?" said Old Ron. "Here, Flossie, let's have a stroke of that little cat and see if some of her luck will rub off on me."

I let him stroke Lucky a few times with his gnarled old fingers.

"Would you like a stroke too, Miss Davis?" I said, out of politeness.

"I'm not very keen on pussycats. They're bird killers," said Miss Davis, but she reached out and gingerly touched the tip of Lucky's tail with one finger. "Don't you go near any of my pigeons, little cat."

"You've fattened those pesky birds up so much I should think Flossie's little kitty would turn tail and run for her life if they flew anywhere near her," said Old Ron.

"She isn't Flossie's cat," Dad said gently. "She's just a visitor."

"She wants to stay, Dad. Look at her!" I said.

Lucky was still snuggled up in my arms, her head

resting comfortably on my shoulder. If I carefully turned my head to one side I could see her expression. She was smiling like the Cheshire cat in *Alice in Wonderland*.

"Well, we'll see if she wants to stick around this time," said Dad.

"She will, she will!"

"Uh-uh, hang on. *Then* we have to go around the neighborhood, making sure no one's lost a cat. We'll ask at the police station too."

"But if no one's reported her missing, can we keep her then, Dad? *Please?*"

"Well, we're not going to be here, are we, sweetheart," Dad said sadly.

"You can keep her over at my place. I've got two cats, Whisky and Soda. One more won't make any difference. A little nipper like Lucky might liven my old ladies up," said Billy the Chip.

"It's so good of you to let us stay at your place, Billy."

"Well, it's a bit old-fashioned, like. I think it needs one of them makeovers. I haven't had the heart to do anything, not since I lost my Marian."

"Ah. Well. Tell me about it," said Dad. "I know just how you feel, Billy."

"Yes, but you're still young, mate, not an old geezer like me. Why don't you think about getting yourself another woman, Charlie?"

"Oh, ha-ha. Who'd want to weigh themselves down with a loser like me?" said Dad.

"I would!" I said.

"Yes, but you're my special princess—and totally prejudiced," said Dad. "No, I don't want another woman anyway. We're fine just the way we are, Floss and me, aren't we, lovey?"

"Your Floss will grow up and be off before you know where you are," said Billy the Chip. "Life can get lonely by yourself, Charlie."

"I'll second that," said Old Ron. "Isn't that right, Miss D?"

"Miss Davis. And I'm never lonely. I keep myself far too busy," said Miss Davis. "In fact, I must be off on my bird trail right this minute." She stood up and started maneuvering her bag of birdseed. She sniffed suddenly. "I shall miss my cup of tea and my little sit-down when the café closes. I've done a little tour of Starbucks and Costa Coffee and Caffé Nero and they're all *much* more expensive."

"And you can't get a decent chip butty in any of them," said Old Ron. "No, we'll have to turn into nightbirds, Miss D, and visit Charlie in Billy's chip van."

"Miss *Davis*. And I'm not going anywhere after dark, thank you very much. It's too dangerous—thugs all over the town."

"I could always escort you, Miss D," said Old Ron.

Miss Davis snorted, not sure whether to take him seriously or not—but she didn't snub his suggestion, and she didn't correct him about her name this time.

Dad cleaned up the café after the party was over while I made Lucky a very soft bed out of my comforter, folded up on the floor of my bedroom.

"So what are *you* going to sleep under?" said Dad, ruffling my curls.

"Oh, I'll be fine with an old blanket or your bathrobe," I said.

"How about giving the cat the blanket or the bathrobe?" said Dad. "You need your comforter, pet."

"Yes, but Lucky's *my* pet. Well, I hope she will be. Dad, what else would she like in her bedroom? She's still quite a little cat. Would she like a cuddly toy, do you think? I could give her Grandma's dog or elephant to snuggle up with. Hey, maybe I could ask Grandma to knit me a mouse. Lucky would like that."

"Knowing your grandma's little problem with sizes she'd probably knit a giant mouse as big as a moose and scare little Lucky to death. I think we'll leave your grandma out of it. Lucky doesn't need any cuddly toys—she's got you, sweetheart."

We watched as Lucky tried out her comforter, playing with it for a minute, rolling around like a frisky kitten. Then she gave herself a little wash, yawned, stretched and lay on her side, paws stretched out. I stroked her back very gently and she started purring.

Her purrs got a little louder, a little slower—sweet little snorty sounds.

"Dad? Is she *snoring*?" I whispered.

"She certainly is, bless her," said Dad. "Come on, let's leave her in peace. All the attention has tired her out. Are you tired too, Floss?"

"I'm not a *bit* tired. It's way too early for me to go to bed, Dad."

"That's what I was thinking. So, now you've got Lucky settled, how about us going out for a little while? I think we both need a little fun tonight. Let's go to the fair, eh?"

"Oh, yes! Can I go on Pearl again?"

"Of course you can."

"And can I have another candyfloss?"

"You bet."

"Bought from Rose's stall?"

"Naturally."

I paused. "Dad, do you like Rose?"

"Of course I do. She's a very kind lady."

"I think she likes you a lot, Dad."

"Nonsense," said Dad, but he looked at me hopefully. "Do you really think so?"

"Definitely!"

"You're kidding me," said Dad, but he was looking down at his old jersey and jogging pants. "Hey, I look like a terrible scruffbag. I'd better change out of these old clothes."

"Well, I'm going to change *into* my old clothes," I said. "I look stupid in this outfit, don't I, Dad?"

"You look very glam and gorgeous, my darling, but not quite *my* little girl. So, yes, you get changed too."

Dad got dressed up in his best jeans and blue shirt and I got dressed down in my old jeans and stripy T-shirt. I checked on Lucky—several times—and left a bowl of food near her and a box of torn-up newspaper as a makeshift litter tray.

Then Dad and I set off for the fair.

It wasn't there!

There was just an empty field with some muddy tracks and litter blowing in the wind. We both stood staring, madly waiting for it to materialize in front of our eyes. But there were no vans, no rides, no carousel, no candyfloss stall.

Dad blinked and shook his head. "Oh, dear. Of course. It's moved on somewhere else. As fairs do. I am a fool. Sorry, Floss."

"Where's it gone, Dad?"

"Search me. There aren't any posters or anything. Poor doll, you've missed out on your ride on Pearl."

"And my candyfloss."

"Yes. Sorry."

"Can't we . . . can't we go and look for it someplace else?"

"Well, where, pet?" Dad said helplessly. He looked

all around and then spotted the pub on the corner. "Let's see if they've got any idea."

We hurried to the pub. I hung around the doorway while Dad went in and asked. He came out sadly shaking his head.

"No one has a clue. Oh, well. Can't be helped. Look, they've got a pub garden. Would you care to join me for a glass of something fizzy, sweetheart?"

Dad had a beer and I had a lemonade sitting huddled up on the wooden furniture. There was a little plastic slide and a playhouse in the garden, Tiger-size. I wondered what he was up to in Australia. Maybe he'd forget all about me in six months. Steve probably *wanted* to forget about me. But I knew Mom was missing me. She kept phoning me, and once or twice it sounded as if she might be crying.

"Dad, what are we going to do about Mom phoning? Will we give her Billy the Chip's number?"

"Oh, dear, I don't know. I—I wasn't actually going to tell her we were moving, as it were. I know she'll think it's not suitable, our living at Billy's." Dad put his pint mug down, sighing. "Who am I kidding? It's *not* suitable, dragging you off to some funny old man's house. Goodness knows what state it's in. He seemed a bit worried about it, didn't he? Oh, Lordy, Floss, I hope this works out."

"Of course it'll work out, Dad." I put my glass down too and felt in my jeans for my pocket-money purse. "Right, it's my round now, Dad. What are you having, another beer?"

Dad laughed and ruffled my curls but wouldn't let me pay. He bought another pint for himself, another lemonade for me, and a bag of chips each.

We walked home holding hands. Lucky greeted us sleepily when we came in, giving us little mews of welcome, as if she'd been our cat ever since she was a newborn kitten.

Fourteen

When I got to school on Monday, Rhiannon was strolling around the playground with Margot and Judy. They had their arms linked, their heads close together. I hovered, not sure whether to run up to them or not.

"She's like *so* boring now," said Rhiannon. "But Mom says I've got to be kind to her, though I don't see *why*. We bought her, like, *the* most exquisite outfit because her clothes are, like, so pathetic."

"And babyish," said Margot.

"And smelly," said Judy.

They all tittered.

"But it was, like, a waste of time because she barely said thank you!"

I started trembling. I ran right around them and shouted, "Thank you, thank you, thank you!" right in Rhiannon's startled face.

"Hey, cool it, Floss!" said Rhiannon, giggling uneasily.

"I didn't want the denim outfit. I didn't want to go out with you on Saturday! I wanted to see Susan and I wish, wish, wish I had!" I shouted.

Rhiannon stopped laughing. Her face hardened, the delicate arches of her eyebrows nearly meeting in the middle. "Yeah, it figures. You and Swotty Potty. You're a real pair. You deserve each other. You be friends with her then, Smelly Chip."

I *wanted* to be friends with Susan, but I wasn't sure she still wanted to be friends with me. I saw her way over at the other end of the playground, walking by herself, tapping each slat of the fence. I hurried toward her but she saw me coming and ran into school.

"Susan! Wait! Please, I want to talk to you," I shouted, but she didn't even turn around.

I ran to the school entrance and rushed to the girls' restrooms, where we'd always met before. I barged straight through two girls giggling together.

"What's up with Floss?"

"Maybe she's got galloping diarrhea?"

They cackled with laughter while I ran up and down the toilets. They were all empty. There was no sign of Susan.

I set off down the corridor, charged around the corner, and ran right into Mrs. Horsefield, nearly knocking her flying.

"Oh! I'm so sorry, Mrs. Horsefield," I gabbled.

"It's good you're in such a hurry to come to school

on Monday morning, Floss," said Mrs. Horsefield. She held me at arm's length. "But you don't look too happy, my dear. You're not running away from someone, are you?"

"No, no, I'm trying to run *to* someone," I said.

"Well, I hope you find them," said Mrs. Horsefield. She paused. "If that someone's Susan, I think I saw her going into the library."

"Oh, *thank* you, Mrs. Horsefield."

"Don't be too long finding her now. The bell's in five minutes."

I set off for the library. Susan was standing by the shelves, fingering her way along the first row of books like she was playing a piano.

"Susan!"

She jumped, and dodged around the other side of the bookshelves.

"Susan, you can't keep running away from me like this! You'll be sitting in front of me in five minutes. Please listen to me. I'm so, so sorry I wasn't completely honest about Saturday. I was just so stupid and I feel awful now. I don't know why I went to Rhiannon's. I didn't have a good time at all. I don't want to be friends with her anymore. I want to be friends with you. Please say you forgive me. Will you come over to my place Saturday and we'll have fun together and eat my Dad's chip butties?"

Susan blinked at me as I spoke, twitching her fingers. There was a little pause when I stopped.

"Do you know, you said exactly one hundred words," she said in a matter-of-fact way.

"Susan, please, did you *listen* to what I was saying?"

"Yes, I listened. You want to be my friend now because Rhiannon's gone off with Margot and Judy."

"No! Well, yes, she *has*, but *I* broke friends with her, I truly did."

"Yes, well, whatever. Only the thing is, Floss, I don't really want to be your second-best friend."

"No, I want you to be my *first*-best friend. *Will* you come next Saturday?"

Susan shrugged. "I think I've probably got something next Saturday." She paused. "I have to go to this conference thing with my parents. Maybe the Saturday after?"

"That won't be any *use*. Oh, Susan, we won't have the café anymore. Please don't tell anyone, but my dad hasn't kept up all his payments and we have to move out and we're going to stay at Billy the Chip's place but it sounds like it's going to be really weird and Dad's going to run his van outside the station and that's going to be weird too and what am I going to do when Dad's out working late and I'm a bit scared about it but I haven't liked to say because Dad's so worried about everything."

"Oh, Floss!" said Susan, and she put her arms around me.

I started crying and she patted me on the back.

"You *won't* tell anyone, will you?"

"Of *course* not! I won't say a word. I'm sure I'll be able to come on Saturday. I don't *want* to go to my parents' conference one bit—they just haven't got anyone to leave me with. Hey, Floss, did you know you said *another* exact hundred words. It's like you've got this weird gift! One hundred is my all-time lucky number too."

"So we're friends now?"

"Best friends," said Susan, giving me a squeeze. "I've wanted to be your best friend ever since I came to this school. Are you sure you're OK about it though? Rhiannon might start being your worst enemy now."

"I don't care," I said, though my heart began thudding at the thought. "I wish I didn't still have to sit next to her."

"Don't worry," said Susan. "If she tries any funny business I'll turn around and yank her off her chair again."

"Yes, she looked so *surprised* when she landed on her bum," I said, and we both giggled.

"She'll be even more nasty and totally mean when she finds out about Dad and me leaving the café and going to live with Billy the Chip. And I don't know what will happen when he comes back from seeing his son. Dad says I should go to Australia to be with Mom, and there's a bit of me that wants to, but I can't leave Dad, I'm all he's got. Well, he's got Lucky too, but she's really my cat. OK, we'll have to see if she belongs to anyone else but I'm hoping like anything she'll be mine."

Susan was counting on her fingers as I spoke. She stared at me in awe. "That's *another* hundred! You are a total phenomenon, Floss."

"A what?"

"A phenomenon. It means you've done something utterly extraordinary."

"A phenonion?" I tried hard but I couldn't say it.

I started mixing Susan up too, so that neither of us could say it without spluttering with laughter.

"Seriously though," I said, wiping my eyes. "Would you say it's a good omen?"

"I'll say!"

"Dad and I keep waiting for our luck to change. Well, *some* good things happen, but most of all I'd like Dad to keep his café. No, *most* most of all I'd like my mom and dad to get back together, but there's no chance of that. I wish there wasn't such a thing as divorce. Why can't people stay together and be happy?"

"Well, people change," said Susan. "Like friends. My parents are divorced."

"*Are* they? So do you live with your mom or your dad?"

"Both. No, they're married to each other now, my mom and dad, but they used to be married to different people. I've got all these stepbrothers and stepsisters. My family's pretty complicated."

"But suppose your mom and dad did split up. Who would you live with then?"

Susan thought about it. I could see her brain trying to puzzle it out, as if it were a complicated sum. She frowned. "I don't know! It must be so difficult for you, Floss."

"I got used to having two homes, but now my mom's house is rented out to strangers and my dad's café is going to be taken over, so I haven't got *any* real home. Dad and I have this joke about living in a cardboard box like street people. I used to sit in a cardboard box when I was little and pretend it was my playhouse. It was my best-ever game for ages. I used to cram a cushion into the box and a little plastic cooking stove and my dolls' tea set and all my favorite teddy bears." I saw Susan was counting again and I caught hold of her fingers. "Don't count my words, it makes me feel weird."

"OK, I won't. Sorry. Tell me more about the cardboard-box house."

"In my mind it had a proper red roof with a chimney, and honeysuckle grew up the walls. I tried crayoning it on the box but it just looked like scribble. There was a blue front door with a proper knocker. If Dad was playing with me, I'd make him pretend to knock on this imaginary knocker when he came calling. He was too big to get in the box with me—the walls would have collapsed—so he always said he'd like to sit in the garden on a deck chair. I'd get this stripy towel and put it just beside the box and he'd lie on it. I'd make him a cup of tea. Not *really*: I'd just put some water in my plastic teacup, and I'd color it a bit with brown M&M's. It probably tasted disgusting but he always drank it right up, his little finger sticking up in the air to make me laugh. I *loved* playing house with my dad."

"I can see why you'd want to stay with him now. My dad didn't ever play with me like that, not in a fun way. He played cards and taught me chess and read to me, but he didn't ever goof around. I played by myself mostly. I didn't make things up like you, my mind doesn't seem to do that, but I *did* play with cardboard boxes, little ones. I made a row of shoebox houses in my bedroom once, and then I started making whole streets with boxes of bricks, and lots of books too—they make very good buildings."

"Show me," I said, thrusting an armful of library books at her.

We sat cross-legged on the library floor while Susan built me a book house. I copied her, and then started making an elaborate tall apartment building. We turned our fingers into people and made them walk in between the houses and climb all the stairs to the high rooftop of the apartments. Then the library door opened suddenly and we both got such a fright that we jumped, and the book apartment building shook and fell to the ground with a great clatter and crash.

Miss Van Dyke stood glaring at us. Miss Van Dyke, the headmistress and the scariest, strictest old-bat teacher in the entire school!

"What on *earth* are you doing, you two girls! This is a library, not a nursery playroom. What a way to treat books! Why aren't you in your classroom? First lesson started twenty minutes ago! Now put those books back this minute—carefully!—and then come with me. You're in Mrs. Horsefield's class, aren't you?"

We nodded, too scared to say a word. Miss Van Dyke marched us briskly along the corridors and then prodded us into our classroom as if we were cattle. Everyone looked up at us, mouths open. Rhiannon's eyes glittered triumphantly. I peeped shame-faced at Mrs. Horsefield. She had given me a gentle warning and I'd let her down horribly.

"These are your pupils, I believe, Mrs. Horsefield," said Miss Van Dyke. "I discovered them in the library building houses with the books, if you please! I wonder why you didn't send someone to look for them. They've been missing from your lesson for nearly half an hour!"

Oh, no, now I'd got Mrs. Horsefield into trouble too. Maybe we'd all have to stand outside Miss Van Dyke's office in disgrace, with our hands on our heads, Susan, Mrs. Horsefield and me.

But Mrs. Horsefield was smiling calmly. "I knew

where the girls were, Miss Van Dyke. They were taking part in my special bonding project."

Miss Van Dyke frowned. "There's nothing about bonding projects in the national curriculum for elementary school."

"I know that, Miss Van Dyke, but sometimes one simply has to use one's initiative to improve classroom dynamics."

I didn't have a clue what Mrs. Horsefield meant. Maybe Miss Van Dyke didn't either. She glared at Susan and me.

"Why didn't you explain, you silly girls?" she said. She marched off, *stamp stamp stamp*, as if she wished we were bugs she could squash with her sensible shoes.

Susan and I stared in awe at Mrs. Horsefield. She raised her eyebrows at us and made shooing gestures with her hands, so we scurried to our seats.

"What are you *playing* at, Smelly Chip?" Rhiannon hissed.

I ignored her. She poked me hard with her bony elbow. I shuffled to the edge of my seat, as far away from her as possible. Susan turned around and gave me a sympathetic grin. I grinned back. Rhiannon could poke a hole right through me and I wouldn't care, just so long as Susan stayed my friend.

PHEW!

Smelly Chip
and
Swotty Potty

Pongy Twit
and
Spotty Botty

THWACK!

OOPS!

Fifteen

Mom rang early the next morning. I sat cross-legged stroking Lucky while she told me that:

1. She had a lovely tan already.
2. The shops in the Victoria Arcade were incredible.
3. They'd been to a concert at the opera house.
4. They'd walked over the Harbour Bridge.
5. They'd seen koalas and kangaroos (but only in Sydney Zoo).
6. Steve was working wonders at the new branch and getting a great team together.
7. Tiger had taken his first staggering steps and had learned to say *"G'day."*

"So much has happened, Floss!" said Mom. "So, darling, what about you? What's your news?"

I took a deep breath. I didn't quite know where to start.

"Are you all right, Floss? Oh, God, what is it? Is Dad looking after you OK?"

Dad was looking at me anxiously as she spoke. I gave him a big smile and a thumbs-up.

"Dad's looking after me splendidly, Mom," I said.

"Then what is it? How's everything at school? Are you up to speed with all your lessons? Is Rhiannon still being friendly?"

"Everything's fine at school. Mrs. Horsefield's being especially nice. Rhiannon's being especially *nasty*, but I don't care because Susan and I are best friends now. She's coming over to play on Saturday."

"How will your dad look after you both when he's got the café to run? How *is* the café? Are you getting any more customers?"

I thought hard. I didn't want to lie to Mom but I didn't want to tell her the whole truth either. "Dad's coping," I said. "And he's expecting lots more customers soon."

"That'll be the day," Mom said unkindly. "Oh, well, Flossie, take care, my little love. I'll ring you next week, OK?"

I covered the phone with my hand and mouthed at Dad, "How can Mom ring next week? We won't be here!"

Dad took the phone from me. "Hi, Sal. I'm glad everything's working out for you. Now listen, I'm making a few changes at the café. We're going to have a different phone number. I'll let you know. What? Oh, just general changes, keeping up with the times, aiming at different customers. Yeah, yeah. Yes, of course, Floss wears clean socks every day—and yes, she washes her hair. What hairdresser? I think she looks cute all curly. Listen, Sal, we've got to go now, she'll be late for school. Bye now."

He put the phone down and mopped his brow. "Phew!" he said, flopping back in his chair as if someone had let all the air out of him. I came and climbed on his lap. He went "Ph-e-e-e-e-w" again, acting it out, while I giggled.

"I am so bad," said Dad. "I should tell your mom exactly what's happening. But if I do she'll insist you join her in Australia. Of course *I* should insist that's what you do. In fact I *am* insisting. We'll phone your mom back and come clean and tell her."

"No, no, no, no, no! Insist all you like, Dad, but I'm staying, OK?" I looked at the clock. "Though I'd better be off right this minute or I'll be late for school. Mrs. Horsefield was so kind to Susan and me yesterday and I don't want to let her down."

Dad let me slide off his lap but he kept hold of me by the shoulders. "What's all this about Rhiannon being nasty to you?"

I shrugged my shoulders under Dad's hands. "Oh, she's just being a bit mean," I said.

Understatement of the century!

Examples of Rhiannon's Extremely Unkind, Unfair and Mean Behavior (in just one day!):

1. She sat at the extreme edge of her seat and held her nose whenever I moved.
2. She called me Smelly Chip over and over again, and got half the class calling me that too.
3. She called my dad Smelly Belly Chip.
4. She told everyone my mom's walked out on me forever.
5. She said I begged her mom to buy me new clothes when we went to Green Glades and said I didn't even say thank you when she spent a fortune on me.
6. She wrote *Smelly Chip and Swotty Potty/Pongy Twit and Spotty Botty* all over the walls of the girls' bathroom. She wrote other stuff too—too rude to include in this list!
7. She shook the desk whenever I started writing.
8. She snatched my best felt-tip pen and stabbed the point on the desktop, ruining it.
9. She tipped my packed lunch onto the floor, accidentally on *total* purpose.
10. She tore the cover right off my math book and scribbled inside it.

I could continue my list, easily reaching 50. Make that 100!

But here's another *lovely* list:

Examples of Susan's Incredibly Sweet and Comforting and Kind Behavior:

1. She kept turning around and smiling at me all through class.
2. She said Rhiannon was a pathetic parrot repeating the same stupid words over and over.
3. She said she couldn't wait to meet my dad next Saturday.
4. She said she wanted to meet my mom when she came back from Australia.
5. I told her about the designer denim outfit and she said it sounded embarrassingly awful.
6. She tried to rub out all the "Smelly Chip and Swotty Potty" rhymes in the girls' bathroom. They remained clearly visible because Rhiannon had used pen, so Susan got her thickest black marker and scribbled right over them.
7. She pushed her chair right back against our desk to steady it.
8. She lent me her own felt tips.
9. We salvaged my banana and my apple and

my Kit-Kat, but my special cheese salad sandwiches (Dad was trying hard to think healthy eating) spattered all over the floor, grated cheese and tomato slices and little leaves of lettuce covered in dirt. Susan shared her tuna and sweetcorn sandwiches with me, and they were delicious. She also gave me half her apricot yogurt (taking turns with the spoon) and a little bunch of black grapes. I insisted she have half my Kit-Kat and half my banana and half my apple. We ended up having a total feast.

10. After lunch Susan mended my math book with Scotch tape while I drew a picture of two girls, one serious with specs and shiny brown hair, one smiling with crazy yellow curls. They were writing an elementary sum on a giant piece of paper: $1 + 1 = 2$ BEST FRIENDS. I stuck my picture over Rhiannon's scribbles and my math book was as good as new. *Better.*

When I had to hand in my math classwork for marking, Mrs. Horsefield smiled and shook her head at the picture. This gave me courage.

"Mrs. Horsefield, I was thinking," I said earnestly.

"I wish you'd think more about your math, Floss,"

said Mrs. Horsefield, going *cross, cross, cross* against each sum.

"Oh, dear," I said. "No, the thing is, Mrs. Horsefield, I wonder if I could move desks so I could sit next to Susan? It wouldn't cause any major disruption, seeing as Susan doesn't have anyone sitting next to her."

"What about Rhiannon?" said Mrs. Horsefield.

"I think she'll be very, very pleased *not* to have me sitting next to her," I said.

"Yes, I gathered you two have fallen out big-time," said Mrs. Horsefield. "You girls! You have more dramas than a soap opera."

"So . . . is that a yes?" I said.

"I'm going to have to think about it. If I let you change desks, I'm going to have a whole posse of little girls wanting to swap places. Probably half the boys will start too."

"Oh, *please*, Mrs. Horsefield."

"Look, I've already done you and Susan an immense favor yesterday. You can't count on being my special favorites, you know."

"*Are* we?"

"I'm a very good teacher and we all know very good teachers don't have class favorites, but if I did, you two *might* be contenders. Now, run along. I'll have a little think about you and Susan and your seating arrangements. Meanwhile, see if she's any better at teaching you math than I am!"

Susan did try and show me stuff but my mind

wouldn't stay still and concentrate properly. We'd start on this sum about six men digging a hole in a field. I'd wonder *why* they were digging this hole. Was it going to be a swimming pool? I saw them in dusty jeans, digging like crazy, and then one of them got a hosepipe and filled up the pool with sparkly water and they all stripped down and jumped in, splashing each other and spouting water like whales . . .

"So what do you think the answer is, Floss?" Susan asked.

I stared at her, because I'd forgotten all about the question.

Susan sighed and rolled her eyes, imitating Mrs. Horsefield. "Could you just concentrate, Floss?"

"I'd much sooner concentrate on you coming over next Saturday, Susan. We'll be in a bit of a mess because Dad and I are moving out on Sunday."

It still didn't seem *real*. Nowadays I kept getting this weird feeling that my home life had turned into the longest, oddest dream. I felt like a boat that had lost its anchor, and now I was bobbing out to sea and the waves were getting bigger and bigger. It felt much safer when I was at school, because that mostly stayed the same.

I *was* late for school that morning. Ten whole minutes. I crept into the classroom and whispered to Mrs. Horsefield that I was very sorry. She wasn't really *cross*, but she did shake her head and sigh at me. It made me feel really bad.

"You're such a teacher's pet, Smelly Chip," Rhiannon hissed. "Anyone else would have got *really* told off. It's just because old Horsey's *sorry* for you. That's the reason anyone's ever nice to you. That's why my mom made me invite you over last Saturday. I didn't *want* you to come. You're no fun. You're a total *loser*, just like your sad, fat Smelly Belly Chip dad."

"You shut up about my dad," I hissed.

She didn't shut up. She said it again. She added bits, poking at me with her ruler. I suddenly snapped. I grabbed the ruler and poked her back hard, right in the ribs.

"Ooow!" Rhiannon screamed.

Mrs. Horsefield got to her feet. "For goodness' sake! Stop that screaming, Rhiannon!"

"I've been *stabbed*," Rhiannon shrieked.

"Let me have a look," said Mrs. Horsefield, sighing. She came over to our desk and looked at Rhiannon's front. She pressed gently all around Rhiannon's waist.

"I think you'll survive this savage attack, Rhiannon," she said. She picked up the ruler. "I take it this was the weapon involved?"

"It hurt!" said Rhiannon.

"I'm sure it did," said Mrs. Horsefield. She looked at me. "Were you the culprit, Floss?"

I nodded. I thought Mrs. Horsefield would shake her head and sigh at me and maybe tell us both off a little bit, but it wouldn't be *serious*. But she didn't shake her head or sigh. She put her hands on her hips and looked very, very, very serious.

"Flora Barnes, I'm ashamed of you," she said coldly. "I'm very disappointed that you're behaving so badly nowadays."

"I'm sorry, Mrs. Horsefield," I whispered.

"Sorry isn't good enough. I can't keep making excuses for you. You waltz into the classroom ten minutes late, and you don't concentrate properly when you are here. I'm going to have to think of a serious punishment."

I bent my head, burning all over. I wanted to lay my head on my desk and weep. I felt so awful. I couldn't understand why Mrs. Horsefield was so very angry with me.

"Please, Mrs. Horsefield, I have a strong feeling Floss was provoked," said Susan.

"You be quiet, Susan. Nobody asked your opinion," said Mrs. Horsefield, totally snubbing her.

Rhiannon was still groaning theatrically, rubbing her ribs, but her eyes were glittering. She was hugely enjoying our humiliation.

"Poor Rhiannon," said Mrs. Horsefield. "I won't have you teasing and tormenting her any longer, Flora. Gather up all your books and pens and pencils, please. Put them all in your schoolbag and stand up."

I stared at Mrs. Horsefield. Was she sending me to the headmistress for the whole day? Was she *suspending* me? Was she EXPELLING me?

The whole class was silent, stunned. Even Rhiannon looked startled. I shoved my stuff in my schoolbag, my hands fumbling. I stood up, shocked and shaking.

"Right. I'm going to move you away from Rhiannon, seeing as you can't behave nicely sitting next to her. Now, where can I put you?" Mrs. Horsefield seemed to be looking all around the classroom for a spare seat. There was only one empty chair. Mrs. Horsefield looked at Susan's desk. She pointed to it.

"Well, Flora, you'd better sit here for now. Susan, move the desk forward as far as it will go, right away from Rhiannon. That's it, I'll have you both beside my desk, where I can keep on eye on you. There now. Sit beside Susan, Flora."

I collapsed onto the seat next to Susan—and Mrs. Horsefield gave me the tiniest private wink.

Galileo

Ellerina

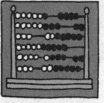

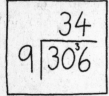
SUSAN
13116
FLORA
63691

34
9⟌30⁶

Dimble

126.00

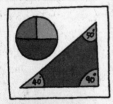

One, two
Buckle my shoe

POLKA
THEATRE

Sixteen

School was heavenly now that I was sitting next to Susan. I even enjoyed math. Well, I didn't exactly *enjoy* it, but it was quite companionable having Susan go through each sum with me and tell me what to do.

We also started a numbers project together in a notebook exactly a hundred pages long. Susan wrote about famous mathematicians like Galileo and Pythagoras. I found out about numerology, and wrote out my name and Susan's name and checked off all the vowels and consonants and found out we were deeply compatible (but we knew that anyway). Susan wrote out neat examples of addition, subtraction, multiplication and division. She even did really difficult stuff her dad had taught her like algebra and geometry. I colored in all her circles and triangles. Susan wrote about the abacus. I invented my own connect-the-dots puzzle. Susan did a wonderful diagram of a calculator. I copied out counting rhymes like "One, Two, Buckle My Shoe."

Mrs. Horsefield said it was excellent and she'd definitely mark it ten out of ten. Rhiannon muttered behind us, "*One, two, don't they make you spew? Three, four, they're such a bore. Five, six, up to nerdy tricks.*"

As if we cared! I started making a list of all the things Susan might want to do on Saturday. The café was closing for good on Friday, so Dad would be free to take us anywhere. I thought about all the special treat days I'd had with Mom and Steve.

On Saturday Susan and I could:

1. Go to Chessington World of Adventures in Dad's van and go on all the rides, even the scary ones.
2. Go to the seaside in Dad's van and have ice creams on the pier and make a ginormous sand castle and go on a boat trip.
3. Go the country in Dad's van and walk up to the top of a big hill and have a picnic and paddle in a stream.
4. Go up to town in Dad's van and go on the London Eye and Dad can row us on the Serpentine Lake and we can play in Princess Diana's park.
5. Go to Bethnal Green toy museum in Dad's van and we can count all the dolls and look at the dolls' houses and play Giant Checkers.

6. Go to Greenwich in Dad's van and run all the way through the tunnel under the river and go to the market and see the *Cutty Sark*.

7. Go to London Zoo in Dad's van and see all the monkeys and the elephants and the penguins and watch them being fed.

8. Go to the National Gallery in Dad's van and choose our top ten favorite paintings and then climb on the lions in Trafalgar Square.

9. Go to the Polka Theatre in Dad's van and ride on the rocking horse and see a play and then have a pizza afterward.

10. Go to the Natural History Museum in Dad's van and see all the dinosaurs and then have tea in the shop over the road and be allowed two cakes each.
    Memo: We *don't* want to go to the Green Glades shopping center.

I showed Dad the list when he tucked me up in bed that night. "What about going to Disneyland in Dad's van?" he said. "Going for a world tour in Dad's van? Flying to the moon in Dad's van?"

"I suppose I got a bit carried away," I said, wanting to kick myself. I'd forgotten just how much most of those days out would cost.

"I wasn't being *serious*, Dad. I was just making a

silly list. You know what I'm like. No, we could just go for a little drive out in the van, maybe for a picnic. Or we could just go to the park. Maybe we'll skip feeding the ducks—Susan might feel she's a little too old, though of course *I* love feeding them. Oh, Dad, if only the fair was still here! Wouldn't that be great! We could go on the carousel. Susan and I could squash up on Pearl together and we could both have a candy-floss from Rose's stall. Maybe she'd invite us all back to her lovely caravan. That would be sooo fantastic."

"Yes, it would be," said Dad. "Only the fair's not here. And I'm afraid I just don't have the cash for the other outings. I've got to be careful with gas too. I reckon we might need a couple of trips to Billy's house with all our stuff, and then I've promised to drive him to the airport." Dad paused. "I went over to Billy's today, Floss. It's . . . it's a bit . . ."

I looked at Dad. "It's a bit what, Dad?"

Dad gestured vaguely, his arms stretched wide. "Well, you'll see for yourself. I'll do my level best to make you a pretty little bedroom somehow. Everything will be OK. Knock on wood." He tapped his head and then glanced around my bedroom. He looked at the faded fairy wallpaper I'd had ever since I was a baby, the curtains falling off the rail, the crooked chest of drawers half painted silver, the pale pink carpet, which was now sludge gray with age.

I sighed. I thought about the time when it was all new and clean and fresh, and Mom and Dad tucked me up in bed together and took turns telling me stories about the fairies flying up the wall.

Dad sighed too. "I'm not much good at the decorating thing, am I, Floss?"

"Never mind, Dad."

"I'm not much good at *anything*, am I?"

"*Don't*, Dad. You're fine. *We'll* be fine, you, me and Lucky." I picked her up and held her close. "Did you meet Billy the Chip's cats, Dad? What are they like?"

"Well, they're huge compared with our little Lucky."

"Oh, no! Do you think they'll bully her?"

"No, no, I think they're too old and tubby to do anything much but sleep." Dad yawned. "Like your old dad. I'm totally exhausted, Floss, and yet I've still got to get to grips with all this packing. I'm so sorry, darling, but I'm going to be busy most of Saturday. I think you and Susan will just have to amuse yourselves."

"But you'll make chip butties, won't you, Dad?"

"I'll make you chip butties fit for a queen. Well, two little princesses."

Dad gave me a big kiss on my curls and he gave Lucky a big kiss on her fur, and then he tucked us both up, me in bed, Lucky in her comforter nest.

I snuggled down with Dog and Elephant. I twiddled Elephant's trunk around my fingers and tucked Dog's limp ear over my nose like a little cuddle blanket. I was becoming very fond of them. I didn't exactly *play* with them, but they were starting to develop personalities. Elephant was called Ellerina, and was a bit flighty. She liked to show off and twirl her trunk in the air. Dog was called Dimble. He quivered at any sudden movement or loud noise. He did his best not to look at all mouselike whenever Lucky was near him.

I couldn't decide whether to introduce them to Susan. She wouldn't tease me like Rhiannon but she might *privately* think me a total baby.

"Do you have any cuddly toys, Susan?" I asked as casually as I could on Friday morning.

"You mean teddy bears? No, I think I had one in my crib when I was very little but I don't have any now."

"Oh," I said, resolving to hide Ellerina and Dimble under my bed.

"I'm not *anti*-teddy. I just don't like the feel of their fur very much. I've got uncuddly toys though. I've got eleven little wooden elephants, one wooden giraffe, one pair of crocodiles with jaws that snap open and shut and three china rabbits—one pink, one blue and one big green one who towers over all the other animals, even the elephants."

"But they're like ornaments. Do you actually play with them?"

"Exactly how could I play with them?" Susan asked.

"You could give them names and make them funny or naughty or shy, and maybe take them out into the garden and play jungles. You could turn your mom's plastic tub into a watering hole and make a big earth mountain for them to trek up and down."

"That sounds a lot more fun than just dusting them," said Susan. "You do get good ideas, Floss." She paused. "Would you mind terribly if we didn't go on one of those special outings on your list this Saturday? I mean, they all sound lovely, and if that's what you really want to do that's fine with me, but I'd sooner make the most of our time together just playing. Is that OK?"

"Of course!" I said, deeply relieved.

Susan paused again. "Look, Floss, this is terribly rude of me, but . . . I couldn't come in the morning too, could I? I so want to have a proper long time together—and also my mom and dad are supposed to be going to this education conference all day. They're both giving speeches and I was going to have to trail along too and lurk in a corner somewhere reading a book, but if you're kind enough to invite me I could be with you."

"Education? Are your mom and dad teachers?"

"Kind of. They teach teachers how to be teachers. They used to be at Oxford but now they've both got jobs near here."

"Are they posh?" I said, and then I blushed because it sounded so stupid.

"They'd die if anyone thought they were posh," said Susan. "They *are* though—my mom even went to boarding school—but they try to act just ordinary."

I didn't quite get this. Rhiannon's mom and maybe even *my* mom were just ordinary and yet they tried hard to pretend they were posh. It was a novelty to think Susan's mom and dad pretended the other way around.

"Well, Dad and I definitely *aren't* posh," I said. "And I'd love you to come as early as you want—that would be brilliant—but the whole place is going to be in an awful mess. Dad and I will be packing everything. We wanted to try to get it all done before you came."

"Can't I help? I'm absolutely great at packing because we've moved heaps and heaps of times."

"OK then, if you really don't mind."

"That's what friends are for," said Susan.

"Did you have a best friend at your old school?"

"Not really," said Susan. "It's always horrible starting at a new school because you stick out so, and I seem to be the sort of person that gets picked on. Rhiannon thinks she's *so* original, but they used to call me Swotty Potty at my old school too. Maybe I ought to legally change my name!"

"My mom wanted me to change my name when she split up with Dad. She wanted me to add Steve's name on with a hyphen but I wouldn't. *He*'s not my dad, he's not anything to do with me, he's just my mom's new partner."

"All these partners!" said Susan. "I tried to do a family tree on this big wall chart but it got so complicated. I did it all in my best italic handwriting, in red ink, but then I had to keep crossing bits out because people kept splitting up. Then my mom's ex-partner kept having new babies with each new lady, so that side of the family tree got much too crowded. It ended up looking such a mess I crumpled it all up and threw it away. That's why I like math so. The numbers don't wriggle about and change; you can just add them up or subtract them or multiply or divide them, whatever, but you always get the answer you want."

"Only if you're you. *My* numbers wriggle all over the place and I never get the right answer unless I copy off you," I said. "OK then, Susan, you come as early as you like on Saturday."

Seventeen

My "early" wasn't quite the same as Susan's. Dad and I weren't even up when the doorbell rang. We stumbled downstairs, me in my nightie, Dad in his old pajama bottoms with a T-shirt on. We opened the door. There was Susan and *her* dad.

We peered at them, mortified. Dad frantically combed his sticking-up hair with his fingers. I rubbed my eyes and pulled the hem of my nightie down as far as it would go, hoping it *might* just look like a dress.

We didn't convince Susan's dad.

"I'm so sorry. We've obviously got you out of bed. How awful!" he said.

He was much older than my dad, more like a granddad, but he was dressed sort of young, in a black T-shirt and jeans and a denim jacket with the sleeves rolled up to try to look casual. His own hair looked as if it needed a good brush. He seemed what

Mom would call scruffy, but try as he might he couldn't make his voice sound anything but ultraposh and sophisticated.

"Yes, I agree, it *is* awful of us. I think I must have slept through the alarm. I've been out of sorts lately. You know what it's like, mate," Dad blurted.

"No, no, I meant *we're* awful, arriving so horrendously early . . . mate," said Mr. Potts. "It's so good of you to say you'll have Susan for the day. I gather she invited herself. But I can see it's the worst possible time for you." He waved vaguely at the cardboard boxes scattered all over the hall, like a giant toddler's building blocks.

"Susan's *very* welcome," said Dad, smiling at her. "Just so long as she doesn't mind a bit of chaos."

"Oh, she's used to that in her own home," said Mr. Potts, and he gave Susan's shoulder a little squeeze. "You know my cell number and Mom's, don't you? Ring if there's any problem. Otherwise we'll come and pick you up about sevenish. Is that really OK?"

He was looking at Dad. He nodded and smiled. Susan nodded and smiled. I nodded and smiled too.

"Thanks again. We owe you big-time. Maybe your Floss might like to come to us next Saturday."

"Oh, yes, please!" Susan and I said in unison, while the dads laughed.

Then Mr. Potts waved and walked to his car, neatly

kicking two Coke cans into the gutter. I could see Mrs. Potts sitting in the front of their car. She had gray hair piled up in an untidy bun and little round glasses just like Susan's. She was wearing a dark red peasant blouse and a big yellow bead necklace. She waved too. I waved back shyly.

"Right!" said Dad. "I'd better get myself washed and dressed pronto, and then see about breakfast. Have you had breakfast, Susan? I'm sure you can manage another, anyway."

"Oh, good! Can we have chip butties?" Susan asked eagerly.

Dad laughed. "You can have a chip butty for your lunch. You might *even* have another for your dinner. But I think we'll draw the line at butties for breakfast. How about cornflakes?"

Lucky came sidling down the stairs, not sure who this new visitor was.

"Oooh, she's so lovely," said Susan, crouching down and holding out her hand. Lucky hesitated and then took two steps forward on her dainty paws, prepared to make friends.

"You are so lucky to have a cat," said Susan. "My dad is allergic to cat's fur. Well, he *says* he is. And Mom fusses about their claws. We've got all these leather-bound books and she says they'd use them like a scratching post."

"Well, we like Lucky's fur. I might wrap her around

my neck in the winter instead of a scarf; she'll keep me nice and cozy. And all our stuff is scratched to bits anyway," said Dad. "I'm a bit of a scratcher myself, come to think of it." He bowed his legs in a chimp stance and scratched his chest.

"Dad!" I said.

"Oops! Sorry. I'd better go and have my shower now. Wash the fleas off."

"*Dad!*" I said.

Dad ran up the stairs making monkey noises. I rolled my eyes and Susan giggled.

"Let's give Lucky her breakfast," I said.

Lucky's cat food looked pretty disgusting—lumpy brown slurp—but she seemed enthusiastic. She ate it up, she had a crunch of her dry biscuits, and she sipped from her water bowl while we hovered over her admiringly. Then she used her new litter tray while we turned our backs discreetly.

I showed Susan how to deal with it.

"It's a little bit disgusting, but nowhere near as bad as changing Tiger's diapers," I said. "Oh, dear, it's weird, I even miss Tiger, though I *don't* miss changing him. Maybe he'll be potty trained when he comes back from Australia!"

We washed our hands and Lucky licked her paws, and then I set out breakfast on the table when Dad joined us, his hair all wet and sticking up from his shower. He was wearing his silliest smiley-face T-shirt and his jogging pants. I'd have died if he wore them in front of Rhiannon, but I felt safe with Susan.

We both had a big bowl of cornflakes for our breakfast. Susan tipped hers into her bowl and then started touching each one with the tip of her spoon.

"What are you up to?" said Dad.

Susan went pink. "I'm just seeing how many I've got," she mumbled.

"We've got plenty of cornflakes, sweetheart. There's another box in the cupboard," said Dad.

"No, Dad, Susan just likes to count things." I smiled at Susan. "I bet you're looking to see if you've got an exact hundred."

"I bet *you* have," said Susan.

"Well, why don't you two silly girls tip your cornflakes onto a plate? They'll be much easier to count then. Do you want a cup of tea, Susan? Do you take sugar? I hope you're not going to count the grains of sugar—you'll go cross-eyed." Dad crossed his own eyes, making a funny face. Susan laughed and made a funny face back.

"I do like your dad," she whispered when we went upstairs.

"I like *your* dad," I said politely.

"Yours is much more fun. And he doesn't mind my numbers thing. It drives my dad nuts. He says it's obsessive-compulsive behavior and I should have therapy." Susan paused. "Do you think I'm a bit nuts, Floss?"

"Not at all. Your dad might be ever so clever but he doesn't know everything. You just like numbers. Same as I like making lists. *Right*, let's make a list of all the things we've got to do today," I said, going into my bedroom.

I made a big thing of looking for my notebook and a pen. I didn't want Susan to be floundering for something nice to say about my bedroom. It looked smaller and shabbier than ever with cardboard boxes everywhere. Susan curled up on the comforter in the corner.

"It might be a bit furry. I'm letting Lucky sleep on it at the moment," I said.

"I shall get as furry as possible and then see if I make my dad sneeze," said Susan.

She reached up to my pillow. Ellerina and Dimble were lurking bashfully underneath, but their little woolly paws were protruding.

"Who are they?" she said, tweaking them.

I made Ellerina pirouette, waving her trunk. Dimble became very shy and hid for a long time, but we gradually lured him out.

"They are so sweet," said Susan. "But they're naked! Let's make them some clothes later on. Put that on your list, Floss."

"Oh, yes! Can you sew properly then, Susan?"

"Well, sort of."

"Did your mom show you?" I asked wistfully.

"No, Mom can't even sew buttons on. My dad

sews a bit. I worked out how to do different stitches and I can join bits together, though I don't always do it properly."

"You are *clever*, Susan."

"I'm not clever at making things up like you are," she said. "You're the one who's so good at pretending that things seem real. Like Ellerina and Dimble. Have you got any other dolls and teddy bears?"

"No," I said mournfully. "I was such an idiot. I threw them all out because Rhiannon made me feel like such a baby. I wish I still had them. I hate it that they're just moldy and sad in some stinky garbage dump. I wish I'd at least given them a proper funeral. Hey, that would have been really cool in a creepy kind of way—a doll funeral! I could have given them each a shoebox as a coffin. It would have been like there'd been a megadisaster in doll-land. Maybe some crazy robot toy ran amok with a machine gun and butchered all my Barbies!"

"We could have a memorial service. That happens a couple of months after the funeral. My mom went to one for the principal of her college. You sing hymns and say poems about the dead person. We could do that for your dolls."

"I'll put that on my list! We'll have a memorial service and we'll make clothes for Ellerina and Dimble. And I know what I'd also really like to do. Have you ever made a friendship bracelet, Susan?"

"No, but I'd love to. I'll make you one, shall I?"

"And I'll make one for you. I've made one for my dad; blue to match his jeans."

We heard Dad thumping up and down the stairs, shifting boxes.

"Shall we help him?" said Susan.

"Yes, let's. We'll put that first on our list. NUMBER ONE: PACK UP THE HOUSE."

I wrote it in capital letters. It wasn't as easy as it sounded. My own things were easy enough because they'd been pared down to the barest minimum by Mom. Susan and I filled one box with my shoes, my underwear, my night things, and my washing things. We filled another box with my home clothes and my school clothes and my princess dress. I was wearing my newly washed and ironed birthday jeans and top. I left the rhinestone designer denim outfit in the wardrobe till last.

"What is *this*?" said Susan, trying on the cap.

It looked comfortingly ridiculous on her too. I reminded her about Rhiannon's mother.

"I suppose it was very kind of her—but I hate it. I look like such a fool," I said.

"Well, you don't have to wear it," said Susan. "Maybe we should put it on the hottest wash in your washing machine and shrink it right down till it fits Ellerina."

"Yes, she'd look really cute in it, and the cap would balance her big ears." I crumpled the outfit up and stuffed it in the box. It felt good, as if it were Rhiannon and I was stuffing her in the box too.

"I can't stand Rhiannon now," I said. "How come I had her as my best friend when really she's my worst enemy? Her and Margot."

Rhiannon couldn't get at us in the classroom now because we'd moved our front desk out of her reach. However, she and Margot and Judy lurked in the corridors at lunchtime and called us stupid names and said rude things and then cackled with laughter. Margot wore the rose quartz bracelet now. Rhiannon must have given it to her. As if I cared!

It looked as if Rhiannon and Margot were definitely best friends now. Judy still trailed around with them, telling ruder and ruder jokes, but Rhiannon and Margot simply sniggered and then ignored her.

"I feel a bit sorry for Judy now," I said. "She's the one who's ended up without a real best friend."

"Don't feel sorry for her. She's been horrible to you and me," said Susan. "She was the one who started up the whole Swotty Potty thing—*and* the Smelly Chip bit."

I paused. I bent my head, surreptitiously sniffing the clothes in the box. Then I buried my head in my chest and breathed deeply, trying to sniff *me*.

"Are you doing *yoga*, Floss?" Susan said.

"No, no, I'm . . . Look, Susan, *do* I smell of chips? Mrs. Horsefield said I should hang my clothes in the fresh air but that's a bit of a problem, unless I find some way of pegging them to my swing. That's my best thing. I'm going to have to get Dad to untie it even though it took him *ages* to get it fixed up."

"I *love* swings. Shall we put swinging on your list?" Susan suggested.

"Well, you can't really swing *properly*. It goes kind of lopsided. Still, of course we can swing. You ever so tactfully changed the subject. I *do* smell of chips, don't I?"

"Yes, you do. You smell absolutely delicious, and if you don't watch out I'll eat you all up," said Susan. She seized Ellerina and Dimble. "Yum, yum, yum!" she said, making their little woolly mouths nibble me.

I doubled over laughing because they were all tickling me. Then I gave Susan a quick hug. "You're the best friend in all the world, Susan," I said. "Let's stay friends forever and ever."

"Yes, forever and ever," said Susan, solemn now. "Can we stay friends right through the summer?"

"Of course we can. We can play together all the time."

"That would be lovely—only some of the time we have to go to our house in France. But I'll write and phone you heaps, OK? You will stay friends?"

"You bet. And even if Dad and I move on somewhere else after staying at Billy the Chip's house, will you still stay friends?"

"Absolutely. Even if you end up going to Australia

to live with your mom. In fact I'll come and visit you and play with the koalas."

"And what about if I go to the moon? Will you come and visit me in your spacesuit and do a dance with me in your moonboots?"

I did a slow, bouncy moon dance. Susan joined in. We danced in and out and around about the cardboard boxes.

Dad put his head around the door and laughed at us. He put an empty cardboard box on each foot and lumbered about doing his own crazy moon dance—and then we all collapsed, laughing.

"I don't know what I'm doing clowning around. There's still so much to be done," said Dad.

"I've just got to pack up my books and crayons and stuff in my pink pull-along suitcase, and then we can help you, Dad," I said.

"We can number each box and write on it what's inside," said Susan.

"You're obviously a girl with a system," said Dad.

Susan was great at getting both of us organized. She found some old brown sticky tape and sealed each box so we could balance one on top of the other.

We finished my room, though we left out clean clothes for tomorrow, and Ellerina and Dimble and my sewing set and Lucky's comforter. She didn't like all this sudden activity and burrowed right underneath the comforter, just her nose and whiskers peeping out.

Dad started to tackle his bedroom while we got

started on the living room. There wasn't really much to take. We packed:

1. The cuckoo clock (though it didn't work). It had been Mom and Dad's wedding present from Grandma, and for as long as I can remember, the hands had been stuck at four o'clock and the cuckoo sulked inside his house, though you could still see him if you opened the little doors.
2. The motorcycle calendar. Dad had inked stars and smiley faces every weekend with *Floss* written in curly writing. Last month he'd written *Floss! Floss! Floss!* in every single box.
3. The photo of Mom and Dad and a baby me at the seaside, all sitting on the sand and licking ice cream. I remembered that day and the heat of the gritty sand and the coldness of the ice cream dripping onto my tummy.

"You were such a cute little toddler, Floss. Look at all your fluffy curls," said Susan. "Your mom's ever so pretty too. She looks so young!"

Mom was cuddled up to Dad in the photo, licking his ice cream instead of her own. Dad was pretending to be mad at her but you could still see just how much he loved her.

I sighed. "I wish I could rewind to when we were all happy together," I said. I sniffed hard. Susan patted my shoulder sympathetically. "We could really do with some Bubble Wrap," she said. "Never mind, we'll have to make do with newspaper."

We were leaving the television because it didn't work properly anyway. I packed all my favorite films (number 4 on the list), hoping that Billy the Chip might have a video player, though if his crackly old transistor radio was anything to go by, he didn't seem up to speed with his electrical equipment.

We were leaving the table and chairs. The tabletop was patterned with coffee-mug rings and the woven seats of the chairs were coming unraveled and scratched your bottom. Even so, I sat down on each one, remembering when we were Mom and Dad and me, with one leftover chair for all my teddy bears and Barbies. They were forever falling off, the teddies too limp to sit up properly, and at the slightest nudge the Barbies jackknifed onto the floor with their legs in the air. Mom would get angry but Dad always helped me get them back on their chair. He'd sometimes put a baked bean or a chip on each of my dollhouse plates for my fidgety family.

"Did your dad really never play pretend games with you when you were little, Susan?" I asked.

"He read to me and did funny voices. And he played weighing and measuring games and guessing words on pieces of card, but that was like baby lessons. My mom played music to me and I had to act it out. Sometimes we played I was a little French girl called Suzanne, but that was so I could count up to a hundred in French."

"You're such a brainybox, Susan," I said.

"Don't!" said Susan, as if I'd insulted her.

"I'm paying you a compliment! You're heaps and heaps smarter than me."

"It's not that great a deal being brainy," said Susan. She sat down on the sofa, sighing.

I went to sit beside her. The sofa sagged badly and the corduroy was shiny with age. There were several big dark stains where Dad had spilled his coffee or his can of beer. We were leaving the sofa too. I wished we could somehow take it with us. It wasn't just because it was where Dad and I cuddled up and watched TV. When I was little, it had been a fairy-tale castle and a wagon train across the prairie and a bridge over the man-eating crocodiles crawling across the carpet.

"I wonder if we could just take one of the sofa cushions?" I said, tugging at it.

"It's a bit . . . tired looking," Susan said, as tactfully as she could. "And it would take up a whole cardboard box all by itself."

"Yeah, I suppose," I said, stroking the sofa as if it were my giant pet.

"Shall we go and see how your dad's getting on with his packing?" Susan said, going for diversionary tactics.

Dad was having similar problems. He was slumped on the edge of his bed, his clothes scattered all over the comforter, so it looked as if there were twenty Dads sprawled beside him. There were Mom things too, clothes I'd completely forgotten about—an old pink terry cloth bathrobe, a sparkly evening dress with one strap drooping, a worn woolen jacket with a furry collar, even some old Chinese slippers, embroidered satin, with one of the butterflies unraveling.

"Dad?" I said, and I went and sat beside him while Susan hovered tactfully in the doorway. "Where did all Mom's stuff come from?" I picked up one of the slippers, rubbing my finger across the satin. I remembered sitting watching television long ago, leaning back against Mom's legs, stroking her satin slippers, feeling the little ridges of embroidery with my fingertip.

"Your mom left them in her half of the wardrobe when she went off with Steve. She didn't want them. I was supposed to get rid of them but I couldn't." Dad sighed, shaking his head at himself. "Silly, aren't I, Floss?"

"You're not silly, Dad."

"I suppose it's time to deal with them now."

"You can still keep them. We can pack them all up in a cardboard box."

"No, no. It's time to chuck them out. Time to chuck half of my stuff too." Dad picked up the jeans that had gotten torn at the fair and flapped the tattered legs at us.

"I thought you were going to keep them as paint clothes."

"Who am I kidding? When was the last time I did any painting, for heaven's sake?"

"You painted my chest of drawers silver."

"And left it half finished."

"I still love it. Can I take it to Mr. Chip's house, Dad? It won't take up much room."

"OK, OK. Definitely, little darling. So how are you two girls getting on with packing up your bedroom, Floss?"

"We're finished, Dad. Susan's absolutely great at getting everything sorted."

"Well, aren't we lucky! Thank you so much, Susan, you're a sweetheart. I wish *I* had a fantastic friend to sort me out," said Dad.

"I'd like to be your friend too, Mr. Barnes," said Susan. "We can start sorting your clothes for you, if you like."

"That's very kind of you, Miss Potts," said Dad. "And *I* could sort out a tasty snack, seeing as you've both worked so hard. Now let me see . . . would you like chip butties—or chip butties—or indeed, chip butties?"

We both put our heads on one side, pretending to consider, and then yelled simultaneously, "*Chip butties!*"

It was a joy to see Susan eating her very first chip

butty. Dad served it to her on our best blue china willow-pattern plate, garnished with tomato and lettuce and cucumber. Susan ignored the plate and the little salad. She didn't use the knife and fork Dad had set out beside the plate. She picked up the chip butty in both hands, staring in awe at the big soft roll split in half and crammed with hot golden chips. She opened her mouth as wide as possible and took a big bite. She shut her eyes as she chewed. Then she swallowed and smiled.

"Oh, thank you, Mr. Barnes! It's even better than I hoped it would be. You make the most wonderful chip butties in the whole world!"

After we'd eaten every mouthful of our chip butties, we sorted Dad's clothes into GOOD, NOT TOO BAD and CHUCK. Susan counted and I made a list.

Dad's clothes:

GOOD—12 items of clothing, including one tie and socks and shoes and underwear

NOT TOO BAD—20 items of clothing

CHUCK—52 1/2 items (the half was an ancient pair of pajama bottoms—we couldn't find the top)

Dad laughed ruefully and started obediently throwing his stuff into a big plastic bag. He took Mom's old clothes, hesitated, and then started chucking them too.

"Maybe we don't have to chuck all of them, Mr. Barnes," said Susan. "We couldn't have them, could we?"

"Do we want to dress up in them?" I asked a little doubtfully.

"No, we want to make them into clothes for Ellerina and Dimble," said Susan.

We borrowed Dad's sharp kitchen scissors and some greaseproof paper to make patterns. It took a *lot* longer than I'd realized, but after two extremely hardworking hours, Ellerina had a sparkly strapless dance dress, Dimble had a fur coat, and they both had pink bathrobes, and tiny embroidered slippers tied to each of their four paws with sewing thread.

"We'll cut the legs right off your dad's ripped jeans and make them little denim jackets, and Ellerina can have a skirt and Dimble can have jeans—he'd look so cute!"

"And caps?" I asked.

"Well, I could give it a go. Just so long as you don't ever, ever, ever wear yours," said Susan. She waggled her fingers. "They *ache* now."

"Mine too. But I wanted to work on our friendship bracelets."

"We can do them another time," said Susan. "We're going to have lots and lots of times. You will come to my house, won't you, Floss?"

"And I'm sure Billy the Chip won't mind you coming to his place. And then . . ." My voice trailed away. I didn't have any idea where we'd be after that. It was so scary not knowing. "Let's go and have a swing," I said quickly. "It goes a bit crooked but you can still swing quite high if you really kick your legs."

We went out to the backyard. Lucky came with us and circled the Dumpsters. I always worried whenever she slipped out of sight, but she bobbed back each time.

I let Susan have first go on the swing, but she wasn't really any good at it, so I stood on the seat behind her and pulled on the ropes and bent my knees and got the swing going. We didn't really go *that* high, but we pretended we were swooping right up in the air, over the treetops, flying far over the tallest tower, up and up and up.

"Wheee! We're right over the sea now," I shouted. "And there's land again! See all those skyscrapers? We're over America!"

"I think it's more likely France," Susan said breathlessly.

"No, no, look, more sea, we're swooping r-o-u-n-d and d-o-w-n and here's Australia! See all the kangaroos? Whoops, there's a boomerang. Who's that waving? It's my mom! Hey there, it's me, Floss. Meet my best friend, Susan."

We both let go of the swing with one hand and waved wildly into thin air.

Eighteen

On Sunday morning Dad and I loaded all the neatly labeled cardboard boxes into the van. Then Dad struggled with my silver chest of drawers and my swing. He crammed in his old CD player and all our pots and pans and crockery and a box of tools I'd never seen him actually use.

He dithered for a long time out in the yard, shifting all the motorcycle parts under the tarps. He laid them all out on the concrete, as if they were parts of a jigsaw puzzle and if he could only sort them all out systematically, he'd be able to construct a splendid Harley-Davidson there and then. He actually moved pieces around as if he were looking for a piece of sky or a flat edge. Then he sighed.

"What am I going to do with it all, Floss?" he said. "I've been collecting all this stuff for years and years, right from when I was in my teens."

"Take it with us, Dad."

"Yes, but what am I going to *do* with it?"

"Make your own custom-built motorcycle, Dad. How cool would that be?"

"Yeah, yeah, if I were still twenty years old—but I'm pushing forty, Floss. I'm a tubby old dad. I doubt I've got the mettle for roaring around the roads on a bike, even if I had one. No, I might as well leave the lot here. Maybe someone else will find all the spare parts useful, eh?"

"But you like them so, Dad. They're part of you."

"You're the only part of me I want to keep forever, Flossie. It's time to move on. It's good-bye to Charlie's Café."

"Let's go around and say good-bye to every room, Dad. Would that be totally nuts?"

"OK, darling, let's go on a little tour of the premises."

We said good-bye to the kitchen and tried to count up how many chip butties Dad might have made, right from the opening day. It was as if thousands of phantom chip butties were whirling all around us like galaxies in outer space.

Then we said good-bye to the café itself. We sat at every single table and we toasted our very special customers in lemonade, our dear Billy the Chip and Old Ron and Miss Davis, but also people we'd remembered for years: the man with a red face who ordered ten chip butties and ate every single one, chomp,

chomp, chomp; the couple who held hands and ordered a big mixed grill to share and then shyly confided that it was their wedding breakfast; the lady who came in with her labrador and ordered one chip butty for herself and one for the dog.

Then we went back upstairs and said good-bye to my bedroom, and Dad told me how he and Mom had taken me home from the hospital when I was born and tucked me up in a little Moses basket. They spent hours and hours trying to get me to go to sleep, and then when I finally nodded off they were so worried they woke me up again just to make sure I was still breathing.

"Do you know, I still sometimes creep in when you're asleep and check that you're breathing," said Dad.

We said good-bye to Dad's bedroom and the bathroom and the toilet, and then we said the saddest good-bye to the living room.

"Let's have one last cuddle on the sofa, Floss," said Dad.

We curled up together and traded memories as we stared at the blank television screen. It was as if films of our family life flickered there—long-ago happy Mom-and-Dad-and-Floss times.

We both sighed. Then Dad kissed the top of my head and said gently, "Let's get on our way, little darling."

Lucky was hiding in her comforter, sensing something was definitely up. She'd taken her time deciding she wanted to come and live in our house, and now we were expecting her to leave before she'd even settled in. She didn't want to be lifted up, and I had to hang on hard to her, comforter and all. She mewed indignantly for me to put her down.

"I've got to hang on to you this time, Lucky. We're going to a new house now. You'll like it just as much, you'll see," I said, though I wasn't sure that was very likely.

Dad drove us very slowly and carefully out of the town to Billy the Chip's house. It was on a big mock-Tudor housing estate, row after row of identical semi-detached houses with black and white panels and crazy paving and clipped privet hedges. I was sure I was going to get muddled as every single street looked the same. I clutched Lucky tightly.

"We're here, pet," said Dad, drawing up outside number four Oak Crescent.

We peered out at the house. The privet hedge was wavering out of control and the crazy paving was sprouting weeds from every crack.

"Poor old Billy. It's obviously got a bit much for him," said Dad. "We'll do our best to tidy it up for him, won't we, Floss?"

"Yes, Dad," I said in a small voice.

I felt like Lucky, who was still mewing piteously in

her comforter. I didn't want to start living in this shabby old house. It didn't seem to have anything to do with me.

I thought of the airline ticket. Dad had taken it out of the kitchen drawer and given it to me to look after. I had smoothed it out carefully and tucked it inside the plastic case of the *Railway Children* video. I'd opened up the case twenty or thirty times over the last couple of days, just to check that the ticket was still safe.

I wasn't going to use it. I couldn't leave Dad. I couldn't leave Susan. I couldn't leave Lucky—though I had asked Mrs. Horsefield privately if you were allowed to take animals on airplanes.

Dad reached out and took hold of my hand. "OK, little Floss?" he said.

I took a deep breath. "OK, big Dad," I said.

We got out of the van. I held on tightly to Lucky. She was so eager to be put down now that we were out of the noisy, scary van and on firm ground again that she clawed frantically with her paws and scratched my neck. I knew it was an accident but it hurt quite a lot, and it hurt my feelings too. I had to blink hard and clamp my lips together to stop myself crying. I knew Dad was peering at me anxiously. I tried hard to make my mouth smile. Dad's own smile was pretty forced too.

We knocked on Billy's door. The knocker was tarnished and the black paint blistered, but there was a lovely stained-glass window set into the door, a big round sun with long slanting rays—the sort I used to paint when I was in preschool.

The door opened and there was Billy squinting in the daylight, looking paler and frailer than ever, but he was proudly wearing a strange new nylon tracksuit and he had a moneybag strapped around his old saggy tummy.

"I'm all set for my trip," he said, patting his purse and holding his nylon arms out for inspection. "What do you think of the new gear? I wanted to be comfy traveling."

"You look real trendy, Billy. Those stewardesses will be buzzing around you like bees around a honey-pot," said Dad.

"Oh, very funny," said Billy, but he looked pleased. "Well, come in, then. Welcome to your new home. I'm afraid it's a bit lacking in modern conveniences. I'm rather set in my ways." He opened the door wider and we stepped inside.

We stayed standing still, blinking in the gloom, staring all around us. It didn't seem as if we'd stepped into someone's home. It was as if we'd moved into a museum. The hall had a little table and an umbrella stand and one of those fat old-fashioned cream phones with a round dial. There was a crocheted mat underneath the telephone, yellow with age.

There were many more crocheted mats in Billy the

Chip's living room. They were on the back of his shabby olive-green sofa and on each arm too. There was a matching set on both green armchairs. There were more mats on the nest of tables and yet more under the china vases on the mantelpiece over the tiled fireplace.

There was a big woolen semicircular mat in front of this fireplace. Two vastly fat tabby cats lay side by side, paws outstretched, heads raised, staring at us like sphinxes. Lucky gave an anxious mew in my arms. I held on to her protectively. Mr. Chip's cats were great tigers compared with tiny Lucky.

More mats were laid out like a card game on the big sideboard, each covered with a photograph. There were old wedding photos. I stared at a strange stiff couple, the man with a little moustache and a wing collar tickling his chin, the lady with her wedding veil right down over her forehead.

"That's Mother and that's Father," said Billy the Chip, gesturing, as if they were real and standing six centimeters tall on his sideboard. He pointed to another wedding couple, a thin awkward young man and a plump woman with her hand tucked in his arm. "And that's me and my Marian." He stroked the glass on the photo over Marian's rounded cheeks.

There were baby photos too; a bare little boy lying on that same semicircular rug.

"That's my boy. He's another Billy, like his dad and

granddad, but he calls himself Will nowadays," said Billy, shaking his head.

"Does he have a chip van in Australia, Mr. Chip?" I asked.

"No, he swore he was never going into the fried chip business. Couldn't persuade him. He did bartending, and now he's got his own wine bar out in Sydney, though I dare say he serves up chips as a bar snack. French fries or potato wedges or whatever fancy name they call them now." Billy sniffed.

"I wonder if Mom and Steve ever go there now?" I said.

"Sydney's a very big city, Floss," Dad said gently. "Your Billy's moved with the times, mate," he said to Billy. "That makes him a smart guy. Much smarter than you and me."

Time had certainly stood still in Billy's house. He *did* have a television, but it was even older than our TV at the café. There was a wind-up gramophone beside it, with a pile of old black records in brown paper sleeves.

"Good God, Billy, have you kept these from your courting days?" said Dad, looking through them. "Hey, these are even before your time, surely?"

"They were Mom and Dad's," said Billy. He gestured with his trembly old fingers. "They moved in here right from their honeymoon. Spanking new, the house was, my mom's dream home. It was considered modern in those days."

It was hard trying to imagine this musty old house as *modern*. I tried picturing a couple dancing to the gramophone, a baby crowing on the rug, laughter and shouting and doors banging—but the house stayed still and silent.

"I'll show you to your rooms," said Billy.

He led the way up the threadbare carpet and then showed us each room along the landing. The bathroom had an old bath with rust stains under the big taps and black chips in the enamel.

"It doesn't look too grand, but I clean it regularly," Billy said, sounding embarrassed.

"It's fine, Billy, and obviously spotless," said Dad, patting Mr. Chip's nylon sleeve. "You're much better at housekeeping than we are. He puts us to shame, doesn't he, Floss?"

There was a main bedroom that had once been Billy's mom and dad's, and then Billy and Marian's, and now it was just Billy's. There was something about that sad big empty bed that reminded me of Dad's bedroom back at the café.

Dad looked relieved when Billy suggested he sleep in the second bedroom, which had always been a spare room with a single bed. It had fraying pink ribbons on the curtains, and the mats all over the dressing table were pale pink to match. There was a firescreen with an embroidered thatched cottage and a faded pink ruffly bedspread. It looked like a room for an old, old lady. My dad looked too big and too fat and too rough for such a room, but he told Billy it was lovely and he was very grateful.

"Now I thought we'd put little Flossie in young Billy's room," said Old Billy.

It was the only room in the house that wasn't stuck in a 1930s time warp. It was a strange boy mixture. There were old soccer posters on the walls and rock music tapes piled up like building blocks, and an elderly Paddington Bear stood in a corner in his duffel coat and boots. Oddly, right in the middle of the carpet, there was a dollhouse. It was a 1930s dollhouse— *two* houses: two semidetached homes making one whole house with a sloping red-tiled roof, black and white paneling, and two front doors.

I squatted down beside it, still hanging onto Lucky, but I was so distracted that she squeezed herself out of one end of the comforter and stood alert, her back arched, her tail outstretched, not sure where she was off to now that she was free at last.

"Look at the dollhouse, Dad!" I said.

There was a hook at one end so I edged it open and the front of the house swung forward. It was fully furnished inside, with little carved wooden replicas of sofas and chairs, tables, baths and beds. One half house had small green cushions on the chairs and little crochet mats as small as a penny piece.

"It's *your* house, Mr. Chip! Yours and the matching one next door!" I exclaimed. "Where did you *get* it?"

"I made it myself, love," said Billy. "It was rather a silly notion. I'd always whittled away at the potatoes in odd moments, carving out a face here, a monkey there, a clown—whatever took my fancy. I'd fry them for the customers just for a laugh, but then when our Billy was on the way I fancied making something more permanent. I took it into my head that he'd be a girl, so I started in on a dollhouse. Silly idea, really. I mean, it's not the sort of thing modern kiddies want to play with anyway."

"*I* would, Mr. Chip," I said.

"Then you play with it all you want while you're here, sweetheart," said Billy.

"Are you sure, Billy? It's a totally awesome work of art," said Dad, kneeling in front of it. "Floss is a very careful girl but I'm not sure she should be allowed to touch it."

"No, no, it's *meant* to be played with. I'd always hoped for a little girl but we only had our Billy—Will. I wondered if *he'd* have a daughter, but Will's not what you'd call the marrying kind, so if little Floss here would like it, then the house is hers."

"Oh, Mr. Chip! I couldn't possibly keep it," I said—though I wanted it desperately.

"Yes, you have it, darling. I promised you a birthday present and here it is. You can carry on furnishing it if you fancy doing so. I made a few bits and bobs and my Marian did the mats, but we felt a bit silly, like, when there was no one to play with them. It's yours, Floss."

"Thank you, thank you, thank you!" I said, and I reached up and gave him a big hug around his wrinkled tortoise neck.

"You've got to stop doing us all these favors, Billy," said Dad. "You've been so good to us."

"You're the ones being good to me, watching over the house and cats while I gallivant off." Billy paused. "I'm not really sure I know what I'm doing, going all the way to Australia. Maybe my lad doesn't want me visiting. We didn't always see eye to eye when he lived here. We didn't part on the best of terms."

"He'll be thrilled to see you, Billy. Boys fight with their dads and leave home to make their own way in life. It's only human nature. But he's a man now and he'll be thrilled at this chance of seeing you."

"Do you really think so?" said Billy, still sounding doubtful.

"Mr. Chip, if I hadn't seen my dad for years and years I'd be jumping right over the moon," I said.

"If you could jump that far you could propel yourself and save on the airfare," said Billy, ruffling my curls.

I don't like it when people do that. It even annoys me when *Dad* does it. But I stood my ground and smiled politely. Mr. Chip said I was a sweet kid and Dad was lucky to have me, and he went all watery eyed. Dad said he knew that, and he had to dab his own eyes with a hanky. I fidgeted from foot to foot, feeling foolish.

Billy insisted on cooking us Sunday dinner.

"I've got a roast chicken in the oven, and roast potatoes. I'm not cooking you chips, because you're the bee's knees when it comes to chips and there's no point competing," said Billy.

"Chip Master of the Universe," said Dad, beating his plump tummy and flexing his muscles.

Mr. Chip's cats had their own lunch out in the kitchen. I got Lucky's special bowl and sprinkled a few dried biscuit balls in it. Whisky and Soda looked up from their own mashed fish bits and eyed Lucky's bowl. Whisky ambled over to it. Soda followed. They licked their lips and mewed greedily.

Lucky barely came up to their furry shoulders. It looked as if one swot of a Whisky or Soda paw would send her flying.

I needn't have worried. Lucky had lived on the streets. She knew how to defend her territory. She gave a ferocious "*Mew!*" and darted forward, wriggling right under their noses, and buried her head in her bowl. She flicked her delicate tail in Whisky and Soda's surprised faces. They slunk back to their own bowls, trying to look nonchalant.

When they'd all nibbled lunch, first Whisky, then Soda squeezed out of the cat flap for a saunter around the garden. Lucky experimented, poking her little head after them curiously. She gathered courage, nudged hard, and then hurtled out into the garden.

I ran to the window and watched her peer around in astonishment, like Alice newly arrived in Wonderland. She circled the center flowerbed, trying to stalk a sparrow, but it flew away mockingly whenever she made a move.

"Is Lucky settling in, Floss?" said Dad, coming over to the window.

"I think so."

"What about you, darling?"

"I think I am too, Dad," I said, though I wasn't really sure.

I didn't *want* to live in Billy's house, although it was mean even to think it as he was being so generous and hospitable. It was so strange and old-fashioned and it smelled musty, like the clothes in charity shops. I hoped *I* wouldn't smell musty as well as chippy. Rhiannon and Margot and Judy went around holding their noses whenever they stood near me as it was.

It seemed so weird that only a month ago I'd taken it for granted that I just had an ordinary detergent/clean clothes/shampoo smell just like everyone else. I had a mom and my own special bedroom in our pretty house. Even Rhiannon had remarked on my cherry-patterned comforter and my matching curtains. Now I didn't have *anything* ultraclean or pretty or matching.

I knew I was being dreadful feeling sorry for myself when Dad was trying so hard and Mr. Chip had been so kind giving me the beautiful dollhouse—but I still couldn't stop two tears spurting down my face.

I bent my head quickly but I think Dad saw. He squeezed my shoulders tightly.

"We'll be fine, little Floss." He lowered his voice. "This is just a temporary measure, sweetheart. We'll find somewhere lovely just for us soon, you'll see. You never know your luck. Something will pop up out of the blue."

I tried to imagine a beautiful home emerging out of nowhere: a coral palace out of the blue sea; a cloud castle out of the blue sky; a Swiss chalet out of a big blue mountain. I blinked and swallowed hard to stop the rest of my tears.

They seemed to stay in my throat. I couldn't swallow Billy's roast chicken dinner. He'd tried so hard to make it a lovely meal for us, but the chicken was still slimy under its skin and the roast potatoes were speckled with little black bits of grit from the oven and the cabbage looked and smelled like old stewed leaves.

I chewed and chewed and chewed. I felt myself getting red in the face.

"Is the roast OK?" Billy asked anxiously.

"It's just delicious, Billy," said Dad.

I felt him nudging me under the table. He was passing me his big hanky. Then he started chatting to Billy about his chip van and where he stored it and the times he opened and shut during an evening—while I turned my head and discreetly spat most of my meal into the hanky, pretending to wipe around my mouth.

When Dad got up to clear the table he managed to dump the hanky quickly at the bottom of Billy's garbage can. I looked up at him gratefully and he wriggled his eyebrows at me.

"How about going out to play in the back garden, Floss?" said Dad. "See if you can spot a good tree for your swing."

I went out of the kitchen door and walked up and down the stretch of grass at the back. There was going to be a big problem. Billy had a flowerbed on either side—although they looked more like weed beds now—but he didn't have any trees at all. He had a few shrubs and bushes but they would have barely supported a toy swing, let alone a real one.

Dad looked up eagerly when I trailed back. Then he saw the expression on my face. His own face sagged.

"It's OK, Dad. I think I'm maybe too old for swinging now anyway," I said quickly.

We spent the afternoon watching television, although none of us were really concentrating on it. Billy kept checking his passport and his flight ticket and his Australian dollars. Dad kept looking around, yawning and sighing and stretching his arms in the air.

He suggested I go and unpack my stuff, but I did that in five minutes.

I knelt down and looked at the dollhouse. It was difficult to know how to play with it when it didn't have any people. I tried cramming Ellerina and Dimble into a room, but their heads hit the ceiling and their legs sprawled in every corner, so they looked like a giant elephant and dog in a very small cage.

I needed to make some proper tiny people. I had a pack of clay that Steve's mom had given me for a birthday present. I took it and started modeling. I made me first, rolling the yellow strip into lots of bobbles for my curls. I put me in the right-hand half of the house. I made Dad, and then a little Lucky. I had to make her purple as they don't make black clay. I made a Susan too, come to visit us, staying overnight in my bed on a special sleepover.

Then I made a Mom. I tried very hard to make the clay Mom very slim and stylish, using the bright pink for her dress. I got a bit sniffly creating her and had to stop to give my nose a good blow with toilet paper. It hurt, because Billy had the weirdest crackly stuff in his bathroom that totally sandpapered your skin.

Then I did a Steve with a pink bullet head and huge muscles on his arms and a tiny Tiger crawling on all fours. I put them in the left-hand house. I made a thin clay door on either side of both adjoining living rooms so that the me-doll could run between houses whenever she wanted.

Then I sat back and sighed.

"Are you OK, Flossie?" Dad called up the stairs.

"Yes, I'm fine, Dad," I said quickly.

"Are you all set to take Billy to the airport?"

"Course I am," I said.

I picked up the pink clay Mom and gave her a big kiss, stroking her very carefully because I didn't want her head or her arms or her legs to fall off.

"I love you, Mom," I whispered. I thought about that airline ticket. In just one day and night I could be with her. I'd stay in a lovely apartment and live in a sunny, glamorous city and everyone I knew would envy me like crazy and no one would ever sneer at me or tease me or pity me.

"Floss?" Dad called.

I picked up the clay Dad and tickled his tummy with my fingernail and made him chuckle and jump about.

"I love you, Dad," I whispered. "Don't worry. I'm going to stay with you, no matter what." I paused. "You never know your luck. Something *might* pop up out of the blue."

Dad and I took Billy to Heathrow. We parked the van and helped him negotiate his way to the check-in desk, and then we went with him as far as the Departures gate. Billy looked so old and frail that Dad asked if we could possibly walk him through to the other side of the airport, but they wouldn't let us.

"Oh, well, I'm sure you'll be fine, Billy, my boy. Just find the prettiest young lady stewardess, hook your arm in hers and get her to help you on your way," said Dad.

"You're the guy who should be hooking up with someone young and pretty," said Billy. "Oh, dear, my tummy's all butterflies! Wish me a safe flight, Flossie. You're the wee girly who brings me luck."

"You'll be safe as safe, and have a lovely time, Mr. Chip," I said.

"Hmm. I don't know about that. If the good Lord had meant us to fly, he'd have given us wings," said Billy. "I've lived well over three quarters of a century without venturing more than six feet in the air, and now I'm embarking on a journey that will take me six *miles* up in the sky. Keep your fingers crossed for the next twenty-four hours that I don't suddenly plummet downward."

"We'll keep our fingers and our toes crossed, mate," said Dad, and he gave Billy a big hug.

I had to give him a hug too, and kiss his white whiskery cheek. Then he toddled off, trying to wave jauntily, though he was terribly tottery on his old bowed legs.

"I hope to God he makes it OK," said Dad. "Tell you what, Floss, if you were traveling with him it would be you looking after old Billy, bless him, not him looking after you."

"But I'm not traveling, Dad."

"I know you're not, darling. Remember though, we've got your ticket safe and sound."

"You might as well tear it up, Dad. I'm not going to use it," I said, taking his hand.

On the drive back from Heathrow, Dad suddenly yelled out and pointed. There was a big field far off, all lit up. There were Ferris wheels and carousels way in the distance.

"It's the fair!" said Dad.

"Oh, wow! Let's go! Oh, Dad, *please* can we?"

"Of course, little darling! We'll find your carousel and you can have another ride on Pearl."

"And we'll find the candyfloss stall and see Rose!"

"Well, that would be great," said Dad, turning right off the main road, toward the fair.

We parked the car and then ran hand in hand, both of us skipping and dancing and whooping—but when we got to the field it suddenly looked all wrong. The vans were lined up strangely, the rides were all different, the carousel had many brightly painted horses with long manes and tails but none of them were pink, and none of them were called Pearl.

We looked for the candyfloss stall. We found three

different ones, but none of them had a big pink teddy bear tied up outside. None of them were Rose's. We were at the *wrong* fair.

We wandered around a little, but it was no use. It wasn't the same at all. We'd lost the heart for it. We just wanted to go home . . . though it was the *wrong* home too.

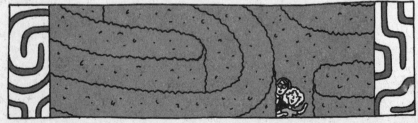

Nineteen

"What are we going to do with you while I'm working in Billy's chip van every evening?" said Dad. "I suppose I should get a babysitter."

"Come off it, Dad," I said. "I'm not a *baby*."

"I could maybe ask Miss Davis . . ."

"*Dad!* She'd cluck her teeth at me and feed me birdseed sandwiches!"

"There's Old Ron. He's a weird old chap but he's harmless and he thinks the world of you, Floss."

"I don't want Old Ron looking after me. He can't look after himself."

"I suppose I could ask if you could stay at Susan's once or twice."

"I'd like that!"

"But I can't ask them to have you *every* night." Dad paused. "Rhiannon's mom was going on at me the other day outside the school—"

"I am not, not, not going to Rhiannon's, Dad."

"OK." Dad sighed. "Well, what *are* we going to do with you, sugarlump?"

"We don't have to do anything. I'll stay here at Billy's."

"I can't leave you all on your own, pet."

"Of course you can. I'll be fine. I'll read and I'll watch Billy's TV and I'll sew clothes, and then when I get tired I'll go to bed. Simple!"

"But what if someone came to the door?"

"I won't answer it. I'm not dumb, Dad."

"I'm sure it's against the law leaving a kid your age on her own," Dad said anxiously.

"Who's going to know? Only us," I said. "Dad, *please* don't worry about me. I'll be fine, fine, fine."

I just about had him convinced. I thought I had myself convinced too. But when it was time for Dad to go out on Monday night, I wasn't so sure.

"I'll be fine," I kept saying.

"Yes, of course you'll be fine," Dad kept repeating, giving me a last kiss, a last cuddle, a last ruffle of the curls.

Then he went out to work. The front door shut behind him. And I started to feel scared.

I was watching a film on television and it was meant to be funny but there were two creepy men chasing after this little kid so I had to switch it off quick. I sat in the sudden silence, ears straining, listening out for creepy men breaking into the house, coming to get me.

Billy's parents frowned out of their wedding photo at me, not liking a stranger sitting cross-legged on their faded old carpet. The house was still filled with their things. Maybe they were still here too, hiding in a dusty cupboard, whispering to each other. When it got dark they'd drift out into the room, silent on their see-through ghost feet . . .

I desperately wanted to cuddle Lucky for comfort, but she'd gone upstairs to lay on her comforter and I couldn't face those creaky stairs by myself. I tried calling her, but the thin sound of my own voice was so strange in the silent house that I clapped my hands over my mouth.

Then I heard it! The gate creaking. Someone walking up the garden path.

I sat rigid on the old sofa, waiting. I heard them outside the door. They didn't knock. There were scrambling sounds. Then I heard the door *opening*.

They were coming right in.

They were coming down the hall ready to *get* me . . . "Floss? Flossie, love?"

"Oh, Dad!" I said. I gave a shaky cartoon laugh: *Ha-ha-ha.* "Hey, what are you doing back home?"

"I know it's silly, I know you're perfectly fine here by yourself."

"Yes, Dad."

"But I couldn't stand it. I kept imagining stuff. I know it's crazy, pet, but would you mind coming in the chip van with me?"

"OK, Dad. I *am* fine here, but if it'll put your mind at rest, then I'll come too. Let's go," I said, scooting off the sofa and hanging on to his arm.

We started up a whole new routine. Every evening I set off with Dad in our van. We'd go to the big garage behind the station, hook the chip van up, and tow it to the curb in front of the station. Then Dad would start the generator and get the fryer heated up while I squashed up in a cramped but cozy nest in the corner of the van, out of sight of the customers. I had two cushions and Dad's old denim jacket to snuggle up in. I didn't need to wear any kind of coat. It was boiling hot in the van from the fryer with its sizzling fat.

I did my homework first, except when it was math, which I needed to do before school with Susan. Then I read for a bit. I started reading all these old Victorian Sunday school books from Billy's house. They were told in a strange old-fashioned way, but the stories were really good once you got into them. They were all about poor ragged children begging on the streets of London. They often had cruel drunken stepfathers and sickly little baby brothers and sisters. They sometimes coughed a lot and then said they saw angels and then they died. I read some of the best bits to Dad in between customers.

"Aren't these stories a bit morbid for you, Floss?" said Dad. "They certainly give me the willies!"

"I *like* them, Dad," I said.

When people started coming out of pubs it got too busy and noisy to concentrate on my books so I made things instead. I made a friendship bracelet for Susan. *Several* friendship bracelets. I made a lanyard keyring for Dad. I fashioned slightly crooked denim jackets for Ellerina and Dimble. I made a little blue denim mouse with a string tail for Lucky.

I tried taking Lucky to the van with us one day, but it was much too hot and cramped for her and she hated it. She seemed much happier left at home. She couldn't care less about creepy men and sad old ghosts.

Dad would give me a little paper plate of chips every now and then, or a can of Coke, but I couldn't drink too much because there was nowhere I could go to the bathroom. After a while I'd start to get achy and my eyes would itch, so I'd put my sewing stuff away and plump up my cushions and rub my cheek against Dad's old jacket and go to sleep. Then at midnight Dad would tow the chip van back to the garage, lift me up into our van, and drive us home. I'd tumble into bed half asleep, one arm out of the covers so I could still reach down and stroke Lucky.

Dad still worried about me being in the van. "Your mom would go crazy if she knew I was keeping you up till all hours," he said. "It's not suitable, I know. Especially when all the lads start coming out the pubs and get a bit mouthy. The language! I think we'll have to put earmuffs on you, little Floss."

I had learned a few amazingly awful phrases, which came in useful when Rhiannon and Margot and Judy were teasing me. They held their noses all the time when I came near. I knew I did smell chippier than ever, but I pretended not to care.

I did try very hard the next Saturday when I went to spend the day with Susan. I got up early and had a bath, although the peeling enamel scratched my bottom. I shampooed my hair as best I could and then tried to brush out all the tangles. My curls had grown a lot. They stuck up all around my head in a crazy fuzz.

I wore my birthday jeans and top and I cleaned my sneakers. Dad made a big effort too. He put on his blue shirt and his best jeans even though he was just going to loaf around at home for most of the day.

He drove me to Susan's house. I was worried that it was going to be a huge great mansion with beautiful polished furniture and very pale sofas and carpets, and I'd have to sit on the very edge of my seat and not eat or drink anything slurpy in case I spilled it. It was a relief to see that it was an ordinary red-brick Victorian villa.

When I got inside I saw it was gloriously untidy, with shoes all over the hall and papers and files stacked high by the phone and books *everywhere* — not just on the bookshelves but in higgledy-piggledy piles all over the carpet and climbing up the stairs and stacked halfway up each windowsill. There were books in the hallway, books in the bathroom, and books all over the kitchen, stuffed in between the saucepans and the spice jars.

The kitchen seemed to be the main Potts living room. There was a television on the counter and fat velvet cushions scattered over the benches on either side of the long table. The actual living room was turned into a huge library study, with Mrs. Potts and her computer and desk and filing cabinet on one end and Mr. Potts and *his* computer and desk and filing cabinet on the other.

They had the big bedroom upstairs. Susan had a very little bedroom with a pine bed and a patchwork quilt and a special shelf for her elephants and giraffe and crocodiles and rabbits. The middle-sized bedroom was *Susan's* study. She had her own computer and desk and filing cabinet, and tons of books on shelves and drawings and posters and maps all over the walls.

"It's so *lovely*, Susan," I said, tiptoeing around, peering at a book here, a picture there. "You've got so many *things*!"

"I wondered . . . would you like to make another book world like we did in the library at school?" Susan asked.

"Ooh, yes," I said.

I watched as Susan eagerly started getting books

down from shelves and tipping out a stack of wooden building bricks all over the wooden floor with a great clatter.

"Won't your mom mind us making such a mess?" I asked.

"She doesn't mind a bit if we're being creative," said Susan.

"Creative?"

"You know, making things up and being artistic."

"I can do that," I said.

So we were happily creative most of the morning, building a land for all Susan's animals. We made a book mountain and had the elephants plodding up it tail to trunk, led by a little Roman toy soldier that Susan called Hannibal. We made a river out of blue and green books, edged with potted ferns and ivy from the kitchen windowsill. The two crocodiles lurked in the river, jaws ready to start snapping. We made Hannibal have a swim and then run away screaming. The giraffe came to have a drink and had a tasty fern sandwich garnished with ivy salad. The pink and blue rabbits had a frolic too, and we sat the giant green one on top of the mountain as a monument.

"We could really do with some more people," I said. "Do you have any clay?"

"I've got modeling clay. Will that do?" said Susan.

It did wondrously. We made a little Roman army for Hannibal to command, and some pilgrim worshippers to kneel at the paws of the Giant Green Rabbit. We made twin giraffe babies for the big giraffe, and lots of tiny baby rabbits for Mrs. Pink and Mr. Blue Bunny. We made half a person screaming in the river, with a severed leg in each crocodile's jaw.

We had great fun acting it all out, but I was still a bit worried about the mess, especially as we'd accidentally smeared modeling clay all over the floorboards. However, when Susan's mom came to see what we were up to, she was so pleased by our bookland that she actually took photos of it. She took photos of us two with our arms around each other and promised I could have copies of all of them.

Then we went in the kitchen with Susan's mom to watch her prepare lunch.

"Though I know I'm not as good a cook as your father, Floss," said Mrs. Potts. "Susan adores his chip sandwiches."

"*Butties*, Mom," said Susan.

"My dad's butties are famous," I said. I started talking about the café without thinking—and then suddenly shut up. It was so awful to think that it didn't exist anymore. It had been my home ever since I was born.

They hadn't just closed it down. When Dad drove me past on the way to school, we saw someone had taken down the HARLIE'S CAFÉ sign. There were workmen in there stripping out the kitchen, tearing everything down. I felt as if they were tearing up all my happy memories too. I didn't say anything and neither did Dad, but the next day he drove to school all around the outskirts of town so we didn't have to go past.

Susan's mom saw I looked a little bit sad. "How about you two doing a bit of cooking too? Have you ever done any baking, Floss?"

"I've made toffee and cornflake crispies and chocolate biscuit cake with Mom," I said. My voice wobbled when I said her name. I think I must have looked even sadder, because Mrs. Potts put her arm around me.

"I wonder if you've ever made bread," she said.

This was a wonderful idea. It was fascinating creaming the yeast, with Mrs. Potts explaining exactly how it worked. Susan helped me measure out the flour accurately. The best bit was the kneading part. I got dough right up to my elbows so it looked as if I were wearing thick white gloves.

I made one loaf and Susan made another. They started to smell utterly delicious as they were baking in the oven, and when at last it was time to take them out they looked wonderful—golden brown with a lovely crust. One had risen just a little higher out of the baking tin and was just a little bit more glossy and golden. Susan and Mrs. Potts said it was *my* loaf. I rather think it was too.

"You've obviously got a real knack as a baker, Floss," said Mrs. Potts. "Next time you come you can try making rolls."

"If only we still had the café, then I could make

newly baked rolls for Dad's chips and we could have a brilliant chip-butty partnership," I said.

It wouldn't work for the chip van. There wasn't space to do anything properly. Dad's chips weren't quite the same anyway. He used the same type of potatoes, the same cooking fat, but Billy's fryer was old and unpredictable. Sometimes the chips burned to a crisp, sometimes they swam limply like white fish in a fatty sea, taking an age to crisp up.

Dad did his best but he couldn't serve his chips with pride. He didn't care for the burgers and sausages he served up either. He didn't have any complaints though. The big lads pouring out of the pubs just wanted something hot and savory to stuff down their throats. They covered everything in bloodred tomato sauce or bright yellow mustard anyway.

"Dad says his chip butties aren't up to scratch anymore," I said sadly.

"Well, I shall always remember mine as the most sublime culinary experience ever," said Susan.

I didn't understand every word she said, but I knew what she meant and smiled at her gratefully.

We had our homemade bread at lunchtime, with cheese and tomatoes and salad, and then Greek yogurt and honey for dessert. Susan's mom told us all about proteins and carbohydrates and vitamins, and Susan's dad told us all about Greece and how bees make honey.

I tried hard to ask intelligent questions like Susan

and ended up giving myself hiccups. Susan's mom told me exactly what little thingy inside me had gone into a spasm and why. Susan's dad told us about some wretched man in Scotland who hiccuped for two solid years. I started to worry I might be an even more wretched girl in England, fated to hiccup her way through life forever—but Susan suddenly leaned forward across the table and shouted, "*BOO!*"

I jumped.

"I bet you can't hiccup anymore now!" Susan said—and she was *right*.

We'd have been very happy to play back in Susan's study all afternoon, but Mr. and Mrs. Potts felt we should go on an outing. They drove us to Hampton Court Palace because Henry the Eighth had once lived there and Susan and I were doing the Tudors in history.

Henry the Eighth had had six wives. Susan's dad told us the names and what happened to them all. Henry divorced his first wife Catherine. My dad divorced my mom. I imagined what it would be like if he got through five more wives.

There were actors dressed up as Elizabethans inside Hampton Court. They gave a talk and then you could ask them questions. Susan asked all sorts of interesting things about beheadings and religion and music. Mr. and Mrs. Potts pretended not to notice but I could see they were bursting with pride.

"You can ask a question too, Floss," Mrs. Potts whispered.

I couldn't think of anything intelligent to ask whatsoever.

"Go on, dear, don't be shy," said Mr. Potts.

I ended up asking the lady how she got her sticky-out skirt to stay all puffed up.

"It's called a farthingale, Floss," Mr. Potts hissed.

I think he was scared they thought I might be his daughter too. The lady didn't seem to think it too silly a question. She held up her skirts so I could see the weird hooped petticoats underneath.

We went all over the palace and Mr. and Mrs. Potts told us heaps of stuff about the Tudors. Susan was obviously fascinated, but I started having terrible yawning fits because it got soooo boring. I tried to keep my mouth shut when I yawned but my eyes watered. Perhaps Mrs. Potts thought I was crying. She put her arm around me.

"I know what Flossie would like to see—the Tudor kitchen!" she said. "Let's go there next."

The kitchen *was* quite interesting, but I so wished Susan and I could have just dawdled around there by ourselves.

The very *best* bit of the Hampton Court trip was going to the maze. Susan's dad had told us this story about some monster called the Minotaur, so we pretended we were running away from this Minotaur. We ran screaming around and around the paths between the high hedges, and every time we came to a dead end and had to turn on our tracks we'd yell, "*The Minotaur! The Minotaur!*" We played we were diving between his cloven hooves or jumping high over his scaly back.

Mr. Potts said we'd got the legend wrong and started to tell it to us all over again, but Mrs. Potts laughed and told him to lighten up.

"The girls are just having a bit of fun," she said, giving Susan's hand a squeeze.

"We're having lots and lots and lots of fun," Susan shouted, her cheeks pink, her eyes shining behind her little glasses.

Mr. Potts smiled at her and held her other hand. Susan jumped up and down between her mom and her dad. The back of my throat went tight. My whole head started throbbing. I'd have given anything in the whole world to hang on to *my* mom and dad's hands and for us to be a family all together.

Then Susan let go of her parents and took my hand. We ran off again, and suddenly without even trying we reached the clearing in the middle of the maze, so we danced around and around in celebration.

Twenty

Mom phoned on Sunday morning. She wanted to know so many worrying details about the café and what was happening. I didn't know what to say. I started telling her all about Susan instead, and wonderfully she got sidetracked for a while. Then she started telling me about this outing they'd had to a special fish restaurant on the waterfront.

"I bet the fries weren't as good as Dad's fries," I said.

"They didn't serve anything as common as french fries there, Floss. This is an extremely upmarket place," said Mom. "But talking of fries, there was an old man at the next table who was the spitting image of that weird old man who haunts your dad's café. You know, the one who had that awful chip van. Your dad calls him Billy the Chip. It couldn't possibly have really been him, not in an ultrastylish restaurant the other side of the world—and yet he was looking at me as if he recognized me too."

"Gosh, Mom, how strange," I said. "Look, I'd better go now, I'll be late for school."

"Floss, it's Sunday."

"What? Oh, yes. Well, my new friend Susan's coming over soon, so I must get ready. Love you. Bye, Mom," I gabbled, and then I slammed the phone down.

"Mom saw *Billy*!" I said to Dad.

"Oh, God. He didn't tell her about the café closing, did he? Oh, Floss, I feel so bad putting you in this position. Maybe we should tell your mom the truth. But then she'd go crazy." Dad put his head in his hands. "She'll go super-crazy when she gets back and finds out we've been camping at Billy's. If we're still here."

"Don't, Dad. We'll sort Mom out," I said quickly. "Let's have a happy Sunday. Can we go for a drive in the van?"

"Certainly, beloved daughter. We'll have a happy, happy, happy Sunday," said Dad.

We drove around in the van for ages. Dad had made enough out of Billy's chip van to buy a full tank of gas. We drove right out into the country and then around and around every little town and village. We always slowed down going past any posters and big fields and parks and recreation grounds. We didn't once say the word *fair* to each other but we both knew what we were looking for.

We didn't have any luck.

We came home feeling a bit frazzled. Of course it *wasn't* home. Still, Dad did his best. He'd bought a packet of English muffins and we stuck them on big forks and toasted them in front of Billy's old electric fire in the living room. Lucky and Whisky and Soda came and basked in the heat on the rug. Lucky lay in between Whisky and Soda. They took turns nuzzling and petting her, tying to outdo each other as foster moms. Lucky smiled to herself, happy to be the center of attention.

All three cats eventually narrowed their eyes, lowered their heads, and started napping. I was tired too, but I had to go off to the chip van with Dad. I washed my buttery-crumpet hands carefully because I wanted to make some more clothes for Ellerina and Dimble. I filled a bag with material scraps and some tissues and toothpicks and some cut-up socks for stuffing. I wanted to make them proper Tudor outfits, complete with petticoats and pleated ruffs. I didn't have the first idea how to go about this but I hoped inspiration would strike once I got cracking.

Dad and I set off to the station. Dad maneuvered the chip van to the curb and got everything set up. The chip fryer was being particularly temperamental, overheating one minute and switching itself off the next. Dad fiddled and swore at it, despairing.

"How am I supposed to cook anything halfway

decent on this broken-down, old contraption?" he said. "Oh, Flossie, Charlie's Café was hardly the Ritz but at least I could cook *properly* back at home. Try as I might, I can only manage lousy food here."

For a long time it didn't look as if anyone wanted any food, lousy or otherwise. We'd been busy on Saturday night and Dad had whistled as he fried, happy that he was keeping Billy's business going and making a bit of cash for us.

But this Sunday we weren't making any cash at all. Dad sighed and fidgeted and shook the surly fryer. Then he came and squatted down beside me, his knees uncomfortably under his chin because he was so big and there was very little space.

"What's that you're doing, sweetheart?" he asked, watching me gluing bits of white tissue to the toothpicks.

"I'm trying to make one of those sticky-out hoop petticoat thingies to go under an Elizabethan gown for my woolly elephant," I said.

Dad blinked. "Ask a silly question," he said. He reached out and ruffled my curls. "You're a funny kid, Floss. Thank God you're so adaptable. Well, I'll keep the blooming fryer bubbling for another half hour or so and then we might as well call it a day. The town's dead, obviously."

Almost as soon as Dad said that a couple walked up to the van and started tapping their money on the counter for attention—then another couple, a little gang of girls, a rowdy mob of boys . . . "So where have you guys all suddenly sprung from?" said Dad, heaving tons of chips into the fryer.

"There's been a green fair down by the river," said one of the girls. "We've been listening to the bands."

"Oh, Dad, the fair!" I said, leaping up.

"It won't be our fair, pet. Green fairs are different," said Dad. "You cuddle down on your cushion and try to go to sleep. It looks like it's going to be a long and busy night after all. We're not going to get home till late."

I tried to finish Ellerina's petticoat first but it totally defeated me. I ended up with little pricks all over my fingers and bits of tissue stuck everywhere. I gave up and had a go at making those baggy knicker things that Elizabethan men wore, but it was difficult fashioning them to fit a saggy woollen dog, so I stopped trying. Maybe Susan would have to be chief dressmaker in our games.

I curled up in a ball, closed my tired itchy eyes and tried to go to sleep. But it wasn't easy. It got noisier and noisier as more and more people came to the chip van on their way home from the fair.

I started dreaming a silly dream about wandering around Hampton Court with Ellerina and Dimble dressed as Tudor courtiers. I'd somehow turned into one of Henry the Eighth's six wives, only he decided he didn't like me anymore and he started shouting at me. I ran away because I knew what happened to the wives who were out of favor. Then all his soldiers started pursuing me and they were all shouting too. I woke up with a start, still shaking.

I told myself that it was only a dream, that I was safe in the chip van with Dad—but I could still hear the shouting. I heard Dad shouting too. I struggled up out of my corner.

"Dad? Dad, what's happening? Are you all right?"

"Get back down, darling. It's OK. It's just some silly lads getting impatient. Pipe *down*, you guys, I'm frying as fast as I can. This isn't McDonald's—there's just me, so you'll have to *wait*."

"Stupid idiots," said this tall guy, who was waiting patiently, his arm around his girlfriend. "Don't take any notice of that lot, mate. You're doing a grand job."

I blinked, then rubbed the sleep out of my eyes. The tall guy was somehow familiar. He had long fairish hair down to his shoulders, a black vest, black jeans, a studded jacket—and large silver biker jewelry on almost every finger.

"It's Saul!" I said, popping up behind Dad.

"Get down, Floss! It's who?"

"Saul!"

Saul saw me and grinned. "Yeah, I'm Saul. How did you know my name?"

"Is she an old girlfriend, Saul?" said his girl, grinning.

"Saul rescued us at the fair, Dad. *Our* fair. He's Rose's son."

"Oh, great!" said Dad. "Well, fantastic to meet up with you again, Saul. Is the fair in our town again?"

"No, no. I'm not actually *with* the fair at the moment. I've moved in with Jenny here," said Saul, giving her a squeeze.

"Stop the chitchat, Chip Man, and get serving!" some stupid guy yelled. His friends started chanting stuff too.

"Hoodlums," said Dad contemptuously, taking no notice of them. "Well, I bet your mom misses you, Saul."

"Yeah, she wasn't too pleased, but she's a tough lady, my ma, she'll cope."

"She's a lovely lady," said Dad, serving up a mega-huge portion of chips to Saul and Jenny. "Here you are, have these on the house."

"Thanks, mate, that's good of you. Imagine you working here in this chip van!"

"It's just a temporary measure. Not quite sure what the future holds. Maybe I should go and see your mom and ask her to tell my fortune," said Dad.

"Here, Chip Man, get serving us, you useless moron!" an ugly guy behind Saul shouted.

"Keep your mouth buttoned, mate, until you learn some manners," said Saul.

"Yeah, so who's going to make me?"

"I might," said Saul, clenching his ringed fingers so they were bunched in a threatening fist.

"Don't get tough with *me*, mate! Who do you think you are, with your girly hair and your jewelry? You're asking to be sorted out good and proper!"

The ugly guy surged forward, all his gang following.

"Now cut it out, fellas. Any trouble and I'm into that station and phoning the police," said Dad.

No one was listening. They were pushing and shoving, shouting and swearing. Then the ugly guy punched Saul on the chin. Saul whacked him one straight back with his ringed fist. The ugly guy staggered, bleeding. He fumbled for something. Then I saw a sudden frightening gleam.

"He's got a knife!" I screamed.

"Oh, God," said Dad. "Watch out, Saul! Look, you stay right here where it's safe, Floss, out of sight. Promise?"

Dad squeezed my shoulder and then went rushing out of the door at the back.

"Dad! Oh, Dad, come back! Don't get hurt!"

I couldn't stay in my corner. I had to peer over the counter to see what was happening. There were people fighting everywhere. Some lads were kicking. Someone was head-butting. I couldn't even see Saul and the ugly guy now. And where was Dad? I prayed he wouldn't get into the fight himself. What if he was hit or kicked? What if he was *knifed*?

I eyed the door, wondering if I dared go after him

to drag him back. But I'd promised Dad to stay in the van.

It wasn't safe anymore though. There were boys banging on it now, so that it rattled and shook. There were thumps and shoves. I cowered right up in the corner again, clutching Dimble and Ellerina.

More fists, more boots. The van shuddered and rocked and tilted.

"Let's turn it right over!" someone shouted.

"Dad!" I yelled.

They all pushed together and the van lurched sideways. The chips sizzled furiously and fat poured out over the fryer. Then suddenly there was an enormous *whoomph!* and flames leaped high in the air.

"Dad! Dad! Dad!" I screamed.

I scrambled for something to throw on the flames but it was too late. They were roaring right up to the ceiling, terrifyingly orange, while filthy smoke swirled all around the van, making me cough.

"*Dad!*" I croaked. The flames and fat were making such a noise no one would ever hear me.

I had to get out! I couldn't even see the door now. I was in a boiling burning whirl of black smoke and orange flame. My eyes smarted and stung. I couldn't breathe. I pressed my woolly toys over my nose and mouth and crouched down, crawling blindly across the floor.

"DAD!" I cried one last time.

Then the door burst open, making the fire roar and spread. There were arms fighting through the flames. Two hands grabbed me and hauled. I was out of the van, still screaming and sobbing, but safe in Dad's arms.

Twenty-one

We had to go to hospital. I was completely fine but they needed to check that I hadn't inhaled too much smoke. Dad had burns on his hands where he'd fought his way forward to grab me. They were both bandaged up so that it looked as if he were wearing white boxing gloves. Dad was very brave and didn't even flinch when the nurse rubbed ointment on, but I started crying.

"Hey, hey, Floss, no tears, sweetheart, I'm fine. Look, I'm being wound up like an ancient Egyptian. Only I'm not a mummy, I'm a daddy!"

It wasn't really funny but I sniffled a little, and the nurse laughed out loud.

"Don't worry, dear, your dad's going to be as right as rain. He'll have to keep his bandages on for a bit but he should heal up nicely. It'll be a good excuse for him to sit back and have your mom wait on him for a week or so."

"Hmm," I said. I patted Dad's knee. "*I'll* wait on you, Dad. You saved my life! You're a hero!"

"Nonsense, pet. I didn't do anything," said Dad.

"Yes, you did, mate," said Saul, poking his head around the cubicle curtain. His arm was in a sling because one of the guys had tried to knife him. "You saved me too, grabbing that punk by the wrist so he dropped his knife," he said.

"I wasn't really thinking straight. I just caught hold of him—and as luck would have it, that's when he dropped the knife," said Dad.

"No, your little girl's right, you're a hero," said Jenny, Saul's girlfriend.

Saul had had to take off all his huge silver skull rings and bangles so she was wearing them for him, jangling and clanking every time she moved her arms. She stroked Saul's sore arm tenderly.

"It's only a flesh wound but it could have been far worse," she said.

Dad and Saul had to give statements to a policeman, though I kept dozing off while they were talking because it was the middle of the night now. I cuddled Dimble and Ellerina, who were a little singed but safe. Every time I went to sleep I heard the ugly raised voices, I felt the thuds, the shaking, I saw the sudden gold-red flare of flame and I started crying. Each time Dad held me in his arms, patting me with his big bandaged hands, soothing me.

"Come on, I've got to get my little girl home," said Dad—and eventually they let us go.

We had no way of getting back from the hospital and Dad didn't have much cash on him, but Saul and Jenny were waiting and they shared a taxi with us, taking us all the way to Billy the Chip's house for nothing.

"If you'd like to come back tomorrow I'll give you the fare," said Dad.

"Think nothing of it, mate. Still, I might come back visiting," said Saul.

They dropped us off and we staggered up the path to Billy's. I had to feel in Dad's pocket for the key and open the front door for us. Lucky and Whisky and Soda were waiting worriedly in the hall, twining themselves around our ankles like furry feather boas, wondering why we'd been out so late.

"Let's get straight to bed, little Floss," said Dad. "It's all right now, baby, we're safe and sound." But as he said it he suddenly started shaking. "Oh, Floss, I can't believe how stupid I've been, dragging you off to that van night after night. You could have been burned to a crisp and it would have all been my fault."

"No, Dad! It wasn't *your* fault, silly. You rescued me. I'm fine, we're both fine," I said, putting my arms around Dad and hugging him tight.

Dad cried a little bit while I patted him on the back. Then his nose started running and he couldn't blow it properly with his poor bandaged hands so I had to help him.

"It's like you're my big baby, Dad," I said.

I had to help him undo all his buttons and shoelaces so he could get ready for bed. When I was in bed myself, Dad lay down at the end with his pillow and blanket so that every time I dreamed about the fire and woke up he could soothe me back to sleep.

He said I could stay home from school in the morning. We didn't set the alarm but we both woke up very early even so. We had to have a special long cuddle just to make sure we were both all right.

"I'll have to phone poor Billy and tell him what's happened to his van," said Dad, sighing. "Goodness knows how he's going to react. That old chip van has been in his family for so many years. I feel so bad. It'll probably break his heart. It seems so cruel to interrupt his vacation and tell him, but I'm worried the police will have to contact him at some stage, so I'd better let him know first."

I carefully made Dad a cup of tea, and he managed to balance it between his bandages and sip from it. Then he dictated Billy's son's phone number and I dialed it for him.

Dad got through straight away but couldn't get a word in edgewise at first. Billy the Chip was babbling away on the other end, telling Dad Sydney was wonderful, his son was wonderful, his son's wine bar was wonderful, the weather was wonderful—and Dad had to listen with an agonized expression, trying to wade into this wave after wave of wonder.

"I'm so glad you're enjoying yourself, Billy, mate, but I'm afraid I've got some bad news," Dad blurted out eventually. "Last night there was a bit of a ruckus with some hooligans. They were trying to tip the van over, and the fat in the fryer caught fire. I'm afraid the van's been burned, Billy. What? No, no, I'm fine, hands got a bit singed, that's all. Thank God Floss is fine too. But I'm not quite sure how we're going to get the van back into action. Have you got proper insurance? Oh, thank God, because truthfully, mate, it's a total write-off. But if you can get the insurance sorted when you're back from Oz then I'll help you buy a new van, get the business up and running again— though I'll have to make some kind of arrangement for Floss: I'm not risking her in a van at night now. What's that? Really? You truly mean that, Billy?" Dad listened. He nodded. He shook his head. He blew his breath out, his lower lip jutting.

"Yeah, yeah. Thanks, mate, but you don't have to. No, no, we'll be moving on soon anyway. Definitely. Well, we've no actual concrete plans but something's bound to pop up out of the blue. OK then. You enjoy yourself, pal. Go for it. Bye then." Dad put the phone down. He rolled his eyes at me.

"He says he wants to stay in Australia and help

291

his son with his bar! It's a boys-only bar too—not really Billy's sort of place at all—but he says he's so enjoying being with his son he wants to stick by him. I don't know whether it will work out in the long term but he seems sure that's what he wants. He's intent on giving up his chip van, whatever happens. He says he's thinking of putting this house on the market too, though we can stay in it for the time being." Dad tried to scratch his head and ended up patting it with his bandages. "Strikes me the world's gone crazy, Floss. Still, I suppose we should be happy for Billy." He raised his mug of tea unsteadily. "Here's to Billy the Chip!"

"Here's to Billy the Chip," I repeated—and Lucky and Whisky and Soda mewed.

"Hey, Dad, what about his *cats*?"

"Well, he says maybe we can find a good home for them. He's thinking of having some firm pack up some of his stuff and ship it to Australia, but he can hardly do that to old Whisky and Soda. I doubt they'd last the journey."

"Well, are *we* a good home, Dad?" I asked.

"We haven't got a good home for *us*, pet, let alone Billy's mangy old cats."

"*Us* meaning you, me and Lucky?"

"Us three, absolutely," said Dad.

I made Dad and me some toast, and fed all three cats. I felt a bit weird not going to school. I was worried about Susan stuck in our classroom in front of Rhiannon without me.

"Maybe I'll go to school after all, Dad, if you feel you can cope OK."

"Are you sure, Floss? You're probably still in a state of shock. I know I am."

"Yes, but you're wounded, Dad," I said, very gently stroking his bandages.

"I can't drive you at the moment, but I'll walk you there, if you like," said Dad. "I've got to go and sort out what's happening to the chip van anyway. And I've got to buy something too—a cell phone! Then I feel I can always summon help straight away if we're in any more trouble. I haven't much idea what they cost, and we'd better hang on to every penny now the chip van business is up the creek, but I thought about selling something. Not that I've got much left to sell, admittedly. I wondered about the cuckoo clock. I know it doesn't work anymore, but it's quite old, and the carving's nice. I could take it into that antique place and see what they offer me."

"But it's your wedding present, Dad!"

"Yes, I know. But your mom never really liked it. And now—well, your mom and I aren't married anymore, are we?"

I swallowed. "Sometimes I wish you and Mom *were* still married, Dad," I said.

"I know, pet. Sometimes I still wish that too. But

your mom's moved on now—literally! Maybe it's time I did too. You won't mind too much if we get rid of the cuckoo clock, will you?"

"I'd much sooner we had a cell, Dad. Can it be half mine too? Hey, even Rhiannon hasn't got her own cell phone yet! I'll be so cool."

We wrapped the cuckoo clock in newspaper and Dad put it in his backpack. There was a specialist clock man in the antique center. He sniffed at our clock a bit, but admitted it was Victorian and hand-carved. He didn't offer that much at first, but Dad argued and eventually he gave him a hundred pounds!

"Wow, Dad! We're rolling in it now!" I said.

"Not really *rolling* in it, Floss," said Dad—but we certainly had enough to buy our mobile phone.

Then we went to the station to have a look at the chip van. It had been towed back into the shed where Billy always kept it. We peered in at it in silence. It was black all over, with half the roof actually burned off. Dad wound his arms around me tightly. We stood for a few seconds and then crept away again.

"I feel like I've let Billy down," said Dad mournfully.

"But he doesn't want his chip van anymore, Dad, he said so."

"He might change his mind. Still, I suppose he can always buy a brand-new van with his insurance money."

We trudged on past the station. I knew where we were going now. Dad looked at me quizzically. I nodded. It wasn't worth walking all around the moon when the direct way to school went straight past our café.

Harlie's Café didn't exist anymore. It was now a Starbucks. Dad stood staring at the smart green paintwork. He stepped up to the window and looked in, past the orange lamps and all the people standing at the counter and sitting at every single table and chair and sofa. He stood still and sighed softly. Then he suddenly waved.

"Look who's in there!" he said. "It's Old Ron and Miss Davis! Look, they're sitting *at the same table*! And getting on like a house on fire as far as I can see. Let's embarrass them terribly and go and say hello."

We went into the café. It was just like stepping into any coffee bar anywhere. I looked up at the ceiling, wondering what was up there now. The girl cleaning the table looked up too, as if worried I'd spotted a leak.

"Yes?" she said uncertainly.

"Who lives up there?" I asked.

"No one. It's just the office and the storeroom," she said.

"It isn't an apartment anymore?"

"I think it was once," she said—like it was a hundred years ago. "But it was in a terrible state. Goodness knows who lived there."

I glanced nervously at Dad, who was thankfully deep in conversation with Old Ron and Miss Davis, gesturing theatrically with his bandaged hands. They were gasping appreciatively.

"Excuse me," I said to the girl, and ran over to join my dad.

Old Ron and Miss Davis were an extremely satisfying audience. They also said how much they missed Charlie's Café.

"I'm on my beam ends, drinking Starbucks coffee," said Old Ron. "Talk about pricey!"

I didn't know what his beam was and where it ended, but I got the gist of what he was saying.

"And Mr. Starbucks doesn't have a clue when it comes to making a good plain cup of tea from a nicely warmed pot," said Miss Davis, sighing.

"Well, as soon as my bandages are off I'll make you as many cups of tea and coffee as you can manage at my place," said Dad, but then he bit his lip. "Well . . . Billy's place. Whatever."

"Is he *really* going to sell it?" said Old Ron.

"So he says. Hey, Ron, if push came to shove, you wouldn't take on his old cats, would you? Whisky and Soda, two very nice old lady friends."

"Well . . ." said Old Ron. "In the general run of things I *might* say yes, but now *I've* got this very nice old lady friend who isn't at all keen on cats." He nudged Miss Davis in the ribs.

She glared at him. "Utter nonsense! And watch what you're doing, I bruise easily," she said, but she wasn't really cross. She leaned across the table at me. "Do they catch birds?"

"Oh, no, Miss Davis, never in a million years. They can't catch anything, they're far too lazy and plump. They don't even crunch up their cat food properly; they just suck all the juice off the fishy chunks. But they're really lovely, kind cats. They've tried to be very motherly to my cat Lucky. I'm sure you'd like them if you met them."

"Well, if there's really no other alternative I won't object if Ronald wants to give the creatures a proper home for their twilight years," said Miss Davis.

"Old Ron and Miss Davis seem to be taking care of *their* twilight years," said Dad, as we continued our long rambling walk to school. "Fancy, all those years of coming into my café and they barely spoke to each other. And then there's Billy the Chip, so stuck in his ways he did the same thing every single day of his life, and yet now he's moved away and wandering around Australia. Your mom too, of course." Dad sighed. "They've all moved on. I've stayed stuck. No, I haven't even done that, I've started going backward. One moment I've got a wife, a child, my own business, and then the next—*poof!*" But Dad was smiling at me. "I've still got the most important little person in my life, that's all that matters. Come on then, Floss. Let's get you to school. You're astronomically late. I hope you won't get a telling-off. Do you want me to come in with you and explain?"

I didn't think this was a good idea at all. "I'll be fine, Dad, really," I said.

"Well, if you're sure, sweetheart. Schools do give me the heebie-jeebies. I always feel like I'm going to be told to stand in the corner with my hands on my head. What's Mrs. Horsefield like, Floss? Bit of an old bag?"

"She's lovely, Dad!"

When we approached the school I saw a class was out in the playground doing PE. *My* class, with Mrs. Horsefield in her prettiest white top and shorts showing all the class how to jog in place.

"My goodness, is she a teacher?" Dad whispered.

"She's Mrs. Horsefield, Dad. *My* teacher. See, I told you she was lovely," I said.

"I'll say. You're a lucky girl, Floss," said Dad. "OK then, pet, you run and join all your friends. I'll come and collect you at going-home time."

I gave Dad a quick kiss and started racing toward the gate into school. Dad waved with his big bandaged hand. Mrs. Horsefield slowed to a standstill, panting a little.

"Floss? Is that your father? Mr. Barnes!"

"Uh-oh!" said Dad. "Looks as if I'm in trouble after all."

He walked along by my side, his arms dangling.

Everyone stopped jogging and stood still, staring. Everyone except Susan. She came flying across the playground and met me at the school gate. She flung her arms around me and gave me a great big hug.

"Hello, Susan," said Dad. "I know you two girls are best friends but do you always greet each other with such gusto?"

"No, no, Mr. Barnes! I'm just so relieved to see Floss. I thought something awful had happened to her. One of the girls in our class said there'd been a fire in the chip van and I was so scared you'd both been burned. Oh, but you *have* been burned, Mr. Barnes. Look at your poor hands!"

"They're fine, dear. I've just got the bandages on to keep them nice and clean. The nurse says they'll clear up completely in a week or so."

"Oh, so you've just got first-degree burns. Thank goodness!" said Susan, knowledgeable as always.

Mrs. Horsefield came right over to us. "OK, Susan, you get back in line, dear," she said. "Are you sure you're all right, Floss? There have been all sorts of terrible rumors running around the school. I tried phoning, but your telephone number seems to be out of order, Mr. Barnes."

"Oh, dear, that would be the old number, yes. Silly of me not to have let you know. I'll give the school my cell number. We're temporarily staying at a friend's house but I expect we're moving on soon, during school vacation."

"Flora's had to cope with quite a few changes recently," Mrs. Horsefield said quietly, careful that the others shouldn't hear.

"Yes, yes, I'm afraid she has, but she's been a little star," said Dad. "She's such a good girl, my Floss. She might not always be up to speed with her lessons. I think she's a bit of a dreamer, like her old dad, but I know she tries really hard, Mrs. Horsefield."

"I know she does," said Mrs. Horsefield. "Mr. Barnes, you do know you can come in to see me any day after school? I always stay on in the classroom for a good half hour or so. If there's anything you want to discuss, any problems, any advice—well, that's what I'm here for."

"Thank you," said Dad. "I wish I'd had a fantastic teacher like you when I was at school."

"Dad!" I hissed.

Dad laughed at me and pretended to punch the tip of my chin with his bandaged fist. "Am I embarrassing you, darling? That's what dads are for," he said. "I'll come and meet you after school, OK?"

He backed off across the playground. When Mrs. Horsefield blew her whistle and got everyone to start jogging again, *Dad* started jogging too, arms pumping, feet pounding. We could see his head bobbing up and down all the length of the school fence. Susan laughed fondly. So did some of the others. Rhiannon and Margot and Judy laughed too, but they were standing with their hands on their hips, eyebrows raised.

"Look at Smelly Belly Chip!" said Rhiannon.

"Like, who does he think he *is*?" said Margot.

"He's so fat! See his big bum! Smelly Belly Waggle Bum!" said Judy.

They all laughed harder. I hated all three of them. When Mrs. Horsefield told us to start running properly I forged ahead, kicked Rhiannon right on her own bum, then Margot, then Judy, kick, kick, kick like a soccer star. Then I charged out of their way before they could get me back.

I couldn't keep out of their way forever. I couldn't keep out of *anyone's* way at break time. Everyone crowded around me in the restroom, wanting to hear all about the fire. The story had already spread rapidly and had become wildly exaggerated. Dad and I had been besieged by thousands of thugs who had deliberately set the chip van on fire with us inside.

"No, no, it wasn't like that at all!" I said.

"So what *was* it like?"

"Tell us, Floss."

"Yeah, come on, Floss, tell!"

So I started telling the whole story myself, and as I got into it I couldn't help doing a *little* exaggerating myself. I had my dad leaping out of the van, knocking knives out of guys' hands kung-fu style. I demonstrated enthusiastically. I had Dad snatching Saul from a serious stabbing, protecting his girlfriend, bashing all the boys and sending them flying.

"Oh, wow, Floss, your dad's fantastic!"

"That's so cool!"

"Did he *really* beat them all up?"

"Of course he didn't!" said Rhiannon. "Old Smelly Belly Bum Chip couldn't bash so much as a baked potato. You're telling whopping great lies, Floss."

"I am not! Well, he might not have hit them all. And maybe there was just *one* knife. But I'll tell you something, and I swear this is true. When the fryer caught fire in the van I was trapped, and I would have burned to death there and then if Dad hadn't braved the flames and fought his way over to me and carried me out," I said.

"Your dad's truly heroic, Floss," Susan proclaimed.

"Yes, isn't he," I agreed proudly.

"Nonsense," said Rhiannon.

"Yeah, like, totally gross," said Margot.

Judy didn't say anything but she made a very rude noise.

"Take no notice of them, Floss," said Susan. "They're just jealous of your lovely dad."

"Jealous!" said Rhiannon. "My dad earns fifty thousand a year in his car business and he's always buying me heaps of stuff and taking us on fantastic vacations, and people say he looks very like Tom Cruise. Plus he doesn't smell, so why should I be jealous, Swotty Potty?"

"Floss's dad loves her tremendously and talks to her as if she's his special friend and plays with her heaps and does funny things to make her laugh and takes good care of her," said Susan.

I squeezed Susan's hand, so moved I could barely speak.

Rhiannon still sneered. "Takes good care of her! You must be joking! My mom says it's appalling. She's thinking about going to social services and reporting Floss."

"*What?*" I said.

"You heard me. Or if you didn't, wash your ears out, and wash the rest of you too so you don't stink so much, Smelly Chip," said Rhiannon.

"Your mom isn't *really* going to the social services about me, is she, Rhiannon?" I said.

"Yes, because she's truly worried about you. First your mom walks out on you—"

"She didn't! You *know* she didn't!"

"And now your dad's café's gone bust and you haven't got a proper home anymore and you look a sight and you smell, and now it seems your dad's dragging you off to his chip van every night and getting into fights and you very nearly end up getting burned to death—your very own words, Smelly Chip. My mom says you need some kind lady to look after you properly. So you wait, the social services will come and get you and put you in care if you don't watch out."

Twenty-two

Rhiannon's words rang in my head all day at school. Susan kept telling me that I shouldn't worry. Rhiannon was just trying to wind me up. No social worker could ever doubt that I had two parents who loved me and cared for me.

I knew she was right, but I was scared all the same. When the bell rang for home time I peered around the school gates anxiously in case there were social workers lurking, ready to capture me. But there was Dad, smiling and waving his bandages at me.

"Look, there's Floss's dad!"

"Hey, Mr. Barnes!"

"Hello, Mr. Barnes. You're a hero!"

Dad grinned at all the kids in my class. Thank goodness he didn't seem to notice the three girls who walked straight past him, rudely holding their noses.

"How have you been today, Floss? You haven't felt funny or had any coughing fits, have you? I've been a bit worried about you," said Dad, cuddling me close.

"I've been a bit worried about *you*, Dad! How have *you* been today? How are your poor hands?"

"They're OK, sweetheart. I've managed fine, though it's a bit of a challenge going to the bathroom! It's not that easy to cook either. I think you might have to give me a hand making tea."

"Glad to, Dad."

"But we're not having chips! I don't want to see a chip fryer for a long, long, long time."

"Are you going to give up being a chip cook, Dad?"

"Well, I've got to *work*, pet, and there's not a lot else I can do. I went down the job center today. The girl there was quite helpful. She even filled in the forms for me, seeing as I've got my hands bandaged. Lucky that, as I'm terrible when it comes to spelling! But she was quite frank about my chances. They're not that great. Still, you never know . . ."

"Something might pop up out of the blue!" we said together as we turned the corner down Oak Crescent.

There was a bright pink car parked outside Billy's house. I'd once seen a caravan exactly that color.

"Dad!" I said.

"What, pet?" said Dad. Then he saw it too. He stopped still, staring.

"Come on, Dad," I said, starting to run.

"Hey! Hang on, wait for your old dad!"

I left him behind and rushed to the car. Saul and

Jenny were squashed up in the back. Rose was in the front, her beautiful red nails tapping a tune on her white leather steering wheel. She had two red velvety roses dangling from her driving mirror.

"Hello!" I shouted.

They all saw me at once. They smiled and started getting out of the car.

"Hello, little Floss," said Rose, and she gave me a hug.

She was wearing tight black pants and a lovely deep pink top patterned with red roses. Her toenails were painted dark red too, peeping out of her high-heeled sandals. She even *smelled* of red roses. I wanted to hang on to her and breathe in her lovely soft, warm smell.

"So where's your dad then, Flossie?" said Rose.

"Just coming! There he is," I said, gesturing.

Dad was ambling along, his arms hanging at his side, head bent bashfully. He looked really odd, as if he were *shy*.

"Well, goodness me, this is a surprise!" he said. His voice sounded weird too, as if he couldn't catch his breath.

He went to shake Rose's hand and then remembered his bandage. He paused awkwardly, half waving in the air.

"Come here!" said Rose, and she gave him a big hug too. "I want to thank you for looking out for my boy."

"I didn't really do anything, honestly," said Dad, going bright red in the face, but looking pleased all the same.

"How are your hands, mate?" Saul asked. He waggled his sling. "Look at us! Talk about the walking wounded!"

"You're a magnet for trouble, Saul, always have been, always will be," said Rose, shaking her head. "But what about you, Mr. Barnes? Are your hands badly burned? Let's go into the house. I want you to show me. I don't trust you strong silent types, you don't make enough *fuss*! I'm so glad Saul remembered the right house after all. I got a bit worried when we first knocked half an hour ago and no one was in. Still, I thought you were probably meeting your little girl at school—and I was right."

"My Floss," said Dad. "Well, come in, come in, all of you."

We trooped into Billy's house. Whisky and Soda and Lucky were waiting in the hall, tails in the air, yowling hopefully for tea. Whisky and Soda backed away and hid behind the sofa, overwhelmed by all the guests, but Lucky was perkily sociable. She gave Saul and Jenny a nod, and actually came and rubbed herself against Rose's shapely ankles.

"Hello, little cat," said Rose, bending to give her a stroke.

"She's my cat. She's called Lucky. Oh, she *likes* you, Rose," I said.

Lucky was daintily licking Rose's toenails as if in homage.

"And I like *her*, darling," said Rose. She carefully stepped around Lucky into the living room. "Oh, what a . . . nice big room," she said uncertainly. "Yes, you've got a lovely huge house, Mr. Barnes."

"Call me Charlie, please. And it's not *my* house. It belongs to an old pal of mine. Floss and I are only here temporarily."

"It's not a *huge* house, Rose," I said, puzzled.

"All houses seem enormous to you if you've been brought up in a caravan," said Rose.

"I love your cozy rosy caravan," I said.

"So do I, dear. Though I know it might seem a bit cramped to some people." She looked at Saul and raised her eyebrows at him.

He laughed at his mom. "I want a bit more space now, Mom. And a proper roof over my head. I want to live with the same girl in the same street. That's not so strange, is it?" He put his arm around Jenny, who smiled and snuggled up to him.

"Well," said Rose, struggling. "As long as you're happy, son."

"So how are you coping by yourself?" said Dad.

"Oh, I get by fine. I always used to run the stall by myself when Saul was little. It's a bit of a struggle sometimes but I manage."

"Tell me about it!" said Dad. "So who's looking after the stall tonight?"

"Monday's always our quiet night, when we've just set up. Liz from the Lucky Darts stall is supposed to be keeping an eye on it for me."

"Where *is* your fair now?" I asked eagerly. "Dad and I have looked and looked for it."

"Have you?" said Rose, looking pleased. "Well, we're over in Felting this week, not too far away. Are you going to come and visit us?"

"You bet!" I said. "We can, can't we, Dad?"

"Of course, darling. Now, let's get some tea organized. Will you be a lovely helpful girl, Floss, and put the kettle on for me? Then, as I can't get at my fingers just now, perhaps you'd also like to dial the pizza place?" He looked apologetically at Rose. "I'd love to cook you a proper meal, but it's a bit awkward just now, as you can see."

"Pizza would be lovely! It's definitely our treat though."

Rose ordered *four* different king-size pizzas, and then ice cream for dessert. I had a big slice of all four pizzas (triple cheese and spinach, chicken and mushroom, pineapple and bacon, and sausage and sweetcorn and tomato) and then a bowl of strawberry and vanilla and chocolate ice cream. Then I felt so full I had to undo the buttons on my school skirt.

Saul and Jenny stayed for a while. Saul let me try on his great big rings. I had a dragon on one finger, a snake on another, three different skulls, an eye ring and frogs on each thumb. They looked *so* cool. But then they said they had to get going because they wanted to see some film.

"I suppose I ought to be going too," said Rose.

"Oh, no, do stay," I said.

"Your dad probably wants some peace and quiet," said Rose.

"I certainly don't!" said Dad. "Please stay a bit longer, Rose."

"Well, I've certainly still got to examine those poor sore hands," said Rose. "We'll take those bandages off and have a look. They've given you fresh dressings, I hope. Let's see how you're healing."

I peered fearfully as she gently unwound the bandages. I was terrified that Dad's fingers would have turned black and cindery like burned toast. It was a huge relief to see they were just a little swollen and shiny red—but very recognizably still my dad's dear fingers.

Rose peered at them carefully, holding his hands in hers.

"Are you reading Dad's palms, Rose?" I asked.

"I might be," said Rose, smiling.

"What do they say? Is Dad's luck going to change?"

"I think maybe it already has," said Dad softly.

He wasn't looking at me. He was looking at Rose.

She stayed very late that evening. Dad let me stay

up but I was starting to feel very tired. I'd had hardly any sleep the night before . . . and a *lot* of excitement. I curled up in a chair with Lucky on my lap. My head started nodding. Dad tucked a cushion under my neck and covered me with his sweater.

I woke up once to wriggle around and rearrange Lucky. I saw that Dad and Rose were sitting very close together on the sofa. Billy the Chip's mother and father were frowning out of their photograph at them, but Dad and Rose didn't look as if they cared one bit.

When Dad came to meet me the next day from school he said, "Guess where we're going!"

It didn't need much power of deduction but I played a game with Dad.

"Are we going shopping? Up to London? The seaside?" I said, trying to seem completely innocent and dumb.

Dad kept going, "No! No! No!" Then he said, "Come on, Floss, where would you like to go most of all?"

I took a deep breath. "THE FAIR!" I shouted.

Dad whooped and punched the air with his bandaged fist and went, "Yay!"

He still couldn't drive, of course, but he'd checked out how to get to Felting on the bus. He'd brought fruit juice and apples and nuts so we had a snack on the journey.

"I thought we'd eat really healthily now so that we can overdose on candyfloss when we get to the fair!" said Dad.

"Does Rose know we're coming?"

"Oh, yes."

"Dad . . . you like Rose, don't you?"

"Yes, of course I like her. You like her too, don't you, Floss? I think she's a very kind, lovely lady."

"Yeah, but I meant, do you fancy her, Dad?"

"Floss!" said Dad. His cheeks were carnation pink.

"That means you do!" I said.

"Now then. Little girls shouldn't be talking about fancying people, not to their dads," said Dad. He paused. "But say I *did* fancy Rose, would you mind?"

"I don't think I'd mind a bit," I said. "So, is Rose going to be your girlfriend, Dad?"

Dad flushed from carnation to peony. "Well, it's early days, darling. I'm not sure a gorgeous lady like Rose would really want to spend much time with a dull old dad like me. We'll have to see. But whatever happens, Floss, you know you'll always come first with me. You're my little princess, and you always will be."

I hitched right across the seat onto Dad's lap and he gave me a big cuddle.

We got off the bus at Felting Junction and found the fair on the village green. We hurried toward it, hearing the hum of the hurdy-gurdy music, smelling the fried onions and warm sugar. It was as if we were walking back into a wonderful dream. But it was all real. There was the Big Slide and the Stargazer ride, the Ghost Train and the Crooked Cottage, the Teacup Whirlies and the Tin Can Alley, the Ferris wheel and the Wacky Waltzer. There was the Victorian carousel, with Pearl galloping round and round, her pink mane and tail flying in the wind. There was Rose's candyfloss stall, with her big pink teddy waving her fat plush paw at us. There was Rose herself, looking lovely in a low-cut pink blouse with a little red enamel rose on a gold chain.

She let me go right inside her van. She even let me pour different colored sugars into her candyfloss cauldron, and then set it spinning so that little wisps of floss started forming. I carefully wound them around and around my stick until I'd made my very own pink, lilac and blue cotton candy.

Dad and I wandered all around the fair, and I had one, two, *three* rides on Pearl, but every ten minutes we came back to chat with Rose. After an hour or so, she got her friend Liz from the Lucky Darts to keep an eye on the candyfloss stall.

Rose took us into her magical cozy caravan for supper. She had red wine for her and Dad, and cranberry juice for me, and little savory tarts and battered prawns and sausages in honey and chicken with peanut sauce and all sorts of chips and olives and crunchy vegetables with dips, and then there was pink iced sponge cake with little red sugar roses and the most amazing giant strawberries dipped in white chocolate.

"Oh, Rose, love, you didn't need to go to all this trouble!" said Dad, but he looked absolutely thrilled about it.

"No trouble at all, Charlie," said Rose. "I like fiddling with little bits. It's not often I have the opportunity, especially now that I'm on my own."

"It's like party food," I said.

"Well, this is *our* little party, isn't it?" said Rose. "And you and your dad could certainly do with a bit of pampering."

Dad found it a little difficult picking all his food up with his bandaged hands, so sometimes I popped a prawn or a sausage into his mouth, and then Rose fed him iced cake and strawberries. We ate and ate and ate, but there was still a lot left over when we were absolutely full. Rose packed all the snacks up in tinfoil and put them in a great big red plastic box.

"You can take them for your lunch at school tomorrow, Floss," she said.

"I shall share them with my best friend, Susan!" I said.

ELLA

Our very favourite teacher

Twenty-three

Susan and I had a positive feast the next day at lunch-time. Everyone looked at our food enviously—especially the cake and the chocolate strawberries.

"Give us a strawberry, Floss," said Rhiannon.

I goggled at her astonishing cheek. "No way," I said firmly. "Here, Susan, have a strawberry. Aren't they delicious?"

"I didn't really want one. I bet they taste of chip fat," said Rhiannon.

"Yeah, Smelly Chip, like we'd risk eating your dad's gross food," said Margot.

"Smelly Belly Bum Chip," said Judy.

They all three held their noses.

I stood up and glared at them. "You three are so *infantile*," I said. "And if you'd only let go of your snotty noses and take a big sniff you would see I don't, don't, don't smell of chips—on account of the fact that my dad's stopped frying them."

"What's he going to do then?" said Rhiannon.

"It's none of your business," said Susan.

"No one asked you, Swotty Potty," said Rhiannon. "So what sort of other work can your dad do, Smelly Chip? That's all he knows about—though he's not much use at that, is he? He lets your café go bust and he lets the chip van go up in flames. My mom says she's going to *have* to go to the social services. She says you need someone to look after you."

I took a step closer to Rhiannon, so we were practically nose to nose. Well, she's quite a bit bigger than me, so were kind of nose to chest.

"You tell your mom she doesn't need to worry about me anymore. She can send a whole *army* of social workers to see me if she wants, but it's a complete waste of time. To start with, I've got my mom, and she'll be coming back this autumn. Then I've got my dad, and he's just great at looking after me. And lastly I have my Auntie Rose."

"You haven't *got* an Auntie Rose," said Rhiannon.

"I have so. She came to see us on Monday and we went to see her on Tuesday and we're going to see each other heaps and heaps. *She* made me my special lunch. She's brilliant at everything. *And* she can tell fortunes. She's got all kinds of extraordinary occult powers and she says I'm highly receptive, so she's going to teach me to channel them properly, and then when I'm up to speed you three had better watch out. Now, would you and Margot and Judy just *get lost* and let Susan and me enjoy our lunch in peace!"

They did just that! They scuttled off, looking quite scared. Even Susan seemed a little disconcerted.

"You said exactly one hundred words *again*. Do you *really* have occult powers, Floss?" she whispered.

"Hey, you're meant to be the brainy one, OK? Of course not!"

"Honestly, Floss, you make things up so they sound so real! So you haven't even got an Auntie Rose?"

"Well, I have, sort of. She's not a real aunt but she's a new friend of my dad's, and she's ever so nice and she *does* tell fortunes and I'm sure she really will teach me if I ask her nicely. And she made the food for us so she is a really brilliant cook, isn't she? Susan, would you mind if I saved that biggest strawberry, the one with the most chocolate?"

"Not at all. It's your lunch, after all."

"It's not for me."

I wanted to save it for Mrs. Horsefield. I put it on her desk at the start of afternoon school.

"This is a little present for you, Mrs. Horsefield," I said shyly.

"Oh, Floss, it looks *lovely*. But I can't eat your special strawberry, sweetheart."

"I've chomped my way through your special iced buns with the cherry on the top. It's your turn for a treat, Mrs. Horsefield," I said.

"Well, thank you very much, Floss," said Mrs. Horsefield. She took a big bite of chocolate strawberry, breathed in and went "Mmmm!" She rolled it around her tongue. "It's delicious!"

"My Auntie Rose made it," I said proudly.

"I didn't know you had an auntie!" said Mrs. Horsefield, sounding delighted.

"Well, she moved away," I said vaguely. "But now she's moved nearer again."

Felting wasn't really *that* near—but Dad and I caught the bus over to the fair again on Friday night. We spent most of Saturday there too. Rose let me serve cotton candy again. I even managed to give the right change to people even though I'm so terrible at math.

Dad hung out with us a lot of the time, but then he went off for a stroll and palled up with Jeff, the guy in charge of the Stargazer ride. He was having a bit of trouble changing a broken wheel. Dad couldn't help much because he still had his bandages on, but he squatted down beside Jeff and peered at all the silver nuts and bolts and talked earnest engine talk.

"Look at them!" said Rose fondly. "Does your dad know much about machinery, Floss?"

"Well, he *thinks* he does," I said.

Rose roared with laughter. "You're like a little old woman at times!" She paused. Then she looked me straight in the eye. "So. What do you think about your dad and me, eh, darling?"

I shrugged shyly.

"I know it's early days yet, but your dad and me, well, we really seem to hit it off," she said.

"Yep," I said.

"And this time, when we move on tomorrow, we're going to make sure we stay in touch."

"That's great," I said.

We both paused to serve two customers pink and lilac cotton candy. Rose went on winding a stick around and around the sugar cauldron even though she wasn't making candyfloss for anyone else.

"I know I'm quite a bit older than your dad," she said.

"Are you?" I said, surprised. "I didn't know that. You don't look it."

"Oh, sweetheart, thank you!" she said. "I also know just how close you and your dad are and that's lovely. I want you to understand, I don't want to get in the way of that. When my Saul was young I had a few boyfriends who were rather hard for him to handle. It caused quite a lot of trouble." Rose stirred and stirred, her cotton candy getting bigger and bigger.

"So is Dad your boyfriend now?" I asked. "He says you're his girlfriend."

"Did he! Do you mind?"

I thought about it very carefully. "I *used* to think I'd mind if Dad had a girlfriend, but I don't seem to mind a bit if it's you. Rose, that candyfloss is simply ginormous now."

"Yeah. Well. It's a special big fluffy floss for you," said Rose, handing it over with a flourish.

I ate it as carefully as I could, but I still ended up with sticky sugar all over my cheeks and spangling my ears and nose.

"You've even got wisps in your hair," said Rose, picking them out carefully. You've got such lovely fluffy curls, darling. You're just like candyfloss yourself." She played with my hair, fluffing it out. "Yes, if we colored it pale pink you'd look like perfect candyfloss."

"Oooh, *could* we?"

"I don't know what your dad would say!"

"I can get around Dad," I said.

"Yes, I'm sure you can, sweetie. But what would they say at school if you turned up with pink hair?"

"We've only got one more week and then it's vacation!"

"All right then. When you're actually on break we'll see about turning you into a real candyfloss, OK?"

I told Susan that Rose had promised to color my hair for me.

"You lucky *thing*," she said. "It'll look prettier than ever. But promise it won't make you go all silly and clothes-mad and boy-crazy like Rhiannon and Margot and Judy."

"I promise, promise, promise, silly!" I said, giving her a hug. "Maybe you could come to the fair with Dad and me one day and Rose will color your hair too."

"My mom would go demented," said Susan.

"Well, we could pretend it was like spraying your hair red for Comic Relief. Oh, Susan, if I get my hair dyed pink I'll match Pearl! She's this horse on the carousel. She's got a wonderful pink mane and tail, and she's snowy white with big blue eyes. She's my absolute favorite, but you can have first go on her when you come to the fair with me. Sapphire's lovely too—she's white as well but with a blue mane—and Amber's great too—he's a glossy brown with a yellow mane and tail."

"You sound like you belong to the fair already," said Susan.

"Oh, I wish!" I said.

I worried that we wouldn't be going to the fair so much the next week because they moved on way past Felting to a town called Bromshaw about forty miles away. But Dad went back to see the doctor on Monday morning and had his burns inspected, and she said they were healing beautifully. He could leave his bandages off and drive the van again.

"It feels so good, Floss," said Dad, waggling his fingers at me one by one. "It's great to have my wheels back too. Let's go for a drive, darling. How about checking out the fair at Bromshaw? I thought it would be fun to see if it looks completely different there."

I looked at Dad. "You think Rose will be selling burgers and Pearl will be stuck onto the Stargazer ride?" I said.

"*No!* Are you teasing me, Floss?"

"Of course I'm teasing you, Dad! We don't need any excuse. Yes, let's go to the fair."

"You can always do your homework in the van."

"I haven't got any homework, Dad. School's out on Friday."

"Oh, lord, yes." Dad sighed. "What are we going to do with you during vacation, sweetheart? I'll have to find *some* kind of job to keep us going, and I very much doubt I'll be able to take you with me." Dad paused. "Maybe it's time for you to go and join your mom, darling. We've had a lovely time together but I've been having sleepless nights, worrying about you."

"Don't worry, Dad. I'm fine. We'll work something out for the summer." I held my hands out in front of my face, palms up. "Aha! Rose isn't the only one who can tell fortunes. I can see a big curvy line on each palm. They're like smiley faces. That means I'm going to be very, very happy."

"I hope so, darling. Listen, I was wondering . . . Susan's dad seems a very nice chap and he did say he owed us. Do you think you could play around at

Susan's some of the time? Once I get a job I can offer to pay."

"That would be great, Dad, though it might do my head in if they kept trying to teach me all the time! But they're going to their house in France."

"I don't know, there's them with two houses and here we are without any."

"Well, maybe it's good to travel light. Like Rose and all the fairground people," I said.

We had another lovely evening at the fair. Eddie, the carousel man, had become such an old pal by now he utterly refused to take my pound for the ride.

"In fact you can do me a favor, Floss. I need to test out all my gallopers to make sure they're all safe and solidly fixed. Perhaps you'd be an angel and ride them each in turn?"

I think he was just being sweet to me but I wasn't going to argue. While I was test-riding every horse on the carousel Dad had another chat with the Stargazer guy, and then he bought burgers and chips from one of the vans and had a long discussion about fat and fryers and types of sauce and vinegar. But *most* of the time we hung out around Rose's stall.

Dad had several goes on Liz's Lucky Darts stall to be polite—and amazingly scored one hundred and eighty. Well, Liz insisted he had, taking the darts out of the board so quickly we couldn't really check. She gave Dad a huge blue plush teddy, the twin of Rose's pink bear.

"Here you are, Floss," said Dad, thrusting a vast armful of bear at me.

"Thank you very much, Dad—but I think I'm maybe getting too big for bears," I said.

"Well, who can we give it to?" said Dad.

"Tiger might like him, but he won't be back for months. Anyway, I've already given him Kanga."

"What about Susan? Is she too big for bears too?"

"She's not really into cuddly toys, Dad."

"Well then . . ." Dad turned to Rose with a big smile. "You wouldn't like to hang him alongside your pink bear, would you?"

"I think that's a lovely idea," said Rose. "We'll hook him up right this minute. Come here, Blue Ted, come and make friends with Pinkie."

"He looks a bit of a *bare* bear compared with her," said Dad. "We'd better get him some clothes."

"Hey, I know an outfit that would be absolutely perfect," I said, chuckling. "A blue denim outfit. I can sew the skirt into shorts easy-peasy. And the denim cap will look really cute tucked over one ear!"

Dad took me on the bumper cars too. I didn't really *like* it much, especially when we got bumped, but I squealed and laughed and pretended because Mike, the owner, let us go on for free as we were friends of Rose. Mike's daughter Ella collected the money on the bumper cars. She was only a year or so older than me but she was much taller, a really tough tomboy girl who leaped lightly from car to car, her money belt tight around her slim hips. She sorted everyone out and swore cheerfully at any boys dumb enough to try to cheek her or chat her up.

We went for an ice cream together while Dad and Mike were having a chat, but I hardly dared say a word to her.

"You don't *say* much, do you?" she said, licking her ice cream with her pink pointy tongue.

I just shrugged my shoulders and licked too.

"You've got a tongue, I can see it," said Ella. "So *speak!*"

"Have you been with the fair all your life?" I mumbled.

"Yeah, my family have always been showmen. Well, my dad used to ride the Wheel of Death, but then he saved up enough to buy his bumper cars." She grinned. "They're mine too."

"That's really cool," I said. "I didn't know children could work at the fair."

"I'm not like a little kid," said Ella. "My brothers work later on, after dark. We all help out. It's what you do at a fair."

"Well, I always helped *my* dad," I said. "He used to have a café. I acted like a waitress at weekends. I even got tips."

"So how come you're so friendly with Rose? Are your dad and Rose an item?"

I shrugged again. "Sort of."

"We all love Rose. She's generally useless at picking men though. They always let her down."

"My dad never lets anyone down," I said fiercely.

"Yeah, he seems like a nice guy," said Ella. "Even though he's a flattie."

"A *fatty*?" I said. "He's not! Well, he's a bit plump but he's not really fat."

"No, I said *flattie*. You're one too. Punters. Customers."

She pretended to smoke her chocolate bar. I copied her.

"I've got real cigarettes if you want one," she said, reaching in her jeans pocket.

"No, thanks. I—I've given up," I said quickly.

She laughed at me, but not unkindly. I decided I liked Ella even though I was a bit scared of her. I hoped we might be friends—though not of course a *best* friend like Susan.

It was so sad at school on our last day before we left for summer vacation.

"I'm going to miss you so, so, so much, Susan," I said, nudging up close to her at her desk.

"I'm going to miss *you*," said Susan, giving my hand a quick squeeze.

Rhiannon made silly kissy noises behind us. We took no notice of her.

"I'll write heaps from France."

"Yes, do! Only *not* in French. I know what you're like, Susan."

"*Moi?*" said Susan, laughing. "I'll text you too on my dad's cell. And even though I'll probably see my cousins out in France, and maybe some of the stepbrothers and stepsisters too, I'll feel so lonely without you, Floss."

Rhiannon made disgusting vomit sounds.

"Perhaps you'd better run to the toilets if you're feeling sick, Rhiannon," said Mrs. Horsefield.

"It's not fair, Mrs. Horsefield, you always take *their* side. It's like they're your special favorites," said Rhiannon. "And they didn't even give you a proper good-bye present, just that babyish homemade thing."

Rhiannon had given Mrs. Horsefield a huge box of chocolates and a bottle of champagne.

Mrs. Horsefield paused. She fingered the blue denim pencil case Susan and I had made her as a good-bye present. We'd embroidered it with pink cherry buns and written *Our very favorite teacher* in chain-stitch.

"You've all given me lovely presents," said Mrs. Horsefield. "I'm very lucky to have such sweet and delightful pupils. As a teacher I try very hard to be impartial. But do you know something, Rhiannon? I'm a human being too. Sometimes you simply can't *help* having favorites."

Susan and I hung back at going-home time so we could both give Mrs. Horsefield a big good-bye hug. Then we had to have *our* good-bye hug and that was so hard. But eventually I jumped in the van beside Dad and waved and waved until Susan was out of sight.

"I hate saying good-bye to people," I sniffed.

"I know, pet. Still, you'll see Susan quite soon, when she gets back from her vacation."

"I wish *we* were going on vacation too, Dad," I said, sighing. "I know we can't help it, and I'm not really complaining, but it's going to be horrible just stuck at Billy's house all summer."

"W-e-l-l," said Dad. "I've got this idea, Floss. We don't have to do it if you don't want to. It's maybe crazy, but how would you like to join up with the fair for a few weeks?"

"*What?* Really? Oh, Dad, I want to, I want to!"

"Rose and I have had a long talk. She's so lovely, isn't she? I can't believe my luck. But anyway, she needs someone to help her out, even though she's so independent. And I've been talking to some of the guys, and they always need someone to help build up and pull down their rides. I'm a bit long in the tooth but they can't always get lads nowadays. I wouldn't make much money, but there's a chance I can help out at the burger stall, maybe making chip butties if there's a call for it. Only you'd stay safe in Rose's caravan, OK! How would you feel about it?"

"Oh, Dad, yes, yes, yes!"

"So you're really up for it, Floss?"

"You bet I am!"

"It's just for the summer vacation, to see how it works out. I don't know what we'll tell your mom. She's always hated fairs."

"We can say we're touring around the countryside for the summer. That's sort of true," I said. "Oh, Dad, it'll be so great! I'm so lucky!" I paused. "Oh, no, what about Lucky?"

"She can come too. She's a streetwise little cat. I think she'll take to a traveling life OK, though Whisky and Soda will have to go to Old Ron and Miss Davis. Rose says we can rig up Saul's old caravan as a very special bedroom for you. You can have Lucky and her comforter in with you. There'll be room for your silver chest. Rose says she'll paint flowers all over it if that's what you'd like. You can have Billy's dollhouse too, and space for your funny woolly toys and books and sewing stuff. And I haven't forgotten your swing. Every site we pitch up at we'll find a good tree and fix it up for you."

"So we won't be flatties anymore? We'll be fairground folk?"

"I suppose so, yes!"

"Fairground kids are expected to help out. Can I help you, Dad?"

"You always do, darling."

"And can I help Rose with her candyfloss stall?"

"She's counting on it."

"Dad. There's just one more thing."

"What's that, Princess?"

"Promise you'll say yes?"

"What is it you want, darling?"

"Can I have my hair dyed pink?"

"What? Absolutely *not*!" said Dad.

But I'm very good at getting around him . . .

About Jacqueline Wilson

JACQUELINE WILSON was born in Bath, England, in 1945, but has spent most of her life in Kingston-on-Thames, Surrey. She always wanted to be a writer and wrote her first novel when she was nine, filling countless notebooks as she grew up. She started work at a publishing company and then went on to work as a journalist on *Jackie* magazine (which was named after her) before turning to writing fiction full-time.

Since 1990 Jacqueline has written prolifically for children and teens and has won many of the U.K.'s top awards for children's books, including the Guardian Children's Fiction Award, the Smarties Prize and the Children's Book of the Year. Jacqueline was awarded an Order of the British Empire (OBE) in the Queen's Birthday Honours list in Golden Jubilee Year, 2002. Jacqueline Wilson's books have sold in excess of 20 million copies in the U.K. and been translated into 30 languages. She is the current U.K. Children's Laureate (2005-07), and for the past three years has been the most borrowed author in British libraries—ahead of all other authors.

An avid reader herself, Jacqueline has a personal collection of many, many thousands of books. She has one grown-up daughter.

www.Jacquelinewilsonrocks.com

GOFISH

QUESTIONS FOR THE AUTHOR*

JACQUELINE WILSON

**What sparked your imagination for
Candyfloss?**
A father queued up at one of my book sign-
ings to get his daughter's book signed. He
said she liked to curl up in the back of his
chip van (selling french fries!) and read my
books while Dad worked his evening shift. I thought this sounded so sweet, so I decided to write a story about a little girl in
similar circumstances. I chose a fairground setting for the latter
part of the book because I love fairs—especially carousels, like
Floss!

**What challenges do you face in the writing process
and how do you overcome them?**
I write quite easily and fluently and I don't have to be in my own
study. I often write parts of my stories on trains traveling to different events. However, I *always* worry whether the story is
working or not, and frequently lose confidence—but I manage
to battle on to the end.

SQUARE
FISH

What tips or advice can you share with students who hope to start writing?

I would *read* lots—not to steal ideas, but to simply stimulate the imagination, increase vocabulary, and see how other writers create their stories.

Do you have a fun writing topic to get students started?

I get children to write an advertisement for themselves: one glowing account, exaggerating every virtue, and one brutal, pessimistic account, stressing every bad point. It's fun reading them out loud. I take part, of course, and I always try to make the teachers join in, too.

If you were not writing, what do you think you would be doing?

I'd be *reading*—and I'd run my own used-book store.

What is your advice to parents for passing the joys of reading on to their children?

I think parents should read aloud to their children right from when they're babies.

How do you decide on themes for your books?

I think of the characters first; and when I know what my fictional children are like, I can work out which theme suits them the most.

How important is research in the development of your books? Can you explain the process as well?

I like to *imagine* things rather than spend time doing a lot of detailed research, but I always check my facts afterward.

Can you tell us about being the UK's Children's Laureate?

I very much enjoyed my time as the UK Children's Laureate. I met many thousands of children, spoke at a large number of events, launched a successful read-aloud campaign, and initiated a traveling exhibition of authors' and illustrators' work. I also got to meet the Queen and introduce her to my fellow authors at her 80th birthday party at Buckingham Palace.

Keep reading for an excerpt from

Jacqueline Wilson's **Best Friends**,

coming soon in hardcover from Roaring Brook Press.

EXCERPT

Alice and I are best friends. I've known her all my life. That is absolutely true. Our moms were in the hospital at the same time when they were having us. I got born first, at six o'clock in the morning on July 3. Alice took ages and didn't arrive until four in the afternoon. We both had a long cuddle with our moms, and at nighttime we were tucked up next to each other in little tiny cots.

I expect Alice was a bit frightened. She'd have cried. She's actually still a bit of a crybaby now, but I try not to tease her about it. I always do my best to comfort her.

I bet that first day I called to her in baby-coo language. I'd have said, "Hi, I'm Gemma. Being born is a bit weird, isn't it? Are you OK?"

And Alice would say, "I'm not sure. I'm Alice. I don't think I like it here. I want my mom."

"We'll see our moms again soon. We'll get fed. I'm *starving*." I'd have started crying too, in case there was a chance of being fed straight away.

I suppose I'm still a bit greedy, if I'm absolutely honest. Not quite as greedy as Biscuits though. Well, his real name is Billy McVitie, but everyone calls him Biscuits, even the teachers. He's this boy in our class at school and his appetite is astonishing. He can eat an entire packet of chocolate cookies, *munch-crunch*, *munch-crunch*, in two minutes flat.

We had this Grand Biscuit Challenge at playtime. I managed only three quarters of a packet. I probably could have managed a whole packet too, but a crumb went down the wrong way and I choked. I ended up with chocolate drool all down the front of my white school blouse. But that's nothing new. I always seem to get a bit messy and scruffy and scuffed. Alice stays neat and sweet.

When we were babies, *one* of us crawled right into the trash bin and played mud wrestling in the garden and fell in the pond when we fed the ducks. The *other* one of us sat up prettily in her stroller cuddling Golden Syrup (her yellow teddy bear) and giggled at her naughty friend.

When we went to preschool *one* of us played Fireman in the water tank and Moles in the sandbox, and she didn't stop at finger painting, she did *entire body* painting. The *other* one of us sat demurely at the dinky table and made clay necklaces (one for each of us) and sang "Itsy Bitsy Spider" with all the cute hand gestures.

When we went to kindergarten, *one* of us pretended to be a Wild Thing and roared such terrible roars in class, she got sent out of the room. She also got into a fight with a big boy who snatched her best friend's chocolate, and *made his nose bleed*! The *other* one of us read Milly-Molly-Mandy and wrote stories about a little thatched cottage in the country in her very neat printing.

Now that we're in elementary school, *one* of us ran right into the boys' bathroom for a dare. She did, really, and they all yelled at her. She also climbed halfway up the drainpipe in the playground to get her ball back—only the drainpipe came away from the wall. They both went *crash, clonk.* Mr. Beaton, the principal, was NOT pleased. The *other* one of us got made an attendance monitor and wore her silver sparkly top (with matching silver glitter on her eyelids) to the school party, and all the boys wanted to dance with her, but *guess what*! She danced with her bad best friend all evening instead.

We're best friends but we're not one bit alike. I suppose that goes without saying. Though I seem to have said it a lot. My mom says it too. Also a lot.

"For heaven's sake, Gemma, why can't you stop being so rough and silly and boisterous? *Boy* being the operative bit! To think I was so thrilled when I had my baby girl. But now it's just like I've got three boys—and you're the biggest troublemaker of them all!"

There's my big brother Callum, who's seventeen. Callum and I used to be friends. He taught me to skateboard and showed me how to dive-bomb in the swimming pools. Every Sunday I'd balance on the back of his bike and we'd wobble over to Granddad's. But now Callum's got this girlfriend, Ayesha, and all they do is look into each other's eyes and go kissy-kissy-kiss. Yuck.

Alice and I played spies and followed them to the park once because we wanted to see if they did anything even yuckier, but Callum caught us and he turned me upside down and shook me until I felt sick.

There's my other brother, Jack, but he's nowhere near as much fun as Callum. Jack is totally brainy, such a nerd that he always comes top in every exam. Jack hasn't got a girlfriend. He doesn't get out enough to meet any. He just holes up in his room, hunched over his homework. He *does* take our dog, Barking Mad, out for a walk very late at night. And he likes to wear black. And doesn't like garlic bread. Maybe Jack is turning into Jacula? I'll have to check his teeth aren't getting alarmingly pointy.

It's annoying having Jack as my brother. Sometimes the teachers hope I'm going to be brainy too and get ten out of ten all the time. As if!

I can do *some* things. Mr. Beaton says I can talk the hind leg off a donkey—and its front leg and its ears and its tail. He says I *act* like a donkey too. I think donkeys kick if you're not careful. I *often* feel like kicking Mr. Beaton.

I get lots of ideas and work things out as quick as quick in my head, but it's soooo boring writing it all down, so I often don't bother. Or I try to get Alice to write it all out for me. Alice gets much better grades than me for all lessons. Apart from soccer. I don't want to boast, but I'm on the school soccer team even though I'm the youngest and the littlest and the only girl.

Alice doesn't like sports at all. We have different hobbies. She likes to draw lines of little girls in party frocks and she writes in her diary with her gel pens and she paints her nails all different colors and plays with her jewelry. Alice is into jewelry in a big way. She keeps it in a special box that used to be her grandma's. It's blue velvet, and if you wind it up and open the lid, a little ballet dancer twirls around and around. Alice has got a little gold heart on a chain and a tiny gold bangle she wore when she was a baby and a jade bangle from an uncle in Hong Kong and a silver locket and a Scottie dog sparkly brooch and a charm bracelet with ten jingly charms. My favorite charm is the little silver Noah's Ark. You can open it up and see absolutely minute giraffes and elephants and tigers inside.

Alice also has heaps of rings—a real Russian gold ring, a Victorian garnet, and lots of pretendy ones out of Cracker Jacks. She gave me a big bright silver-and-blue one as a friendship ring. I loved it and called it my sapphire—only I forgot to take it off when I went swimming and the silver went black and the sapphire fell out.

"Typical," said Mom, sighing.

I think Mom sometimes wishes she'd swapped the cribs around when we were born. I'm sure she'd much rather have Alice as a daughter. She doesn't say so, but I'm not dumb. *I'd* sooner have Alice as my daughter.

"I wouldn't," said my dad, and he ruffled my hair so it stood up on end. Well, it was probably standing up anyway. I've got the sort of hair that looks like I'm permanently plugged into the electric outlet. Mom made me grow it long but I kept losing my silly bows and bobbles. Then it got a bit sticky when I went in for this giant bubble-blowing contest with Biscuits and the other boys and *hurray, hurray* my hair had to be chopped off. Mom cried but I didn't mind one bit.

I know you're not really meant to have favorites in your family, but I think I love my dad more than my mom. I don't get to see him much because he drives a taxi and so he's up before I wake up, taking people to the airport, and often he's out till very late, picking people up from the pub. When he *is* home, he likes to lie on the sofa in front of the television and have a little snooze. It's often a long, long, long snooze, but if you're feeling lonely, you can cuddle up beside him. He pats you and mumbles, "Hello, little Cuddle Bun," and then goes back to sleep again.

My granddad used to drive our cab but he's retired now, though he helps out when the car-hire firm needs an extra driver. They've got a white Rolls for weddings and Granddad once took me for a sneaky drive in it. He's lovely, my granddad. Maybe he's my all-time absolute *favorite* relative. He's always looked after me, right from when I was a baby. Our mom went back to work full-time just as Granddad retired, so he's acted like my babysitter.

He still meets me from school. We go back to Granddad's apartment, which is right at the top of the high-rise.

You look out of Granddad's window and you see the birds flying past—it's just magical. On a clear day, you can see for miles and miles across the town to the woods and hills of the countryside. Sometimes Granddad narrows his eyes and pretends he's looking through a telescope. He swears he's squinting all the way to the sea, but I think he's joking.

He jokes a lot, my granddad. He calls me funny names too. I'm his little Iced Gem. He always gives me packets of iced gems, small doll-size biscuits with white and pink and yellow yummy icing.

This annoys Mom when she picks me up. "I wish you wouldn't feed her," she says to Granddad, "she's going to have her dinner the minute she gets home. Gemma, you mind you clean your teeth properly. I don't like you eating all that sugary stuff."

Granddad always says he's sorry, but he crosses his eyes behind Mom's back and makes a funny face. I get the giggles and annoy Mom even more.

Sometimes I think *everyone* annoys my mom. Everyone except Alice. Mom works in the makeup department of Joseph Pilbeam, and she gives Alice all these dinky samples of skincare products and little lipsticks and bottles of scent. Once when she was in a really good mood, she sat Alice down at her dressing table and gave her a full grown-up lady's makeup. My mom made me up too, though she told me off for fidgeting (well, it was tickly) and then my eyes itched and I rubbed them and got that black mascara stuff all over the place, so I looked like a panda.

Alice's makeup stayed prettily in place all day long. She didn't even smudge her pink lipstick when she had her dinner. It was pizza, but she cut hers up into tiny bite-size pieces instead of shoving a lovely big slice in her mouth.

If Alice wasn't my very best friend, she might just get on my nerves sometimes. Especially when Mom makes a big fuss of her and then looks at me and sighs.

Still, it's great that Mom *does* like Alice because she never minds if she comes for a sleepover at our house. My mom has banned big birthday sleepovers forever. Callum doesn't care as the only person he'd like to sleep over is Ayesha. Jack doesn't care either. He's got a few nerdy friends in school, but they don't communicate face-to-face, they just e-mail and text each other.

I've got heaps of ordinary friends as well as my best friend, Alice. Last birthday, I invited three boys and three girls for a sleepover party. Alice was top of the list, of course. We were supposed to play out in the garden but it rained, so we all had a crazy game of soccer with a cushion in the living room (well, not quite *all*—Alice wouldn't play and Biscuits is terrible at games). Someone broke my mom's wedding present Lladro lady *and* burst the cushion. My mom was so mad she wouldn't let any of them sleep over and sent them all home. Except for Alice.

I'm still allowed one-special-friend sleepovers so long

as that special friend is Alice. So that's great, great, great because as I've probably said before, Alice is my very best friend.

I don't know what I'd do without her.